A Patriot's Betrayal

Andrew Clawson

Cover design and illustration by Books Covered

ISBN: 978-1477589014

Get Andrew Clawson's Starter Library FOR FREE

Sign up for the no-spam newsletter and get two novels for free.

Details can be found at the end of this book.

Epigraph

Who sows virtue reaps honor

~ ~ ~

Leonardo da Vinci

Prologue

Tonight, death's silent footsteps stalked the countryside, and the weather was perfect.

Thick snow flew sideways through the night air, crystallized flakes careening on frigid wings. A thick blanket of snow covered the rolling hills of Virginia's scenic countryside and touched the surging Potomac River. Jagged chunks of the frozen river floated atop the waterway, icy testaments to nature's raw power.

On the crest of one hill, covered in winter's embrace, sat a stately mansion aglow with light, a beacon of warmth and humanity amid the winter storm's chaos. Icy winds howled outside thick glass windows, frigid tentacles blowing with force enough to send lamp flames dancing. Shadows flitted across oak walls as pellets of hail began to crash. A roaring fire provided comfort and light, though no such warmth could be found among the inhabitants.

A massive bed dominated the room. A sprawling feather mattress covered the man lying in it now, a man with thin hair white as the snow outside. Deep coughs wracked his body, each one accompanied by a sharp clicking sound as he fought for air. The room was empty save for his wife sitting beside him.

A moment later the bedroom door swung open and the man's personal physician stepped through. Sadness hooded the doctor's eyes as he leaned in close, listening to his patient's labored breathing.

"Sir. You must drink this. The fever has yet to break."

A once-powerful hand reached for the proffered cup. The patient winced at the bitter taste, though he drank it all.

"I pray this alleviates your pain, sir."

Two words were the only response. "'Tis well."

The man's wife sat silently beside her husband, merely smiling when the physician took her hand and assured her everything would be all right, though the truth was plain for all to see.

One hour later, George Washington was dead.

The doctor relayed this news to a rider waiting at the front door. Clad in a thick woolen coat, the rider, a silversmith by trade, nodded once and walked back out into the brutal cold. He secreted a small book wrapped in oilcloth in his saddlebag. It had been given to him only yesterday by his oldest friend—the great man whose corpse now lay warm inside. The rider had pledged to deliver the small volume to a man in Philadelphia, several hundred miles away.

As Paul Revere tore down the path, clumps of dirt flying from his mount's hooves, he had no idea that the doctor who had delivered the news would soon be found floating in the Potomac River, the truth of what had transpired this evening silenced forever.

Chapter 1

The city hummed with life at all hours of day and night. Headlights moved like ants in a farm over the serpentine roadways, mirroring trade routes laid out hundreds of years ago to carry freight on the rivers.

Rittenhouse Square, one of Philadelphia's most exclusive neighborhoods, was an oasis of green amid a sprawling expanse of concrete and asphalt. Couples walked hand in hand through the brisk spring air, and people trailed dogs pulling at their leashes as the animals savored the sounds and smells of the outside world.

Some of these people walked by a van parked on a side street several blocks away, bathed in a warm yellow glow cast by street lamps overhead. Two men sat inside, watching a specific building. Signs plastered on the vehicle advertised an electrical business that wasn't listed in any phone book or tax record. The driver studied a third-floor window across the street. A lone figure had been visible moving around the apartment for over an hour. Despite the central location, this area of the city was quiet at night. The occasional pedestrians who did pass strolled by quickly, their breath visible in the cool March air.

The driver turned to a man seated beside him. "All right. You ready to do this?"

The passenger studied the street for potential witnesses. "You know it. Let's roll."

Without another word, the two men got out and walked up to the four-story brownstone apartment that was home to, among others, Professor Joseph Chase. Professor Chase was a member of the history department at the University of Pennsylvania, a respected academic whose specialty was Colonial America. They had been told that Dr. Chase lived alone, was not married, and did not have any military or martial arts background. Whoever this poor bastard was, someone wanted him dead, and that someone was willing to spend a hundred thousand dollars to make it happen.

A set of lock-picking tools made short work of the front door, both men keeping their heads down so the security cameras wouldn't get a shot of their faces on their way upstairs. They stopped outside Chase's door, where each pulled out a pistol with an attached suppressor.

"You pop that lock and I'll move in. Keep an eye on the hallway while I take him out. We promised them no witnesses."

The lock gave way with a click. One man crept inside, light touching his shoes as he headed down a hallway toward where the target had last been seen, in a room facing the street outside. A heavy rug padded his steps, and he stopped outside another room in which a man sat in front of a desk, his eyes on a computer monitor.

A grandfather clock ticked in one corner, slicing off one of the few remaining seconds of Dr. Chase's life. Books and manuscripts occupied every inch of surrounding floor, tabletop, and chair, a stereotypical academic's office. Dr. Chase never turned around as the gunman walked in and stopped mere feet from the professor before pulling out a disposable cell phone and speed-dialing the only number it contained.

Joseph Chase's desk phone rang.

"Who the hell could that be?" He grabbed it from the stand. "Joseph Chase speaking."

Pfft. Pfft.

Two bullets slammed into the back of Chase's skull, and then his lifeless body slumped over the desk. The assassin retrieved Dr. Chase's laptop computer, as specified in his agreement, and two minutes later relocked the professor's front door and returned to the van.

The driver turned to his partner as he stuck the key into the ignition. "We should throw that damn computer in the river. The last thing we—"

His words were cut off when the engine turned over and two pounds of C-4 strapped to the van's undercarriage detonated. For a brief second, the city street was bathed in a fiery glow as the van rocketed ten feet in the air before slamming back down, a burning shell of twisted metal with two charred corpses inside. Debris clinked on the asphalt as wide-eyed residents peered out of windows at the demolition. A wailing siren soon came to life in the distance, growing louder as the van's shell burned.

Two hundred feet down the block, a man sat in his car surveying the destruction. Satisfied no one could have survived the inferno, he pulled out of his parking spot and headed away from the carnage, taking out his cell phone.

A heavy voice answered on the first ring. "Is it done?"

"Mission accomplished," the man replied.

The line went dead. He put his phone down and concentrated on driving as several city police cars flew past, headed to the explosion.

A minute later a smile cracked his face.

Chapter 2

Philadelphia, Pennsylvania

Red and blue lights pierced the darkness, washing over paramedics as they loaded two charred corpses into body bags. The zippers slid shut as Philadelphia detective Kristian Nunez arrived at the scene. A uniformed officer motioned for Nunez to pull his fire-engine-red 1968 ragtop Mustang past the sawhorse barricades, behind which smoke drifted in ghost-like tendrils from the burned-out remains of a vehicle.

Nunez shook his head. Another beautiful day at the office.

"Detective, over here."

Nunez turned toward a nearby ambulance. A dirty and disheveled officer in blue sat inside the open back doors with an oxygen mask attached to his face and bandages on both hands.

"I was the first responder, sir." The officer looked all of twenty years old.

"How you doing, son?"

"Been better, sir. Just wanted to let you know what I found."

Nunez took out a notebook and waited quietly, pen in hand.

The officer waved one bandaged hand toward the smoking metal. "When I got here, this damn van was a huge bonfire. I see one guy in a front seat, and I can't tell you why, but I tried to pull him out. Only after I got this"—he held up his hands—"did I realize the guy was already roasted. Didn't see anyone else in the area when I arrived, and right after I got burned the cavalry showed up."

"Thanks, Officer. You take care of those burns."

Just as he turned to seek out the lead sergeant, another uniformed officer jumped in his face.

"Detective, you've gotta get over here. We found another stiff."

Nunez hustled into the building and up a set of marble stairs. He ducked under a flapping string of yellow police tape that barred Professor Chase's front door and found the crime scene, the details of what had transpired all too clear. A pool of blood covered the desk and spilled onto the floor. Books lined the walls, hundreds of them alongside pictures of the newly deceased: shots from Stonehenge, Buckingham Palace, all complemented by Joseph Chase's smiling face. Nunez glanced out a window as a search and rescue team pulled the driver from inside his van's burned-out shell.

He checked his preliminary notes. No signs of forced entry on the apartment door, though any competent thief could bypass the deadbolt with one hand. From the burn marks on the victim's skull, it appeared Dr. Chase had been working at his desk and was shot from nearly point-blank range.

The poor bastard never saw it coming.

Nothing seemed to be missing other than a computer. A power cord dangled from atop the polished walnut desk. Chase's wallet was on a nearby table, several hundred dollars inside. This was no random robbery. Someone had come here with a purpose.

The officer who had spoken with Nunez outside walked up beside him and cleared his throat.

"Our initial report was confirmed. Deceased is Joseph Chase, age fifty-five, single, no children, lived alone. He's a professor at Penn. Afraid that's all we have right now, Detective Nunez. No prints so far, no discarded cigarette butts, hairs, clothing fibers, bullet shells, nothing. Whoever did this was careful."

"I figured as much," Nunez said. "This is too clean to be some junkie off the street. Usually we'll find everything except the perp's wallet lying around when we get a homicide, but this is different. Somebody knew what they were doing."

"Unless whoever did this is now roasting outside."

A grim smile flickered across Nunez's face. "Excellent point, Sergeant. If that's the case, we have a whole new set of problems to deal with."

Nunez's phone vibrated. One of the IT guys was calling, hopefully with some good news.

"Nunez here."

"I just saw the building's surveillance footage," an officer on the information technology team said, "and they got most of it on tape. We have two guys entering the apartment, then leaving three minutes later with a laptop. They take the stairs to ground level, walk to their van, and *boom*, no more bad guys."

"Do you see anyone else around the van?"

Maybe they'd get lucky and spot somebody planting an explosive on the vehicle.

"Negative, sir. They parked for about ten minutes, just sitting there, then walked into the building. Nobody gets anywhere near that vehicle from the time they park until it goes sky-high."

"Damn. Get those tapes and bring them in. We'll have to go over them more thoroughly in the lab."

Nunez flipped the phone shut.

"Looks like you were right, Sergeant. The two men who shot Dr. Chase are the same two you found outside. We've got a real mess on our hands here."

After an hour of processing the scene, Detective Nunez walked outside with a storm brewing on his face. Every uniformed officer avoided his hunched figure, a sea of blue parting as thunderclouds barreled past.

Chapter 3

Philadelphia, Pennsylvania

Inside the Philadelphia branch office of the Central Intelligence Agency, a man sat behind his government-issued desk and thought distinctly ungovernment-like thoughts. Maybe it was a good thing when the thugs and degenerates killed each other.

He closed the report and slammed it on his desk, frustrated with the meaningless investigations that consumed his days.

Who cared if one gang in Kensington was taking over more turf to sell drugs? The dealers were like a Hydra. Cut off one head, and two more grew in its place.

His ringing desk phone pulled him back to reality.

"Dean."

He listened for a few moments before hanging up. An email popped onto his screen. Moments later a different report was in his hands, and for the first time all day, CIA agent Nicholas Dean had found something worth his time.

A car had exploded in Rittenhouse Square. Preliminary reports indicated the accelerant was a C-4 plastic.

Finally, something exciting. The incident summary, taken straight from the city's police database, indicated two stiffs had been found in the burned-out van. Interesting, but that wasn't what he cared about. What got his attention was the third body, a college professor of some repute, found shot to death in an apartment across the street.

A security camera had caught two men walking out of the dead guy's building and immediately getting blown sky-high when their van turned into a fireball.

A humorless grin crossed Nick's face. This was a lot better than dealing with idiot dope fiends who fancied themselves as gangbangers. He picked up the phone and called a friend in Langley.

"Brent, its Nick Dean. I need you to send me any reports we have that involve C-4 explosive in the past year, whether it was detonated, used in the commission of a crime, or any that was reported missing or stolen. As soon as possible, and I know—I owe you one. Thanks."

Five minutes later, several pages of reports from Brent shot out of his printer.

Nick studied them for a while, listening to the wall clock tick as he read. Once he'd finished, Nick made a brief phone call to the Philadelphia chief of police and then walked out of his office and climbed into his government sedan. He had the name of the investigating detective on the dead professor homicide and permission from the chief to liaise on the case.

After the events of 9/11, a push had been made for government agencies to open the lines of communication in the hopes that an increased information flow would aid in preventing another disaster. After the dust had settled and the forced friendships between Type A personalities had been declared in rambling and mostly unenforceable mission statements, one of the few initiatives that had actually gone forward was Nicholas Dean's position. Normally constrained by the FBI's monopoly on all domestic activity, the CIA had gained a tenuous foothold on American soil with the establishment of Agency liaison positions with FBI field offices.

As the CIA's lone agent operating in the Philadelphia area, Nick's post was a lonely one. He could call in support from Langley when needed, but those occasions were rare. Nick joked that the FBI tended to treat him like a mushroom: feed him shit and keep him in the dark. As such, Nick had made the best of it and developed relationships within the Philadelphia police department. He wouldn't label them as friendships. No, these were more of the acquaintance variety, people who said hello but didn't really want to know how you were doing.

The chief had approved Nick partnering with one of the city's best in homicide. Whether or not Detective Kristian Nunez wanted a government agent along for the ride was a different story.

Dean would worry about that later.

Leaves painted black in the moonlight fluttered on a soft breeze, small trees in the parking lot backlit by the city lights. His tires spun as he shot out of the parking lot, headed toward Philadelphia police headquarters. If he was right, Detective Nunez had just landed in the deep end and had no idea what was coming next.

Chapter 4

Philadelphia, Pennsylvania

Even at this time of night, traffic had backed up on the Schuylkill Expressway. Red brake lights cast a melancholy glow on each driver stuck in the mess. Nobody moved but some had a better seat than others. Detective Nunez, for one.

His Mustang elicited envious stares from nearly everyone it passed. However, Detective Nunez stared at the traffic with hard eyes as he drove, glowering at the dark night sky while he inched toward headquarters at Seventh and Race, a circular concrete edifice nicknamed "The Roundhouse."

The nerve center for the department's operations, it housed an arm of every specialized area the police utilized. Right now, he had questions enough for all of them.

Why did two professionals murder a college professor in cold blood for his computer and then walk outside only to be blown apart? Where would someone get the explosives used to destroy the van and its occupants, and just who the hell could pull that off?

A buzz reverberated, his cell phone at it again. The damn thing never stopped.

"Nunez."

"Detective, this is Officer Benson at dispatch. A CIA agent just walked into the building and requested to speak with you immediately. Shall I patch him through?"

Nunez nearly rear-ended the motorcycle in front of him.

"Did you say CIA?"

"That's correct, sir. I'm not sure why he's here, but he wants to speak with you as soon as possible."

"When did he get there?"

"Just now, sir."

"Tell him I'll be there in five minutes. Show him to my office, please."

"Yes, sir."

Nunez hit the switch for his unmarked car's blue and red lights and, in a minor miracle, traffic actually parted.

Minutes later, the Mustang roared into The Roundhouse's underground parking garage, Nunez's stormy mood growing darker by the minute.

When he made it upstairs, the office door bearing his name and rank was open, the lights shining from within. Detective Nunez turned the corner and found himself face-to-face with a human bulldozer.

Chapter 5

Pittsburgh, Pennsylvania

Puffy white clouds dotted the sky on a beautiful day, unseasonably warm for spring in western Pennsylvania. In Pittsburgh's Squirrel Hill neighborhood, sunlight filtered through kitchen windows and a group of children shrieked as they raced down the sidewalk. A flock of hardy birds that had shunned their southern flight chirped as frost melted to dew on fresh shoots of green grass.

Inside one red-brick-fronted apartment, a man sat at a table, his face white with shock.

Parker Chase couldn't believe what he was hearing.

"How did it happen?"

The female police officer who had called cut straight to it.

"Your uncle was shot during a robbery. Right now, it appears that he was merely in the wrong place at the wrong time."

That was impossible. Who would want to kill his uncle?

"A robbery? What did he have worth stealing?"

"The only thing we can verify as missing is his laptop, though it's difficult to be certain, given that he lived alone."

"Do you have any idea who it was?"

"Not exactly," the officer responded. "This may sound a bit strange, but we believe the men who shot your uncle are now deceased."

"Already? He only died last night. What happened?"

"We believe the killers died in an explosion immediately following the murder. As I said, the investigation is still in the preliminary stages. When we learn anything else, I'll be sure to pass it along."

A thousand questions raced through his mind, but she silenced them with one sentence.

"Not to be blunt, Mr. Chase, but as the next of kin, do you have any idea where the funeral will be held? I can have the morgue arrange for delivery of the body if you'd like."

Reality smacked him in the face. Nothing was going to change the fact that his uncle was dead.

But Parker had some experience in arranging funerals.

"It will be here in Pittsburgh. He was born here."

The woman perked up, probably happy she didn't have to do everything for him. "Once you choose a funeral home, contact the morgue and pass the information along. In-state delivery should take no more than three business days."

Just like ordering a Christmas gift.

"Thank you, Officer. I'll be sure to let them know."

A numbness settled over Parker when he hung up. How could this have happened? Two days earlier he'd spoken to his uncle about visiting him in Philadelphia.

Now he was dead.

As his gaze wandered across the kitchen walls, the sunlight seemed dull and bland, all the warmth drained away. Joe was a distinguished professor at the University of Pennsylvania, an immensely respected academic. Internationally renowned for his work on the American Revolution, he was something of a rock star in academic circles.

As these thoughts raced through his mind, Parker's cell phone vibrated.

He sighed deeply. Who was bugging him now? He glanced at the screen, and the chasm of emptiness inside him flooded with emotion at what waited.

Erika Carr.

Of course she would know about Joe's death. They were both employed by Penn, and in the close-knit world of academia, she must have heard the news. There was no other reason. She certainly wasn't calling to chat. They hadn't spoken in over a year, not since their split, and though they had tried to be friends, it was never going to work.

A deep breath did little to clear his mind. *May as well get it over with.*

"Hello?"

Silence. Maybe she had pocket dialed him. "Hel—"

"Parker. It's me."

With those familiar words, his stomach dropped.

"I just heard about Joe," Erika said. "I'm so sorry, Parker. I can't believe it."

"Neither can I. The police only called a few minutes ago."

"Oh, my goodness. I had no idea. I'll let you go."

Despite the way his chest tightened whenever she came to mind, he was surprised to find he wanted to talk.

"No, it's fine. I don't really know what to think right now." True, but the questions came quickly. "Why would anyone kill Joe just for his computer?"

"What do you mean, just for his computer? Is that why he was murdered?"

"The cops said that so far the only thing missing is his laptop. It sounds like he was working in his study when someone broke in, walked up and shot him."

Erika gasped.

"They also said the two bastards who did it got blown up outside his building; some kind of car bomb."

Pain was reflected in every word. "There was a report on the news about an explosion in Rittenhouse early this morning. But why would the murderers have been killed after they shot Joe?"

"I can't begin to guess." Parker rubbed a hand through his hair. "The cops said they'd call if they learn anything else."

Parker walked over to the window and looked out at the setting sun. His usually tranquil neighborhood seemed sinister and dark, a pall cast over everything in sight.

"I can't imagine how hard this is for you," she said

Her voice gave rise to a new wave of emotion as he found himself drawn to thoughts of their recent past.

Little more than a year had gone by since their split, and time had done nothing to heal the wounds. His father had died shortly after, pushing any chance to process their breakup into the back seat while he grieved, and it had stayed there ever since..

"Is there anything I can do?" she asked.

How easy it would be to say he needed her; he knew she would come. She would offer him whatever support he needed, but in the end, it wouldn't be what he truly wanted. He had never dealt with anything like this, and certainly never with anyone like her. He didn't know what to do.

"No." He forced himself to bury it away. "Thank you, though. I'll be fine."

Erika made a halting noise, as though she wanted to say something, but then stopped. A moment later she coughed, once. "If you're sure," she finally said. "Please let me know when the funeral arrangements are made. If it's all right with you, I want to be there."

"I will," he said, though the last thing he wanted to do was face her when he was down.

"If there's anything you need, call me."

"I will. Take care."

He wanted to say so much more.

But he didn't.

"Good-bye," Erika said. The line went dead.

Parker stared out at the plush green grass and wondered who would want to kill his uncle. A single tear slid down his face, the only outward sign of sorrow he would allow himself. He hastily wiped a sleeve across his face. It didn't become a man to cry.

Chapter 6

Philadelphia, Pennsylvania

Erika Carr wept silently in her office.

Joseph Chase had been a distinguished professor at Penn, greatly admired and a colleague she'd seen daily. With a razor-sharp wit and kind heart, he had been popular with students and faculty, a great guy to have a conversation or a drink with. To Erika, he had been all that and more. He had been a tangible connection to her past, a subtle memory that brought comfort and joy.

Upset as she was, her despair didn't hold a candle to what Parker must be going through. She had been hesitant even to call him when she'd heard. It had been nearly a year since they separated. Calling him out of the blue after Joe died couldn't go over well. Yet, she'd dialed his number.

Images of happier times filled her vision. For eight wonderful years she and Parker had grown together, from their first meeting as freshman, through college and eventually living together in Pittsburgh.

After the first round of grad school, when she had accepted the position at Penn, their relationship had come to a crashing halt; the distance between Pittsburgh and Philadelphia had been simply too great. Picking her career over a relationship hadn't been easy, but deep down she had hoped that in the long run bygones would be bygones and they could at least maintain a cordial relationship.

That plan had evaporated when Parker's father had died days after she moved.

Even now it was surreal: Parker had called her to relay the news that his father was dead, killed in a fall from his tree stand while hunting. After that, Parker had become withdrawn and distant. He stopped returning her calls. She still worried about him, living alone, no family at all. Erika worried that Parker would blame himself again, illogical as it may be. That kind of self-imposed pressure didn't always sit easily on a person's mind. Even an outgoing guy like Parker could change with the kind of weight he carried on his shoulders.

Parker's mother had died giving birth to him, a horrible accident out of anyone's control. He and Erika had been together for over a year before Parker, drunk after a night out, had told her the story of how his father had lost a wife while gaining a son. He never spoke of it again, and only through conversations with his father did Erika learn of the guilt Parker carried. Without his father's input, she would never have guessed that the affable and testosterone-laden man she loved had buried his pain deep inside. On the outside, he was the quintessential all-American guy. Football scholarship, intelligent, charismatic, and handsome. Inside, though, it was a different story.

She dabbed at her cheeks with a tissue, eyes blurry as she tried to focus on the papers littering her desk.

Like every assistant professor at the university, part of Erika's responsibilities included teaching classes. Dozens of papers awaited her attention, a task she alternately relished and despised. Interacting with some of the nation's brightest young minds kept her sharp and stimulated, though grading the same test nearly a hundred times grew tiresome.

Full professors, men and women like Joseph Chase, taught sparingly, instead devoting their energies to research. Academia was as cutthroat as the business world, and as the old saying went, it was publish or perish. Penn was internationally renowned as a leading producer of scholarly research materials, and that was why they paid the senior faculty members the big bucks.

Dr. Chase had been a leading authority on American history, consistently producing cutting-edge work. If the spotlight was shining brightly on the university, donors took notice.

Despite the macabre circumstances, Erika couldn't help but wonder who would be appointed to fill Joseph's position. Say the department chair were to offer her the spot: she'd be foolish not to accept. Realistically, she had far too little experience to be considered, but the intrigue of departmental politics would make life interesting for a while.

As red ink trailed from her pen, Erika glanced at the framed photo on her desk, taken during their senior year of college. Even now, Erika couldn't help but smile at the snapshot of Parker and her on the field after his last game, eye black running down his cheeks in rivulets of sweat, the world at their feet.

Chapter 7

Philadelphia, Pennsylvania

Nicholas Dean took center stage in Nunez's office, a force of nature come to life.

Six and a half feet tall, Nick weighed in at two sixty, every ounce of it solid muscle. He hadn't lost a pound since his days as the undefeated heavyweight boxing champion of the US Navy, a title he had only relinquished upon his honorable discharge following Desert Storm. Today, beneath his trim mane of chestnut hair, Nick's expression betrayed nothing.

"Detective Nunez, I presume," Nick said at last.

"What are you doing here?"

"My name is Nicholas Dean. I'm the Central Intelligence Agency liaison in Philadelphia."

"So I heard."

Detective Nunez brushed past the unwelcome guest and fell into his chair, the rickety wooden contraption squeaking in protest.

He did not invite Agent Dean to sit down.

"You didn't answer my question," Nunez stated.

Agent Dean looked at the two vacant chairs across from Nunez.

"May I have a seat?"

Nunez waved toward one. "Don't get too comfortable."

"Detective," Dean said as he sat, "I'm not trying to step on your toes. I'm here because I've been told that C-4 plastic explosive may have been used to destroy a van in Rittenhouse last night. I'm here for the same

21

reasons you are: to figure out who detonated it and how to stop it from happening again."

Nunez said nothing, his olive-toned jaw set in stone.

"I would appreciate you allowing me to participate in your investigation. Of course, you would be provided with unfettered access to all Agency databases for the duration."

Nunez narrowed his eyes. "Are you trying to bribe me, Agent Dean? Do you think that you can buy your way onto my team by 'allowing' us to access your precious databases?"

"I'm doing no such thing, Detective. If you don't want to work with me, it would be little trouble to cut you and your men out completely. In case you weren't aware, several batches of C-4 explosive have gone missing from federal facilities this year. One phone call to the right people and you are removed from this investigation."

Heat filled his chest as Nunez rose to his feet. "You're a tough guy, huh? Throwing your federal badge around like you're a big shot?"

"I'm not trying to be difficult. I'm merely stating the facts." Agent Dean held up one hand. "Listen, Kristian. I don't want a pissing match. Both you and I know it won't do any good, and in the end, everyone loses. I want to work with you, to figure out where the hell this stuff came from and make sure no one else dies."

For a moment, the air grew thick. Neither man moved until the detective sighed, and then put up his hand, palm out.

"Listen, Agent Dean—"

"Call me Nick."

"All right. Nick, you have to realize what it looks like from my end. Every day, my department is bombarded with new cases. Usually it's run-of-the-mill stuff—shootings, carjackings, stuff like that. We don't hear a word from any of the feds. As soon as this happens, a case that might register on the national radar, some big shot from the government swoops in and wants to run the show." Nunez stood and began pacing behind his desk. "How do you think that makes my men feel?"

"Believe me, Kristian, I understand where you're coming from. I'm not trying to take over your case. I just want to work with your team and solve this."

Nunez's gaze fell to a framed photo on his desk.

"You know who this is?" He flipped the picture around, allowing Nick to see Detective Nunez and a dark-haired woman with porcelain skin arm in arm. "This is my wife. She's the reason I get up for work every day, why I deal with the scumbags in this city. If you can help make this place safer for people like her, then I don't have a problem working with you."

Agent Dean nodded and shook Nunez's proffered hand. He tried and failed to suppress a grimace. The man's grip was like iron.

"I'll be back this afternoon with my gear," Nick said. "Think you can find a desk for me?"

"I'll have one brought up here. I want to keep an eye on you."

Agent Dean nodded his appreciation and rose to leave. Just before he walked out, Nunez called out.

"Hey, Nick."

"Yes?"

"Don't make me regret this."

Chapter 8

Philadelphia, Pennsylvania

From thirty-five stories in the air, if you look east over the Delaware River, New Jersey stretches to the horizon. After two centuries of water traffic, the once-sparkling river now possesses a grayish hue. Even on warm and sunny days only the most optimistic of souls takes solace in the great waterway.

Preston Vogel was one of these souls.

When he stared out his floor-to-ceiling window at the river flowing slowly south, he saw ships of every shape and size, bound to and from ports that spanned the globe. All day these ships came and went, year-round, carrying thousands of tons of every product imaginable, from coal to cars, fuel to fur coats, each one generating revenue. Many of the vessels were owned and operated by his company, Vogel Industries.

Based in Philadelphia, it was one of the world's largest conglomerates, with holdings in real estate, oil refineries, steel production, and railway transport.

Preston ruled over a financial empire valued in excess of twenty billion dollars. Such wealth made him an influential man in the most powerful country the world had ever known, a businessman to be reckoned with.

He was also regarded as one of the coldest bastards on earth.

At the moment, Preston Vogel was focused on a ringing telephone.

He picked up the receiver. "Hello?"

"The professor is no longer with us."

"Excellent," Vogel replied and hung up, satisfied now that his upcoming meeting could proceed as planned.

The push of a red button brought his buxom assistant scurrying.

"Brooke, is everyone here?"

"Yes, sir. All four of them are in the conference room as you requested."

Twenty-six years old, tall and slender, Brooke was quite the young lady. With an Ivy League education and a ruthless desire to succeed, Brooke had been hired five minutes into her interview. Needless to say, she had soon become one of his favorite employees for a number of reasons.

"Tell them I'll be right in."

Today marked the beginning of his most ambitious venture ever, one that would ensure Vogel Industries' continued prosperity for decades to come. One man had stood between Vogel and his goal, but that man was no longer a problem.

Now, finally, he could begin.

Chapter 9

"Gentlemen, welcome to Philadelphia." Preston nodded to his four invited guests.

The four men seated around the massive conference table appeared diminutive in contrast with the oversized furniture. Appearances, though, could be deceiving.

In addition to comprising the five largest shareholders of Vogel Industries stock, all in attendance had one additional attribute in common.

Together, they constituted the membership of an organization that had existed for over two hundred years. Led by a man with vision and poise, a man with a ruthless desire to achieve his goals, no matter the cost, the group was an international powerhouse.

That leader?

Preston Vogel.

"Thank you for being here today. We are at a crossroads, gentlemen, and it is imperative that we move decisively, as we are now faced with the opportunity of a lifetime."

The four men waited, unaware of his plans.

"It has become apparent that America's increasing dependence on foreign oil is untenable. Every year a different crisis emerges that illustrates the instability of our current arrangement. A single dictator should not be able to disrupt the entire energy market." He paused, taking a sip of water. "I'm excited to inform you that Vogel Industries is now in position to ensure America remains energy independent, now and forever."

"Exactly what are you getting at, Mr. Vogel?"

Linwood Graves's soft, melodic voice floated through the air, a diminutive tone in stark contrast with the thick-shouldered man.

"I'm glad you asked. I invited you here today so that we can enact change to stave off the largest crisis our nation has faced in decades. I have the solution to a problem, and that problem, as I said, is America's current dependency on foreign oil. Every day, the United States requires over twenty million barrels of oil to power industry, produce goods and services, and fuel our transportation needs. Over ten million of those barrels are imported *each day*. Our production is half that, a daily deficit of five million barrels, a ratio that is wholly unsustainable."

Preston studied each of them as he spoke, gauging their response. As the elected leader of their group, he was free to direct their actions, but with a majority vote, they could stop him from proceeding.

Given the fact that his four fellow members were generally skittish, hesitant to take any risk, Vogel needed to convince them now.

"Gentlemen, we do not need foreign oil. The answer to ending our nation's dependency on it lies beneath the Arctic National Wildlife Refuge."

Graves was the first to respond. "You're talking about drilling, aren't you? Preston, do you have any idea how much work would be involved to do that?"

Good. None had rejected it outright, and now he could move onto the logistics and revenue projections. If anything could garner their support, it was profit.

"Correct, and I certainly do. While it will take approximately a year to fully commence operations, the US Department of Energy has estimated that the value of oil produced from the Arctic Refuge would be three hundred billion dollars. Give or take a few billion."

Silence surrounded him as four men wrapped their minds around all those zeros.

A nasal, tinny voice sounded from the table.

"From a business perspective, it makes sense. But how are you going to drill in a federally protected reserve? It would take an act of Congress to allow this."

Short, pale, and balding, Chesterton Rupp was a weasel of a man. He did, however, possess a keen mind and was often at odds with Preston's ideas. Vogel put on his best politician's smile, though if Rupp had been paying attention, he'd have realized it was a shark smiling down on him.

"I realize that what I'm proposing is illegal under current federal law. I assure you, though, that I have the utmost confidence this can be addressed. As we speak, my dear friend from Tennessee, Senator Hunter, is educating his constituents on the benefits our proposal would bring to every voter in America. If you recall, he is the current chairman of the Appropriations Committee."

Rupp and Graves both frowned at the news.

Deacon Bancroft, their fourth member, spoke up.

"Preston, I'm not sure you realize just how difficult and fickle elected officials can be."

"Deacon, I understand that our elected officials are only as reliable as your last donation, but you must realize that I'm not proposing we undermine the country's economy. Instead, I propose to bring jobs back to America, to employ men and women whose lives have been filled with despair. Tell me, what politician would stand in the way of such an idea?"

Bancroft's eyes narrowed.

"Perhaps you are correct."

These men were independent, rich and used to being in charge. Which is why before the meeting Preston had decided he'd be taking this bull by the horns.

Don't give them time to think.

"I have taken the liberty of assembling a business plan from start to finish."

As Preston walked around the table, he handed each man a packet outlining how he planned to move billions of gallons of oil from the frozen tundra of Alaska to refineries in America. Splashed in bold across the first page was a summary of their anticipated profits.

"Finally, gentlemen, remember that while each of us will benefit handsomely from this endeavor, the true beneficiary will be the organization we have been blessed to serve."

As always, there was no question of disagreement. Not from a group with roots stretching back to before the Revolution.

In Boston, the year was 1765. Britain's colonies in the New World had been under siege from increasing royal taxes and legislation for years. A group of men banded together, intent on halting this economic assault by

King George on his subjects.

This coalition included men like Paul Revere, John Hancock, John Adams, and his cousin Samuel. Among the leading merchants, artisans, and tradesmen of the era, they envisioned a future free from the tyrannical restrictions levied by their unwanted leader. Word spread of their actions, and within a year's time their membership numbered in the thousands, a presence in every colony. This diverse collection of activists was known as the Sons of Liberty. Even today various patriotic organizations carried the moniker as a testament to their forefathers.

However, during this time of rapid expansion in the eighteenth century, a select few leaders established a secretive order within the larger cooperative, unknown to all but the organization's elite.

They were known as The Guild.

These men covertly directed the actions of the entire coalition, subtly moving forward with a discreet duality of purpose. Their mission was an unbridled success, and in the aftermath of England's surrender, this secretive cabal had shaped the future of America so that their influence extended across nearly every industry and avenue of commerce. Consequently, each man had been enriched beyond his wildest dreams.

Today, in Philadelphia, the direct descendants of The Guild's original leaders sat together.

"Preston, you know we must put this plan to a vote before we commit."

The beady eyes of Chesterton Rupp fixed on Vogel.

Membership was passed from father to son, and only then if the son was deemed worthy. Occasionally, a member would decide that he no longer wished to participate, no longer wished to contribute his services for the betterment of the brotherhood. Invariably, his mind was changed when faced with the reality that disassociation meant death. Once accepted into the fold, the commitment was for life.

Unfortunately, this also meant that all five members were afforded a vote. Vogel's family had been acknowledged as the leader since the group's inception, but its members were accepted as leaders among equals.

"Of course, Mr. Rupp. I simply wish to ensure everyone is fully educated on the venture."

And maybe you'll be run over by a bus tonight, you little prick. One could hope.

There was a reason membership was a lifelong commitment. All present shared in the knowledge of a hidden truth, a secret that had allowed them to flourish for centuries. However, this knowledge would devastate their operation should it ever leave the brethren. It was for this reason that, last night, Preston had ordered the murder of a renowned scholar, an academic who had unwittingly placed himself directly in The Guild's crosshairs, as he had come far too close to exposing their buried secret.

"Do you have any news on last night's proceedings?"

Linwood Graves voiced the question on everyone's mind.

"All is well. The professor is no longer a concern."

Heads nodded, and a few of them grinned faintly. This was not the first time they'd silenced an outside threat.

"And the messengers?"

"I believe they have retired, effective immediately." Preston himself had orchestrated the timely explosion of their van. "Gentlemen, I have a press conference scheduled tomorrow to announce our venture. I move that we put this issue to a vote. Are there any objections?"

Each man shook his head slowly.

"All in favor?"

Slowly, four other hands rose to join his.

"Excellent. It is decided."

The group's designated historian, who had remained silent throughout the gathering, dutifully recorded their vote in a ledger.

"Thank you, gentlemen. Please do not let me detain you."

After they were gone, Preston filled a crystal glass with bourbon and then called for his head of security.

The amber liquid burned his throat as he drank. A warm, delicious burn. Thank goodness that was over and the other Guild members had left. How he despised those men.

The door opened and Vogel Industries security head Frank Keplar strode into the room, his face a stone-cold mask.

"Those spineless bastards," Preston ranted. "Not a single one of them is half the man I am. Only the Vogel line has maintained strength and honor through the years. Those worms do little but worry and suck our resources dry. If it weren't for me, there would be nothing left."

Frank said nothing. It was not his place to speak. While he too had been afforded his position through his father's lineage, the need for a security chief had only come into existence in the past century, after Vogel Industries had come to dominate the marketplace on multiple fronts.

One unfortunate byproduct of their success was that the Vogel family had made some dangerous enemies. These enemies, men whose lives had been ruined by Vogel's great-grandfather through cutthroat acquisitions, had attempted to murder Preston's ancestor in retaliation for their losses. Only through sheer luck had he survived, and through necessity, the position of security chief had been created. Over the years, the position had expanded from a single man to include dozens of operatives, men who answered to Keplar, who was prepared to do whatever was asked of him in defense of Preston Vogel and his fellow Guild members.

"Have you heard anything?" Preston needed to make sure the police had no leads, nothing to tie this murder back to him. Unfortunately, not all police officers were for sale these days, but Frank Keplar still had his sources.

"My man at the station tells me they have nothing so far," Frank said. "However, the government is taking at least a cursory interest in the matter. A CIA agent just arrived this morning and has been meeting with the lead detective on the case, a"—he consulted his notes—"Detective Kristian Nunez. It doesn't seem to be anything serious, but we'll keep our ears open."

This was not what he needed, not on the eve of his most ambitious business venture ever. Preston couldn't afford distractions at such a crucial time.

"Keep an eye on the government agent. I don't want any surprises."

"Yes, sir."

"What else have you learned about Professor Chase?"

"He was a bachelor, never married. He has a nephew across the state in Pittsburgh with whom he communicated regularly. The kid's dad, who was Chase's brother, died recently. I don't anticipate any difficulties from him."

"Excellent. Update me as soon as you learn anything else."

Preston flipped a switch and the room's curtains retracted into the ceiling. While the stress of these past few days had been immense, it had served to invigorate him as well. A renewed energy flowed through his veins, and Preston felt like a man half his age. Having just celebrated his sixtieth birthday, Vogel was acutely aware that time stopped for no man.

As he gazed out on city hall and the capstone statue of William Penn, Preston ran through the details of his upcoming speech for the hundredth time, aware that public perception could be won or lost with this announcement. All thoughts of last night's bloodshed faded as he considered the most effective way to deliver his message and ensure The Guild continued to thrive in this new millennium.

Chapter 10

Pittsburgh, Pennsylvania

It had been a whirlwind few days since Joe died, mostly spent arranging the funeral and dealing with a tidal wave of condolences. Parker was mentally and physically exhausted, and now his biggest client was threatening to move a ten-million-dollar portfolio to a new wealth management firm. To top it off, Parker was stuck in his car, talking in his parking lot.

"Mr. Toretti, sir, I completely understand your frustration. However, you have to realize that it's extremely difficult to make money when the market has dropped over five hundred points in the past three months alone. The economy will bounce back, but it won't happen overnight."

His best client wasn't used to hearing bad news. As the founder of one of the largest gas well drilling companies in the state, Roger Toretti had plenty of experience telling people what to do.

"I don't give a rat's ass about the markets, Parker. I want results. If you keep losing my money, I'm through with you guys."

The man was worth fifty million, and he kept track of every penny. His earnings were down through the first quarter, and while he had boatloads of cash, one thing he did not have much of was patience.

"I'll do whatever it takes to turn this around, sir," Parker replied.

"You better."

The line went dead.

What a prick. The last thing he wanted to deal with right now was Roger Toretti's ego. Parker pounded the steering wheel before climbing out of his

33

car and heading inside, thankful to be home.

When he had started out as a financial consultant, they hadn't included *punching bag* on the list of qualifications. Over time he'd learned there was often a direct inverse relationship between the amount of money a person had and their ability to control their temper.

Inside his apartment Parker almost tripped over a pile of leftover funeral programs. He plopped his bag down by the front door and kicked his shoes off beside it as he picked up the mail. Joe's service had been a simple, efficient affair, a reflection of how the man had lived his life. While Parker had known the funeral would be difficult, he hadn't considered how he'd react to seeing Erika, beautiful as always, among the hundreds of mourners. It hadn't been easy, and they had barely spoken.

After the service, she had said good-bye and vanished. No idle chit-chat, no time to catch up, nothing. She'd just left.

The mail landed on his kitchen table, unopened. Right now he needed a beer.

As he savored the crisp lager, the same thought that had been running through his mind all day carried on its unending loop.

His uncle was dead. It was just Parker now.

Anger welled up like an exploding volcano, white-hot and unstoppable as a freight train. He smacked the table, giving it a good whack and hurting his hand in the process. To make matters worse, his beer went tumbling down, spilling everywhere.

"Parker, you are an ass," he muttered.

The mail was soaked. Upset and feeling more than a little stupid, he got to his feet and began swiping the sopping envelopes and flyers into a soggy heap, and nearly missed it.

A manila envelope caught his eye. Those tight, carefully constructed letters. He knew that handwriting.

It almost looked like...

No way. It was impossible.

The letter was from his uncle Joe.

Chapter 11

Philadelphia, Pennsylvania

Gray and blue shirts fell like trees in a hurricane. Torn-off limbs were strewn about the ground, fresh grass on this mortal field.

Cannon fire shook the earth, as—

A ringing phone snapped Erika back to the present.

She sighed as the mental image of a Civil War battle tale she'd been reading faded away. It was a firsthand account, written the night of the battle by a survivor. She set the brittle paper on her desk.

"Erika Carr."

"It's me."

Parker sounded as breathless as she felt.

"Parker?" she said, heart fluttering. "What's up?"

They had spoken at Joe's funeral, a brief conversation, but their first in nearly a year.

"I'm going to be in Philadelphia tomorrow," he said. "I have to run by Joe's place and take an inventory of things, see what can go and what I'll want to keep. After I get done, I was wondering if you'd mind going over the list with me, let me know if there's anything I shouldn't get rid of."

"Sure. I'd be happy to help."

"Thanks. I also have to get into his office, see what's in there. Would you be able to help me with that? You can take a look at what he has, see if you want anything."

It seemed callous to her, but the reality was, what else would Parker do with Joe's stuff? Parker was a finance guy, not a historian. He wouldn't know a first edition print if it smacked him in the face.

"I can get a key to his office, and I'd be happy to inventory the contents. He did have some valuable things in there."

"Thanks. I really appreciate it."

And that was it. "What time will you be here?" Erika asked.

"I'm not sure yet. It shouldn't take more than a few hours to go through his apartment. Would early afternoon work for you?"

"That's fine. I'll be in my office tomorrow afternoon, so stop by whenever you get here. Joe's office is right down the hall."

"Sounds good. See you soon."

He hung up before she could say good-bye.

Long after she turned her attention back to the Civil War tale, the butterflies in her stomach flapped with abandon.

Chapter 12

Parker hung up the phone.

The envelope had been postmarked the day Joe was killed.

He re-read the single page written in Joe's distinct script.

"Dear Parker,

I am writing because you're the only person I can entrust with this message. We have always shared a special bond, one that I value beyond measure. I must confess, it is against my better judgment that I write this letter. As incredible as this may seem, I assure you I am utterly serious.

I recently had the chance to study artifacts related to George Washington. Two weeks ago, I discovered something terrible in a diary written by his personal assistant, Jared Sparks. Several times in the document, in the months leading up to Washington's death in 1799, Sparks noted instances of unusual behavior by the general relating to his private journal. You should know that after Washington's death, Jared Sparks took all of Washington's papers to Boston, and they eventually made it to the Library of Congress. Amongst all this paper, however, neither Sparks nor any subsequent curator has ever located Washington's journal.

What interests me is a passage in Sparks' personal diary in which he recounts a conversation he had with Washington. Apparently, the general mentioned how a group of individuals, men who considered themselves patriots, would destroy what Washington called "his greatest triumph."

Sparks never learned to whom Washington had referred, but suspected the general's

37

bitter opposition to this group could be found in Washington's missing journal.

Parker, I believe this group is now after me, as I have found the key to locating that journal. I think I know the location, but need help to retrieve the book.

If my conclusions are correct, this journal contains information that will shake the very foundations of our country, and I believe men will kill to keep this secret. Send an email to my work account with a secure way to contact you. Again, I must emphasize the seriousness of this situation. Whatever you do, be wary of any unusual activity you may experience, for I know not what will come to pass from my recent activities. If I do not hear from you, I wish you the best. Regardless of your decision, destroy this letter immediately.

J. C.

P.S. I often recall our times together, our journeys to Boston and other destinations, focusing on what treasures we gained.

It was like talking to a ghost.

As he read the neat, concise script a second, and again a third time, each word became not just ink on paper, but the voice of Joseph Chase, and it conveyed a warning of dire import. Try as he might, he could only focus on the fabled surname leaping off the page.

Washington.

What could Joe have found that would shed any new light on the great man? Why did it matter now?

These and a thousand other questions filled his mind, important and alarming and serving no purpose at all. *Losing your mind isn't how you solve a problem.*

If he was going to get anywhere, he would have to think logically, one step at a time.

Step one, organize those thoughts. He grabbed a piece of paper and began to write.

First, what had his uncle discovered about George Washington? And who was Jared Sparks? He'd never heard of the guy.

Fortunately for Parker, he knew just the right person to help him. Unfortunately, that person was his ex-girlfriend. No matter. Fate didn't always hand you the most convenient tools.

Armed with a plan, he grabbed a fresh beer from the fridge, the hair on his arms rising ever so slightly. He sat back down at the table and reached for his laptop.

Thank goodness for modern technology. What fifteen years ago would have required an epic expenditure of time and energy could now be completed in a matter of days.

Darwin would have killed for a high-speed connection.

Without much to go on, he figured he might as well begin with a broad search, so he queried "George Washington mystery" and was rewarded with over fifty-one million hits.

Whoa.

Three hours and a massive headache later, he'd learned one thing.

He didn't have a damn clue where to start.

This didn't make any sense. Joe's uncanny prescience regarding his demise showed he had known trouble was on the horizon—and that he might never have an opportunity to share what he'd learned. Joe must have realized Parker wouldn't know what he was writing about. There was no way he'd leave Parker hanging like this, with no idea where to locate the "key" he had referred to.

But Joe had been a renowned scholar at one of the most prestigious institutions of higher learning in the western hemisphere. Parker, simply put, was not. Joe wouldn't have expected him to know how to follow the trail without help.

H groaned, running a hand through his hair. *Maybe I missed something.* He read through the letter again, focusing on each sentence individually.

This time, a lone phrase stuck out.

"I often recall our times together, our journeys to Boston and other destinations, focusing on what treasures we gained."

Why would Joe mention traveling to Boston? They'd toured the city after one of Parker's college football games, Joe serving as the unofficial tour guide. Over several days he'd seen countless landmarks and learned the history behind dozens of buildings and alleyways. His uncle had even purchased a desk crafted of wood harvested from a—

That was it.

Joe had purchased a desk made from an old shipwreck in Boston harbor, a vessel that dated from the late eighteenth century and had sunk in the shallow body of water. The mere thought that this boat had taken part in a Revolutionary War battle had been enough, and Joe hadn't blinked at the five-figure asking price.

It had to be. Joe had loved that desk. Was he subtly pointing to it? If he'd thought people were after him, maybe he'd been worried they'd intercept his mail as well.

And the use of *"treasures"* was odd, not normally something he'd expect Joe to say.

Weak, but it was a start. If Parker was correct, somewhere in or around that desk a clue waited, one about the mysterious secret that had killed his uncle.

Which meant that if he was going to make any progress, it would be at his uncle's apartment.

He was in over his head, but at least he realized it. Thank God for Erika and her expertise, he thought. As much as he didn't like it, she was far more qualified than he to conduct a search.

Three hours later he drained the last of his third beer. No way around it now. It was time to move. He stuffed a few days' worth of clothes in a suitcase, moving faster and faster, his heartbeat picking up, the cool wave of energy coming back. What could Joe have found that had, up until now, eluded detection since the eighteenth century? And where would it lead?

The harsh gong of his doorbell sounded. Parker turned for the stairs, but his uncle's final message made him stop.

"… I must emphasize the seriousness of this situation. Whatever you do, be wary of any unusual activity you may experience, for I know not what will come to pass from my recent activities."

Better safe than sorry. He peered out of a window. Below, an unfamiliar man stood on his front porch.

The guy glanced up. Parker whipped the curtain closed.

The hell with it.

Parker walked downstairs to the staccato thump of knuckles on wood and whipped open the door.

Damn. The guy was huge. A veritable monster.

And under his coat, a holstered pistol.

Chapter 13

Sunlight glinted off the polished steel grip of a very large, very real handgun.

But instead of being jammed in Parker's face, the gun was quickly covered beneath the man's suit jacket.

"Parker Chase?"

There was no one else in sight. He was alone with this giant. A full head taller than Parker, the man was a well-dressed, walking eclipse.

"That's me."

"Nicholas Dean, Central Intelligence Agency."

A badge flashed in his face.

Parker exhaled. It appeared this was not an assassin sent to continue the systematic eradication of the Chase line.

"Is there something I can help you with?" Parker asked. He didn't move from the doorway.

"I'm investigating the murder of Joseph Chase, and have some questions for you. May I come in?"

"Wait a minute—you're with the CIA?"

Dean nodded.

"Why's the CIA interested in my uncle's murder?"

"Mr. Chase, it's my belief that you may be in possession of information vital to this case."

Could this guy possibly know about Joe's letter?

Curiosity outweighed caution, so Parker stepped aside and invited Agent Dean inside, his heart pounding. As the thickly muscled agent took a seat on Parker's couch, his hard face betrayed nothing.

Even if the guy somehow knew about Joe's letter, Parker wasn't going to spill his guts straight away. Let Agent Dean show his cards first.

"I assume you've been informed of the circumstances surrounding your uncle's death?"

"To a certain extent."

Agent Dean nodded and then threw a curveball. "Are your parents alive, Mr. Chase?"

What did that have to do with anything?

"No. My mother died when I was born, and my father recently passed away."

Parker forced those memories aside, unwilling to deal with that set of demons right now.

"I understand that you and your uncle were quite close," Agent Dean continued, "and I'm hoping you can help me out. I've run into a dead end. We believe that the men who killed your uncle, and there were two of them, died immediately after the murder when their van exploded."

So far, so good. Nothing about any clandestine letters.

"I can't say I'm sorry to hear that, but what's it got to do with me?"

"The van was destroyed by military-grade C-4 plastic explosives. That's why I'm here. There's a chance the C-4 was stolen from an army base, and as you can imagine, the federal government takes the theft of this material very seriously."

"And you think I can help you how?"

"Your father had only one sibling, correct?"

"My uncle Joe."

"Were you and your uncle close?"

What was he getting at?

"Yes, especially after my dad died."

"Did your uncle ever mention anyone with whom he had a problem, anyone he was afraid of?"

"Not that I remember. Everyone liked my uncle. He was pretty easy to get along with."

This was the truth. Joe had treated people the way he wanted to be treated.

"Did your uncle use drugs?"

"Joe? No way."

"How about gambling? Could he have been in debt to anyone?"

"No. My uncle was on the level."

"Then why did two men shoot him in the head?"

"I thought you were supposed to figure that out."

Dean's eyes narrowed. "Mr. Chase, I'm not insulting your uncle. All I want to do is find out who killed him and how that C-4 got into the wrong hands."

"I know," Parker said, taking a deep breath. "It's just difficult with Joe dying like this. If I knew anything, I'd tell you. I honestly have no idea why anyone would want to kill him."

"What about his work? Did you ever talk to him about what he was doing? I ask because the only item missing from his apartment, as far as we can tell, is his computer."

Parker drummed his fingers on one leg. "Nothing that comes to mind. We would talk about history sometimes, or he would show me around Philly when I visited. He was always doing some kind of research, and to be truthful, it usually was way too obscure for my tastes."

Agent Dean's pen hung above his notebook, unmoving.

"I appreciate your time, Mr. Chase." He flipped his notebook shut and held out a business card. "This is my number. Call me if you think of anything else."

Parker followed him to the door, but just before Dean walked outside he stopped and turned around.

"If I need to contact you, what's the best number?"

Parker gave him his cell.

"Will you be leaving the state anytime in the next week?"

"I'm not planning on it. I'll be in Philadelphia tomorrow, at my uncle's apartment. I need to go through his belongings, see what I'm going to do with the place."

Agent Dean's eyebrows went up.

"Are you the beneficiary of his will?"

"Unfortunately, yes. I wasn't aware until his attorney contacted me yesterday."

"I see. If you think of anything, call me."

"You'll let me know if you figure out who did this, right?"

The agent nodded and then headed toward the parking lot. For such a large man, he was light on his feet.

Parker closed the door, suddenly exhausted. Agent Dean hadn't mentioned anything about a letter. Apparently his secret was safe.

A glance at his watch made him get moving. Nearly five o'clock, and his Krav Maga class started in twenty minutes. There would be hell to pay if he was late.

Parker had read about Krav Maga while in college, and after graduation he'd attended one class on a whim. Originally developed by Israel as a personal defense system for its soldiers, the instinctive, practical martial art had struck a chord with his competitive nature, and he'd signed up on the spot.

Nearly half a decade later, Parker had progressed to the penultimate brown belt level.

With a glance at his half-empty travel bag, he threw on a set of workout clothes and hurried out the front door, grateful for an opportunity to exercise his muscles instead of his mind.

Unseen by Parker, Agent Nicholas Dean walked back to his government sedan and stopped.

In the adjacent parking spot was Parker's SUV. Agent Dean moved between the two cars and stooped down, rear bumpers on either side.

After a few moments, he stood again and got behind the wheel of his vehicle, driving away from the apartment complex, only to stop moments later.

Parked on a desolate street, he waited.

Chapter 14

Philadelphia, Pennsylvania

Try as she might, the epic battle Erika had visualized minutes ago eluded her.

Talking to Parker had destroyed her focus.

Why couldn't she get him out of her thoughts?

Three sharp knocks sounded on her office door. She imagined that Parker had somehow made the four-hour drive in twenty minutes.

"Come in."

Unless Parker had shrunk five inches, dyed his hair jet black and been at the beach for a month, it wasn't him.

"I'm looking for Dr. Erika Carr."

Dressed in a nondescript gray suit, with a slight bulge beneath one shoulder, her visitor was the Dominican version of Joe Friday.

"That's me. May I help you?"

"I'm Detective Nunez, with the Philadelphia police."

"Good morning, Detective." Erika gestured to a chair across her desk. "Have a seat."

The detective scanned the room as he sat down.

"Dr. Carr, I'm sure you're aware that a member of your department was recently murdered. I'm conducting the investigation and need to ask you a few questions about Dr. Chase."

"Certainly, Detective. Whatever you need."

"I'll make this as brief as possible. First, could you tell me about your relationship with the deceased?"

Erika explained that while she worked in the same department as Joe and had seen him on a daily basis, as an assistant professor, their interactions had been minimal. Joe had done little in the way of "traditional" professorial work. He hadn't taught many classes and had spent most of his time either researching or delivering lectures on his findings.

The detective asked his questions, but it must have become apparent she had little idea about Joe Chase's life outside the office.

"One last question, Dr. Carr. Do you know of anyone that Dr. Chase may have socialized with, people he may have spoken to outside of his professional circles?"

The obvious answer jumped out.

"Recently it would have been his nephew, Parker. They grew quite close after Joe's brother died."

"Did you ever meet Parker?"

She felt her cheeks warm.

"Parker and I met in college and were together for nearly a decade. Our relationship ended less than a year ago."

Nunez nearly jumped out of his seat.

"Excuse me? You used to date his nephew?"

"Yes."

"Is that so? Please, tell me about your relationship with this man Parker."

"I went to school on a volleyball scholarship. Since Parker was on the football team, our paths crossed." Her mood lifted as she spoke, the memories brightening her spirits. "He asked me out, one thing led to another, and we stayed together for about eight years. We were living together in Pittsburgh while I finished grad school, and when I was offered this position, I accepted."

"When was that?"

"About a year ago. I moved here; he stayed there."

"What is Parker doing now?"

"He works in finance, manages money for his clients."

Nunez scribbled in a tiny notebook.

"You mentioned that Joe's brother is dead. I take it this was Parker's father?"

"Yes." Her cheer vanished with the memory. "His father was killed while he was hunting about a year ago. He fell out of a tree stand and broke his neck."

"Was foul play suspected?"

"No, it was an accident. One of his friends found him five minutes after he fell, but it was too late."

"Have you seen or spoken with Parker recently?"

"I saw him at Joe's funeral, and we spoke on the phone a few times. He's actually coming to Philadelphia tomorrow to go through Joe's office. He asked me to help catalogue the contents."

Detective Nunez didn't respond, instead putting his pen down and looking around.

"Ms. Carr, do you know if Dr. Chase had any enemies, anyone who would want to harm him?"

"No, not at all. Joe was a kind man, maybe a bit straightforward when it came to work, but never mean or hurtful. The only people he didn't get along with were all professionals, and even then, they had the utmost respect for him."

His gaze seemed to bore through her skull, reading her thoughts as they formed.

"I believe that's everything."

Detective Nunez stood and extended his card.

"Thank you for your time. If you think of anything else, please call me immediately."

She nodded and followed him toward the door. As he walked out, she spoke.

"Detective."

He turned.

"Are you going to catch whoever is behind this?"

Nunez nodded.

"That's what I do."

Chapter 15

Philadelphia, Pennsylvania

A media contingent waited on the ground floor of Vogel Industries' downtown headquarters. Cameramen fiddled with equipment while reporters received last-minute updates. The buzz was practically visible in the gleaming lobby, an opulent homage to capitalism. On a raised dais, the podium waited for Preston Vogel.

Thirty stories above the crowd, Preston tightened the knot of his tie.

Preston's surprise news conference had attracted every major network in the country, and anticipation ran high in the conference room downstairs mostly because nobody knew what to expect from the enigmatic businessman.

Traditional, established, and respected was how most people described Vogel Industries, unless the person actually knew Vogel. They would describe him as ruthlessly cunning, a visionary unable to accept anything short of total victory.

Vogel walked over to the waiting elevator, rehearsing his address in his head. In truth, the plan was simple: if Vogel Industries could lower the price of gasoline by injecting domestic oil into the market, millions of Americans would benefit from the sudden drop in cost.

One pleasant byproduct?

Immense public support.

Vogel would claim he was reducing America's dependence on foreign oil. That this solution was only temporary was not his problem. Once the masses realized this wasn't permanent, their money would already be in his pocket and their support secured.

Things were coming together nicely.

He zipped down to ground level, and the crowd quieted when his assistant took the stage.

"Ladies and gentlemen, your attention, please."

Red lights on news cameras flashed to life. They were live.

"Thank you for joining us on such short notice." More clicks, and one reporter coughed quietly in back. "It is with great pleasure that I introduce Mr. Preston Vogel."

Preston oozed confidence as he ascended the stage. Quite literally, the bright lights shone on him.

"Welcome," he said, standing behind the podium. "I have invited you here today to witness history. I believe that, with your help, America can enact changes that will stave off the largest crisis our nation has faced in decades. Today, we have the power to change the course of history, to help America stand on her own two feet again. I have a solution to a problem, and that problem is America's current dependency on foreign oil."

Murmurs raced through the crowd.

"The United States requires nearly twenty million barrels of oil daily to power industry, produce goods and services, and fuel our transportation needs. Our production is approximately nine million barrels per day. The remaining eleven million barrels are imported *each day*. In other words, more than half of the oil we use is imported, which means dollars leaving America for foreign lands. I don't have to explain that this ratio is wholly unsustainable for any true patriot.

"In the last fifty years, America has seen unprecedented growth, yet the world's greatest nation is unable to sustain itself without foreign support. America should not be at the mercy of any other nation. Merely because another government finds itself in possession of massive oil reserves is not reason enough for Americans to bow to that government's whims. Ladies and gentlemen, we do not need foreign oil."

Even the camera clicks stopped now.

"The answer to America's unacceptable dependency on foreign oil lies beneath the ground of the Arctic National Wildlife Refuge, and with your help, I can bring this solution from Alaska's barren tundra to your neighborhood. No more will we fall victim to skyrocketing gas prices, and no longer will we continue to line the pockets of foreign royalty while millions of our fellow citizens are unemployed."

Preston took a sip of water.

"My proposal to remove this abundant natural resource will allow the men and women of this country to directly aid in ensuring we remain the greatest nation on earth, beholden to none, while improving not only their quality of life, but also the lives of those around them. Americans working to keep America strong is what I offer, and with your help, we can make this dream a reality."

There was no immediate reaction from the crowd; a sea of thoughtful or, in some cases, stunned faces gazed silently back up at him. He had given them every reason to believe in him, to follow him in hopes of saving a few bucks while making America great again.

Financial independence and patriotism. No one could argue with that.

However, for Preston, of course, this wasn't about pride or altruism. This was about making money, but to do so, he needed the public's backing. Much in the same way that the president answered to farmers in Iowa, Preston needed the public and, by extension, Congress, to support his plan. Without a revocation of the congressional ban on drilling in the Arctic Refuge currently in place, he would never earn a dollar. So he was using one of the oldest tricks in the book: a little misdirection, and no one would realize he needed them more than they needed him.

Hands shot up now as reporters vied for his attention. Shouted questions filled the air.

Preston had taken the precaution of briefing a local reporter on some appropriate questions. With the eyes of the nation upon him, he wanted a few softballs to knock out of the park.

"Mr. Waller, with the *Inquirer*." The bespectacled, balding reporter affected a stern countenance. "Mr. Vogel, would you please explain exactly how your proposal will impact America's current dependency on foreign oil?"

"Certainly. While it will take approximately one year to transport materials, build, and begin operations, studies have estimated the oil produced from the Arctic Refuge will reduce America's net expenses on imported crude by up to three hundred billion dollars, simultaneously reducing the foreign trade deficit. This venture will keep those billions of dollars in the country, to pay the salaries of the thousands of jobs that will be created. In addition, secondary markets such as automobile production and transportation will realize immediate benefits through reduced oil-related expenditures.

"Ladies and gentlemen, this isn't just a business venture. This is an opportunity to regain control of our economy, to assert independence from foreign markets. This is a path to a brighter future."

Again the room rang with calls for his attention. Confident he had them all under his spell, Preston pointed at a pretty young reporter.

Too late he noted sis assistant off-stage frantically slashing her hand across her throat.

Shit.

"My name is Megyn King, with the National Resources Defense Council."

How had this tree-hugging activist been allowed to attend?

"Mr. Vogel, would you explain how trashing the pristine landscape of this federally protected wildlife sanctuary to *attempt* the removal of oil, which amounts to only a fraction of this country's oil needs, will solve our problems? What about the countless species of wildlife and fauna that depend on this land's fragile ecologic balance to sustain life?"

This was being broadcast live. No time to let this little girl push him around.

"Ms. King, thank you for your question." Preston offered a smile you'd give to an annoying child. "As to your assertion that we would 'trash' the refuge, only eight percent of the preserve will be available for exploration. Furthermore, fewer than two thousand acres will be occupied by drilling platforms. Over ninety percent of the preserve will be untouched, remaining in the same pristine condition it is today."

Ms. King was not impressed.

"How can you be so presumptuous as to think you can destroy one of America's most valuable ecologic preserves when, on several occasions, Congress has acted explicitly to defend this area from unscrupulous predators such as yourself?"

The smug look on her face would have been infuriating but for one thing. She didn't know it, but the fiery activist had unwittingly gifted Preston the perfect opening for introducing the most precarious aspect of his plan, the one stumbling block that could derail the entire process.

"An excellent question, my dear."

Her grin vanished.

"I have spoken with the Department of the Interior, the agency tasked with oversight of our National Parks and Preserves. Once the chairman realized the potential impact of this venture on the economy, his decision was simple. As we speak, a bill is being drawn up that would open select areas of the Refuge for drilling while maintaining a safe environment for all indigenous wildlife and plant life. With the support of citizens such as you and me, this bill will pass and the American consumer will soon be experiencing the benefits of Vogel Industries' newest venture."

The tree hugger was stunned and, mercifully, silent.

Time to wrap this up.

"Thank you all for coming. My assistant will be happy to answer any other questions."

Brooke stepped behind the podium as he departed. Tomorrow he was hosting some of the aforementioned congressmen in his suite at a Phillies game, and he needed to perfect his pitch for their support, as well as cut checks to their upcoming reelection campaigns. In truth, the men were a collection of arrogant buffoons, but they knew that million-dollar donations didn't come in every day.

As Preston's elevator rose skyward, he caught sight of Independence Hall and his thoughts turned to Dr. Joseph Chase. It was too bad for the professor that his research had strayed so close to The Guild. One more death in the protection of their order was nothing. In every war there were casualties, and it had been an easy decision to have him eliminated. It wasn't the first time Preston had killed for his cause, and it certainly wouldn't be the last.

Chapter 16

Central Pennsylvania

Vast swathes of rolling hills dotted with budding trees flew past as Parker cruised east on the Pennsylvania Turnpike. A scenic drive, no doubt, but his thoughts lay far ahead.

Since leaving his apartment, he'd been consumed with the possibility of finding something hidden in his uncle's ancient desk. However, if Joe had indeed stowed something away for him to find, that something had gotten him killed. Would he be able to identify whatever Joe had hidden, if it even existed? He was a financial advisor and sure as hell not qualified to interpret anything he found.

The only person he trusted to help was Erika. Good thing, because she was also the only person on his list.

A few short hours later, the Philadelphia skyline broke the horizon, William Penn standing guard atop city hall. Parker never saw the dark blue sedan that trailed several miles behind, just as it had ever since he'd left his apartment.

Chapter 17

Philadelphia, Pennsylvania

A city bus roared down the street, newspaper pages trailing in its wake. Leaves sprouted on tree limbs, and from the open window of a car parked in Rittenhouse Square, a radio broadcast floated on brisk spring air.

"It's a deep fly ball to left, and that ball is outta here! The Phils take the lead!"

Willy Harris smacked his steering wheel. About time those bums started hitting the ball. With all the money they'd shelled out this off-season, the team was expected to light up the scoreboard on a nightly basis. A bicyclist whizzed by, and for the thousandth time this week, Willy glanced at the four-story brownstone to see who was walking inside. Same old gray-haired frog he'd seen a dozen times, tottering down the sidewalk, ready to croak.

Why couldn't this place have some fine-looking women? Just a bunch of middle-aged people and retirees for him to keep track of, day after day. It was a shit job, but he was glad to have it. They didn't exactly post ads in the paper for what he did.

Willy grabbed his smokes off the dash and lit up another lung dart. Twelve hours a day he'd sat watching the place, with nothing to do but smoke and listen to the radio.

His assignment was simple: watch the front door, and when anybody walked inside, wait to see if the button turned red. When he'd taken this job, his boss had given him an infrared motion detector, one that you put on a door to tell if anyone opened it. His first day here, Willy had walked into the building and stuck the transmitter on the doorknob of the apartment he was watching. The thing was tiny, maybe the size of a dime, paper thin, and pressure sensitive. If anyone opened the door, the receiver in his car would turn red. When the button turned red, he called his boss.

Willy didn't know why he had to watch this building, and he really didn't care. Every twelve hours another one of the "freelance" guys he worked with came to relieve him so he could grab some sleep.

He got out to finish his smoke and stretch his legs. His arms pushed overhead, and as he stood on his toes pins and needles cascaded down the cramped limbs. All the while, the .40-caliber Smith & Wesson stayed invisible beneath his jacket.

Wiry and of average height, Willy didn't stand out, but the gun was a magnet for attention. He didn't really care if anyone saw it, as he had a concealed carry permit in his wallet for the piece. If the cops were to search his vehicle very thoroughly, however, they might get lucky and find the pair of Heckler & Koch USP 9mm pistols secreted away in a false-bottom compartment under the driver's seat. Those were unregistered, used for jobs when the client required extra discretion. It wouldn't be good if the cops found them, not with his prior felony conviction for assault.

Besides, this was one of the ritzier areas of town, so who knew what some trophy wife out walking her pooble, or puddle, or whatever damn kind of trendy dog she had, would say if she caught sight of his gun.

He stubbed out his smoke just as a guy he hadn't seen before walked into the building. Tall, athletic-looking dude, maybe late twenties. His radio told him the Phils were coming up to bat again as he settled back into the car, counting the minutes until his relief showed up.

His jacket vibrated. Willy reached for his phone, only to realize it was in the other pocket.

The receiver was buzzing, red button shining brightly. No one had said the stupid thing vibrated.

His pulse quickened as he struggled to recall every detail about the guy who'd just walked in. Short dark hair, casually dressed. He hadn't been carrying a bag of any type.

Three rings passed before his boss picked up.

"Yes?"

"The alarm just went off," Willy said.

"Any recent activity?"

"Yeah, a guy just walked in a minute ago." Willy described him.

"Stay where you are. If he leaves, follow him. I'm on my way."

The line went dead, and Willy shut off the radio, eyes never leaving the brownstone. Whoever that guy was, his day was about to get a whole lot worse.

Chapter 18

Traffic was bumper to bumper in the city, thousands of cars filling the streets in a city where millions of people moved about every day. A cacophony of engines, brakes, doors and mechanical noise to accompany the living, breathing mass of humanity.

As Parker navigated toward Joe's apartment, one particularly loud beep blared from behind, the impatient driver furious that Parker would have the audacity to make him wait while he parallel parked. Ever so slowly his SUV settled next to the curb as Parker took his time. Tires screeched and his friendly wave was rewarded with a single-fingered salute as the guy peeled off to stop at the red light fifteen feet ahead.

Welcome to the city.

Once he got out and started walking, however, everyone he passed on the sidewalk not only failed to abuse him, but several even offered a welcoming smile. Apparently the city of brotherly love was just that, so long as you weren't behind the wheel.

As he stood on the steps of his uncle's building, dying sunlight glinted off the key in his hand. The building didn't have a doorman, so Parker let himself in and walked to the second floor. He stopped outside Joe's front door, fiddling with the key. What had appeared a sure thing five hours ago under the bright lights of discovery was now tenuous at best.

Had Joe truly sent a message from beyond the grave?

As he stood, the day's last rays of sun filtered through a window, warm on his face, highlighting the single page in his hands.

"I often recall our times together, our journeys to Boston and other destinations, focusing on what treasures we gained."

What were the chances he was right? Less than he wanted to admit.

I didn't come all this way to turn around. A moment later, he pushed open the front door to his uncle's apartment. Inside he found the familiar surroundings, and it seemed as if Joe were down the hall in his study, anxious to talk, not buried in the ground, his voice silenced forever.

His feet sank into a thick rug as the door clicked shut. A muted illumination filled the hall as he flipped on the lights and headed down the hallway, past pictures of his uncle at various spots around the world.

Stained a deep shade of brown, the desk sat in Joe's office, which smelled faintly of disinfectant, a remnant of the cleaning service Parker had contracted with to tidy up the mess.

Nearly ten feet wide and half as long, it contained plenty of places to hide something. Parker counted eight drawers that he could see, so even though he doubted his uncle would be so obvious, he figured they were as good a place as any to start.

Fifteen minutes later he had sifted through every drawer twice, clambered underneath and poked, slapped, and punched the thing several times. All he had to show for it was a broken fingernail that would probably fall off in a few weeks. He'd found nothing remotely interesting. A checkbook, some presentation materials, old photographs, the usual detritus one would expect.

Stymied, he considered hidden drawers or false bottoms. Maybe Joe had fashioned a hiding place himself. When each successive knob or handle failed to twist, and repeated knocking revealed a very solid, well-made desk free of hidden areas, Parker was ready to give up.

All this way for nothing.

His shoulders seemed a little heavier as he sat on the desk and leaned back. As he stretched, his fist jammed against something solid and electric waves of pain shot up his arm.

What the hell was that?

He'd hit one of two gold pens standing in their holders on the desk. The damn thing hadn't budged.

He grabbed it by the base and pulled, but it refused to move. He pushed the identical pen and stand next to it, and it promptly toppled over. Maybe the first stand was glued to the desk. He tried to remove the pen from its base, but it stuck fast, solid as a rock. Muscles straining, he tried again until it suddenly gave way and slammed down.

A grinding noise came from beneath the desk.

Parker ducked down. A panel had opened in the footwell scarcely six inches across. He hadn't spotted the nearly invisible compartment during his search.

He leaned in further, and the breath caught in this chest. There was something inside.

It was a book.

With delicate care, Parker removed the small, leather-bound volume and studied the cover. *What in the world?*

Worn leather covered the book, smaller than a paperback novel. Inside he found page after page covered with Joe's precise script. A few had drawings or diagrams, of what he couldn't tell. As he flipped, a folded sheet fell out.

When Parker picked it up, he saw that numbers had been scrawled in one corner, but strangest of all, a diamond-shaped pattern had been cut from the center.

What was it? Perhaps the answer lay hidden in the secret compartment at his feet.

Booming knocks came from the hallway.

Parker froze, heart racing. He set the book aside, crept to the door and looked through the peephole to find two men standing outside. One was short and slender, with an arrogant sneer on his face. The other was tall and thick, obsidian hair cropped close to his fair skin. His eyes were stone cold.

Chapter 19

Philadelphia, Pennsylvania

Vogel had instructed Frank Keplar to station a man outside Joseph Chase's apartment building as soon as the police tape was taken down.

When Keplar got the call that someone was inside the apartment, he sprinted to the parking garage. Fifteen minutes later, he parked down the street from his waiting watchman.

Keplar approached the vehicle from behind. The driver's-side window was open; Keplar leaned in and asked, "Is he still in there?"

Willy jumped, his head banging on the roof.

"Dang, boss. You scared me. Yeah, he's still there. Been inside for about twenty minutes now. What's the word?"

Frank didn't answer as he pulled out his phone.

Preston answered on the first ring.

"What?"

Voices were audible in the background.

"Someone's entered the apartment," Keplar said.

"Who is it?"

"Not sure, but we're going to find out."

"Hold on a second." The din of conversation faded.

"Go inside. Tell them you're with the insurance company, building security, something like that. Find out who he is and what he's doing there."

"Yes, sir."

"See what he's getting into," Preston said. "If anything catches your eye, call me immediately."

"Is there something in particular I should be looking for?"

"Anything he touched, moved, looked at, *breathed on*. Call me after you get in there."

"Understood."

Willy sat idly by, cigarette smoke trailing out the car window.

"Put that damn cancer stick out," Keplar barked at him. "We're going inside."

"What's the plan?" Willy asked as the glowing red butt bounced on the sidewalk.

"You and I are with building security. We received a report of an unknown male in Dr. Chase's apartment and are checking to ensure the safety of the other tenants. Keep your mouth shut and eyes open. Don't let him see your piece unless we have to use it. You have a suppressor on?"

Willy nodded.

"Good. We wouldn't want to alarm the neighbors."

Pedestrian traffic was steady at this hour, and a constant stream of drivers chatting on cell phones rolled by, all of them staring vacantly ahead as they gabbed. None of the zombies even glanced at the two men who crossed the street.

A gust of wind sent twirling pieces of trash past their feet as the pair hustled up the front steps of the brownstone. The door to Joe Chase's apartment, halfway down the second-floor hallway, was shut. Frank banged on it, acting as if he actually belonged there.

"Who's there?" a man asked from inside.

"Building security. Open the door, please."

The door swung open to reveal a well-built man in his late twenties, taller than Frank or Willy.

"Sir, we received a report of suspicious activity. I know this isn't your unit, because the owner was killed last week. Would you mind telling me who you are and what you're doing in a dead man's apartment?"

"My name is Parker Chase, and this is my uncle's place. I'm here to gather his things."

"Are you the next of kin?"

"Yes."

"I see. Do you mind if we come inside? I need to call my supervisor and confirm everything is in order."

Parker hesitated.

"It will only take a moment, sir. After I verify your story, we'll be on our way."

Parker finally nodded and opened the door for them to come in.

It was dark inside with all the windows closed. The only light came from an open door down the hallway, and Frank walked toward it, brushing past Parker.

"I'm going to need to see your identification, sir."

While Parker dug through his wallet, Frank and Willy looked around.

Bookshelves lined the room, orderly and filled to capacity. Several oil paintings decorated the walls, and an overstuffed leather couch completed the impression of a nineteenth-century men's club.

"Here's my driver's license," Parker said.

Willy took the identification as Frank circled the room, one eye on Parker the entire time.

"What do you intend to remove from the apartment, sir?"

"Some of his personal effects."

Frank caught Parker glancing at a large desk. A book lay on top.

Frank reached toward it, and Parker flinched.

Gotcha.

"May I ask what this is?"

"Joe's notebook."

Handwritten notes filled the pages of what looked like a journal, a bunch of incomplete sentences, circled words and drawings.

Frank looked at his phone.

"Please gather what you wish to take with you. I'll need an inventory for my records."

Down the hallway, Frank dialed Vogel, the journal in his grasp.

"What's going on in there?" Vogel asked.

"Chase's nephew is here. Says he's going through his uncle's stuff. When we walked in, the only thing the kid had out was a journal of some kind. Nothing else was out, just this—"

"What's in the journal?" Vogel barked.

"A bunch of notes, some hand-drawn pictures."

Frank flipped through the book as he spoke.

"Quite a few references to George Washington and some other names I don't recognize."

"Listen very closely. Bring that journal directly to me. Don't tell anyone about it; don't stop anywhere. I need to see it immediately. Did you hear me?"

Keplar confirmed he had. "What about the nephew?"

"He doesn't leave that room. I can't take the chance he may know what he has. Do you understand me?"

"Yes, sir."

The line went dead.

All this over some dead guy's diary?

Back in the office, Parker was leaning against the huge desk, watching every move the other two made.

"Mr. Chase, I'm afraid I have some bad news. I can't let you take this journal."

The kid's mouth fell open.

"What are you talking about? That belongs to me."

"You won't have any use for it soon. Apparently your uncle got involved with something far out of his league, and he had to be dealt with."

Lines creased Parker's forehead. "What?".

Frank nodded at Willy, who pulled out a pistol and aimed it at Parker's chest.

"Good-bye, Mr. Chase."

Willy pulled the trigger and a deafening blast filled the room.

Chapter 20

Thunder roared in Joe's office.

Parker jumped back and was shocked to see two red holes open in the shorter man's chest. The other guy dove behind a bookcase. Only then did Parker realize the shots had come from the hallway.

Two men burst through the door with guns blazing. Leading the charge was the gargantuan CIA agent from yesterday.

Parker's would-be killer clawed at his chest as he crumpled, the life draining from him via a pair of ragged wounds.

The other one leaned around the bookcase and returned fire, which sent both cops scrambling behind the couch for cover. Bullets tore into the rich leather and a white flurry of shredded padding flew about the room.

As shots scorched the air, Parker peered out from beneath the desk. It was time to get the hell out of this mess. The muscled government agent and his friend had the other man pinned down, but the single gunman had retrieved his dead partner's pistol and was holding his own for the moment.

The only exit was directly in front of him. To his left was the CIA, and to his right the fake security guard.

If he ran now, he'd be gunned down instantly.

Time was running out. Eventually one of these shots would find their mark. If the government colossus and his friend lost, Parker was dead. A stray bullet could do it too. Several loud *thunks* in the desk made the decision for him.

Time to go.

Parker caught sight of Joe's journal, on the floor and within reach.

Whatever it contained, that book was leaving with him.

Now all he needed was an opening. As if on cue, one of the guns clicked on an empty magazine. The surviving assailant ejected the spent clip, and before he could reload Parker made his move.

He burst out from under the desk and shoved a chair at the fake security guard, scooping up the journal as he moved and hurtling toward the office door. He glanced at the two men crouched behind the now shredded couch providing perfect cover fire.

A bullet shattered the photo next to his head. Glass sprayed like rain as pain exploded like a firebomb on his shoulder. He never stopped moving as he bolted from the building, blood seeping from where the bullet had shredded through skin.

Chapter 21

As Nick watched, Parker raced past the two cops, his wounded shoulder leaving bloody residue on the wall. Both lawmen continued to fire at the remaining gunman, slugs sizzling above his partner's corpse.

Trapped behind the couch, Kristian risked a glance around the side.

When he did, a bullet went right through his eye and the back of his skull exploded.

Nick saw it all in slow motion. Tiny droplets of blood dotted the wall, a Jackson Pollock painting from hell. Kristian slumped to the floor, his remaining eye open in a vacant, accusing stare. His body bounced on the ground, twisting around, but all the while that one eye stayed locked on Nick, a dead man watching.

He blinked, but the shots kept coming, and time reasserted itself. His adversary darted from behind the pockmarked bookcase with guns blazing.

Plaster rained down as the bullets sailed overhead.

Nick dove around the couch and fired blindly as the killer raced past. Footsteps pounded down the hallway and out the door, the staccato beat fading to nothing.

Nick jumped to his feet to give chase, took one step, slipped in a pool of blood and crashed to the ground.

Stars filled his vision when he tried to get up, sending him back to a knee. No chance of catching that guy now, not with his head spinning like this. He reached for his phone and ensured paramedics were en route.

When he hung up and looked around, a scene of utter devastation waited. The room had been torn apart.

Five minutes later police cruisers filled the neighborhood for the second time that week. Every window was open, neighbors whispering and pointing at the law enforcement show gathered below.

An ambulance screeched to a stop out front, joining a half-dozen police cars. It wasn't much later that two EMTs came out of the building, carrying the body of Detective Nunez on a stretcher, a white sheet draped over his corpse.

Back inside, Nick sat on the apartment floor, eyes glazed over. It was a hell of a scene. The first five cops who'd walked in had stopped dead in their tracks, none of them ready for the Brian de Palma shootout scene they encountered.

Everyone left him alone, at least until after the body was gone, when a grizzled detective began interviewing him.

"Agent Dean, why were you and Detective Nunez here? This was a closed crime scene."

"As part of our investigation, we interviewed the former owner's nephew."

Nick wiped a sleeve across his forehead, smearing a crimson streak of war paint over his eyes.

"The nephew, Parker Chase, lives in Pittsburgh. While I was interviewing him yesterday, he indicated he would be traveling here today to inventory his uncle's possessions. Detective Nunez and I thought it would be a good opportunity to follow up on a few questions we had, so we came here unannounced. When we walked in, that guy"—he pointed at the corpse—"was pointing a gun at Parker. We shot him, and then this happened."

His arms rose to indicate the surrounding destruction.

"Would you take me through everything, one step at a time?"

Nick gave a summary of the shootout while the detective took notes.

"I suppose that's everything for now."

He put a finger inches from Dean's nose.

"I know you federal boys think you're big shit, but I don't give a damn about your jurisdiction or your office. Don't even think about leaving town until I'm done with this case."

Nick nodded. He wasn't looking for a fight.

A processing team appeared, geared up in white suits and plastic shoe covers, ready to search for the trace evidence that so often broke these cases. Before CSI could lock down the scene, though, Nick stood and walked through the room while everything was fresh, undisturbed.

His path retraced every step Parker Chase had taken.

Chase had been standing in front of the massive desk when they'd walked in, one of them leveling a gun at his chest. Parker had vanished behind the desk when the shooting started, and he'd stayed there until his mad dash for the door.

Nick walked behind the bullet-riddled desk and sat down; pieces of stuffing drifted down from the ripped chair. Nothing stood out, nothing grabbed his eye. Only wood chips and white couch stuffing everywhere. He leaned down and put his chin on one hand.

What was that?

Nick squinted into the footwell. A small shelf was visible underneath the desk. When he leaned closer, Nick could see small brown specks of something inside the space.

Brown specks that looked like leather, specks the same color as the book Parker had scooped up as he raced outside.

"Hey, you."

Nick shouted at one of the evidence technicians.

"Get over here. You need to take a look at this."

Chapter 22

Footsteps pounded down the sidewalk, rubber slaps echoing off row-house walls. Amid the din of Philadelphia, no one paid any mind to the bedraggled young man who sprinted by.

Parker stopped running when his legs threatened to give out a mile later. A weaving, directionless course had taken him far from Joe's building, and for the moment, he was safe. He was also thoroughly lost.

Bent over, gasping for air, Parker took stock of the situation.

On the bright side, no one was shooting at him. He checked his pocket and found the solid bulk of his uncle's book still there. Score one for the good guys.

His luck continued as an empty cab came into view. Right now, he needed to get somewhere safe to figure out what the hell was going on, and there was exactly one person in the city he trusted.

Parker dialed Erika's number, his earlier trepidation at a reunion suddenly unimportant. What had Winston Churchill said? The most exhilarating thing in life is to be shot at without effect? That cigar-smoking Brit knew what he was talking about. Bullets flying like raindrops had definitely put the situation into perspective for him, and suddenly seeing his ex wasn't so scary.

She answered on the first ring.

"Erika Carr."

"It's me."

"You're here already? How was your trip?"

"Very interesting. Where are you right now?"

"I'm at my office. Is everything all right? You sound out of breath."

"Not really. I'm fine, but I have to see you. Is anyone else in your office?"

"What's going on?"

"I'll explain everything when I get there. Just make sure we have some privacy."

She didn't sound happy about it, but Erika gave him the address and hung up.

Once the taxi was moving, Parker slouched down in the back seat, wary of everyone they passed. Who knew what had happened to the trigger-happy security guard? It would be just his luck that they'd drive right past him, and Parker would be served up like a paper target in a shooting gallery. Razors of pain stabbed at his shoulder, a small smear of blood leaking from the wound onto the plastic seat cover.

His plan was to show Erika the book, see if she had any idea about what it could be or what made it worth killing for. From what little Parker had seen of the contents, there didn't appear to be a treasure map where "X" marked the spot. If she could help him out, great. It wasn't like he had other choices. But if she couldn't, and all he ended up with were more questions, then he had no idea what to do, and no one to help him figure it out.

As the taxi rattled toward her office, Parker closed his eyes and thought of nothing. Better that than to imagine what might be next.

Chapter 23

A bloody and disheveled Frank Keplar stood in stark contrast to Preston Vogel's lavishly appointed office.

"Are you sure there's no way for the police to connect us to your dead thug?"

Preston couldn't believe his ears. Keplar had not only failed to retrieve the journal, he'd killed a cop and left a potentially incriminating corpse behind.

"Yes, sir. Cash exchanges only; no electronic trail."

"You heard the police scanner. There's nothing worse than killing one of their own."

Preston massaged his temples. Berating Frank wouldn't change anything.

"Did the other officer get a good look at your face?"

"No, sir. We were exchanging fire the entire time. I never got a good look at them, either."

While Preston was confident that Frank was not in danger of being identified, what both infuriated and intrigued him was the mysterious book Parker had been found with. He had to assume Chase was still in possession of the book, the contents of which could prove disastrous. Joseph Chase had been eliminated precisely because of his research and, based on what Frank had seen, it sounded like Dr. Chase had recorded a portion of it in that journal.

"I need you to locate Parker Chase and retrieve that book. From what you saw, I believe it may contain information that could prove lethal to Vogel Industries."

Frank said he would.

"Have one of your men hire an investigator to dig into Parker Chase's background. We need to locate anyone he might run to for help. And put a man on his house and office."

Preston dismissed his security chief with a wave.

Once he was alone, Vogel picked up the phone. No need to leave this all up to Keplar.

"Mr. Chase is in possession of information we need to contain," Preston said when the call was answered. "He cannot be allowed to continue where his uncle left off. If you discover his whereabouts, call me at once."

For the first time since he'd learned of Joseph Chase, Preston was worried. Guild leaders had kept the past buried for over two centuries. He would not be the man who stood by and watched the downfall of their proud organization. Once they picked up Parker's trail, the knowledge Joseph Chase had unearthed would soon be reburied in a shallow grave.

Right next to Parker Chase.

Chapter 24

On the streets of Penn's campus, cool spring air brought goosebumps to his skin as Parker walked among a collection of the some of the brightest students in the country. Waning sunlight flashed off dormitory windows, amber fireflies glittering atop the Schuylkill River.

Once he located the towering building that housed the history department, Parker consulted a directory to find his old girlfriend.

E. Carr – Second floor.

Filled to bursting with display cases and bulletin boards, the dimly lit building contrasted with his modern, sleek offices in Pittsburgh. It seemed the past weighed heavily on the confines of those determined to unlock its mysteries.

He rounded a corner and voices caught his ear, floating down the hallway as he approached Erika's door. One was unfamiliar, smooth and southern. The second, however, he knew. A smile crept across his lips as he walked up to her door and found Erika chatting with a well-dressed older man. He had bright silver hair worn long, and his crisp suit contrasted sharply with Erika's sweatshirt and jeans.

"That sounds interesting, Erika. I look forward to reviewing your work. I have a feeling the academic community will owe you a debt of gratitude after you publish this research."

"Thank you, Dr. Newlon. I'll send the draft over by Friday."

As he watched, Erika studied the document on her desk, the paper illuminated by a powerful viewing lamp. She flipped the page, and as she read, pulled a stray lock of hair behind her ear.

~ ~ ~

"Erika."

Dr. Newlon had just left her office, and now a familiar voice came from the doorway.

She looked up and found Parker watching her.

On impulse she rushed over and enveloped him in a tight embrace. Just as quickly, she pulled back, studying the man she'd known so well. Or, at least she thought she did.

"You look *terrible*. Is everything all right?"

She touched his ripped shirt, and her fingers came away wet and sticky.

"Yeah, I'm fine."

"What is this? Is it—oh my goodness."

The ragged wound on his shoulder took her breath away. Blood oozed from torn skin as he brushed past her.

"What happened? We need to get you to a hospital."

"No, I'm fine. It's just a scratch."

Parker fell into a chair across from her desk, a storm brewing on his face.

"Shut the door," he said.

Erika did, mind racing as she walked around behind her desk, taking in her bloodied ex. She turned a framed photo to the wall when he wasn't looking.

It was a shot of them, taken after his last collegiate football game.

"What happened to your shoulder?"

He sighed and rubbed his eyes.

"You're not going to believe this."

As Parker detailed the past few days, Erika bounced from shock to fear, with some anger and sorrow sprinkled in between. One of the men who had helped save Parker's life sounded exactly like the Detective Nunez who had interviewed her only yesterday.

A strange pairing. What had a city detective been doing with a CIA spook?

She nearly fell out of her chair when Parker said he'd been struck by a bullet, but after closer inspection the wound appeared to be minor. At least as minor as a gunshot wound could be.

"After I ran out of Joe's apartment, I hopped in a cab, and here I am."

Before she could respond, he removed a book from his pocket.

"This is what I found in Joe's desk. He hid this for me to find."

Finally, amid this madness, something she could handle.

Erika gently took the notebook as years of training kicked in. It was a beat-up little book, albeit an expensive one. Black leather, worn from extensive handling, but nothing unusual. The paper was of high quality, lined and covered in writing. She recognized the script as having been written by her mentor, Joseph Chase. She also noted several drawings—of what, though, she was unsure.

"And this," Parker continued, "is the letter Joe mailed before he was killed."

Parker laid it on her desk. Her eyes flew over the concise script, a message from beyond the grave.

"Washington ... Jared Sparks," Erika murmured. "I've heard of him. Joe never said anything to me about this."

"He must have only just learned someone was after him," Parker said. "I doubt Joe would mention it to anyone without serious proof."

Erika fell silent. The book and the tale behind its discovery were amazing, but where did it leave Parker?

"Do you have any idea who those guys were? The men who tried to kill you?"

"I've never seen them in my life. The one who got shot never actually spoke, just pulled out his gun to shoot me. I would have been dead if it weren't for those cops."

"How did the police know you'd be there?" Erika asked. "They could have called you if they needed to talk."

"Good question. I don't know. Plus, they showed up just when that guy pulled out his gun, almost like they were waiting outside for something to happen."

"Do you have any idea who the two men called?" Erika asked, now in full investigative mode.

"No, the one guy walked away. I couldn't hear anything he said. Whoever it was, they wanted this journal."

She flipped through the book as he spoke.

"There aren't any dates here, just bits and pieces of information. It's almost like a running summary of what Joe was thinking at any given time.

It all appears to be recent."

"Why would he write down information in a book when he could save it on his computer or send an email?"

"Maybe because he thought someone would dig through his electronic files or steal his computer," Erika said.

His face lit up.

"Joe's computer was the only thing stolen from his apartment. He may have compiled this book as an insurance policy."

Erika laid the book on her desk and turned it so Parker could follow along as she read.

"There are some dates with these entries."

At the beginning of most of the entries, Parker noted a sequence of numbers preceding the actual notes.

"Are any of them recent?" he asked.

She pointed at a set that read *20-5-1798*.

"This one is from May 20th."

"May? That's almost a year ago. Check near the end."

"Parker, it's dated May 20, 1798."

He frowned. "That doesn't help."

"It looks as though these are entries from another source that Joe copied. Look, here you can see where the copied passage ends, and Joe references a page number."

"What did he make a copy of?" Parker asked. "And why make the copy by hand when he had access to a scanner or copier? That doesn't make any sense. There must be over a hundred pages in here."

Only once he said that did she finally get it.

"You're right," Erika said, snapping her fingers. "It doesn't make sense, unless it's the only choice you have. Excellent observation. I didn't think of it until you said that."

"Said what?" he asked.

"Joe went through the trouble of writing all this by hand because it was the only way he could do it."

His face was still blank. "Erika. Stop for a second. I have no idea what you're talking about. What did I say, and why couldn't he copy this stuff?"

She took a deep breath and leaned back. "Did the detective tell you about my interview?"

"What interview?"

"Detective Nunez was here yesterday, asking about Joe."

"What did he want to know?"

"Stuff about his background, or did he have any enemies. I was upset when we spoke, so it never occurred to me to mention a package Joe recently received from the Library of Congress. It was a book of some kind, and Joe spent a lot of time in his office while it was here."

"What does that have to do with this journal? You think he was taking notes?"

"No, I think he was *transcribing* it. Depending on the age or condition of what he was copying, he may have been unable to photocopy it due to the potential for damage. Exposing old paper or ink to modern duplication processes can damage the material. Because of this, historians are forbidden from using modern technology on such fragile items outside of a strictly controlled setting. If these notes are really from a book that's over two hundred years old, which according to what I'm reading, they are, Joe wouldn't have been permitted to do anything besides look at it."

"Is there any way for you to find out what book he was studying? There must be a record of it around here somewhere."

As he spoke, a passage in Joe's notebook caught her eye.

"Hold on a second," she said. "That might not be necessary. Check this out."

She traced the words that had grabbed her attention: *My esteemed uncle.*

She turned without another word and began typing on her keyboard. Parker couldn't see her monitor, and she knew he had the patience of a five-year-old.

"Care to share what you're doing?"

"I suppose." She hit enter and confirmed her suspicions. "Just as I suspected. Look at this."

Erika turned her monitor around so Parker could see the screen.

"Bushrod Washington died in November 1829. The last dated entry in this book"—Erika flipped through the pages—"is from November 1, 1829."

The triumphant look on her face diminished only slightly when he replied.

"Who the hell is Bushrod Washington?"

"Bushrod Washington was George Washington's nephew—and the son that George never had. Not only was he an associate justice on the Supreme

Court, he was Washington's sole heir."

"You think the book I found in Joe's desk is a copy of something this Bushrod guy wrote about George Washington?" Parker asked.

She nodded. "I'd guess that Joe was studying a journal or diary Bushrod kept, and while doing so he uncovered information about President Washington. It makes sense based on everything that's happened."

"What kind of information did Joe copy?"

She had flipped the book back around and was slowly studying the pages.

"If we're right, it looks like Joe only copied passages that Bushrod wrote concerning his uncle George. A few of them date from when Washington was in office, up to 1797, but most of them are from his retirement in Mount Vernon from 1797 through 1799."

"Anything in there that tells us why Joe was so interested in this book?"

"There are some notes, but not many."

Parker walked around and stood next to Erika. She saw him sneak a quick glance at the photo she had turned around when he came in.

"You can see where the passages break off and Joe makes his own notes, but they look haphazard, as though his pen couldn't keep up with his mind."

"Well, maybe he was in a hurry or didn't know what he was looking for."

Both of them were silent as they studied the book. Passages from what they assumed were Bushrod Washington's writings had been copied along with corresponding dates, with some of the passages more obvious as to their meaning.

An entry dated November 1792 referenced Washington's reelection, and a later entry from the same month in 1794 related the signing of the Jay Treaty to normalize trade relations with Britain and keep America out of war.

Judging from the dates, Joe had sporadically copied entries from the time Washington spent in office, but had copied later passages more frequently. The time period covering Washington's retirement in 1797 until his death two years later comprised nearly half the notebook's total content.

"Why would Joe pay so much more attention to the few years when Bushrod was around his uncle in Mount Vernon?" Parker asked. "It's not like Washington was doing anything noteworthy. He was retired."

"Actually, George Washington was as involved with the shaping of our nation in his final years as he'd ever been."

Erika consulted her monitor as she spoke.

"You're right about Washington's original intent. By all accounts, when he retired, Washington looked forward to living the lifestyle of a gentleman farmer, to supervising his estate. Mount Vernon produced grain and other crops, even spirits, and required daily management. For his first year out of office, Washington was able to focus on his personal life. That all changed in 1798 when it appeared America would be going to war with France."

"I thought France helped us defeat the British? Why would they start a war with America?"

"The French Revolution in 1789 changed their political landscape," Erika said. "And they were also upset when America stopped repaying our war debt after the French king was overthrown. At the time, the French had been seizing American ships trading with Britain in what was likely an attempt to settle that debt."

"I'd think we would have supported the new French government, seeing how we had just revolted against a monarchy ourselves."

"You'd think so. Anyway, when it looked like war was imminent, John Adams came to Mount Vernon and offered Washington the position of senior officer of the army."

"When did Adams do this, exactly?"

"He made the offer in July, 1798. Washington accepted that month and served until his death on December 14, 1799."

"Look at this." Parker pointed to an entry dated *4-7-98*.

"President Adams arrived today accompanied by Abigail. Uncle George and Pr. Adams retired to the study for an extended period, emerging long past sundown, the strain obvious on their countenances."

A later entry dated July 5 continued the narrative.

"President Adams again called upon U.G. at sunrise. The men took breakfast in the study and remained therein for the duration of the day. Pr. Adams and U.G. were absent for the midday meal, also failing to take supper in the dining hall. It was again long past sundown when they retired."

In the last passage, the word *sunrise* had been underlined several times.

"Adams must have made one hell of an argument to get Washington to come back."

Erika nodded.

"I wouldn't want to do it, but I'm not George Washington. You have to remember he had poured the past thirty years of his life into establishing our democracy. I doubt he could ignore his sense of duty and love for what he'd created."

"What's so important about this?" Parker pointed to the lone underlined word.

"I'm not sure. Keep an eye out for any other references."

The next several pages detailed an increasingly troubled General Washington as he struggled with the offer presented by President Adams. Adams had left on July 6, and after Washington brooded for nearly a week, a messenger from President Adams had arrived at Mount Vernon. Washington had spoken with him privately in his office and emerged a changed man. In high spirits, Washington had left for Philadelphia the next day.

Erika pointed to the entry as she read. Joe had scribbled four question marks beneath the passage. "This is interesting. Looks like Joe thought so as well."

"What would make him so excited about going to Philadelphia?" Parker asked. "Do you think Washington was holding out for money? Maybe Adams didn't offer him enough money to come back, but then changed his mind and paid up."

"I doubt it. Washington was a wealthy man, and money was never something he chased after. Initially he tried to refuse his salary as president, and only accepted compensation to make certain the position was accessible to men who weren't already rich. Chances are we'll never know unless Bushrod made specific notes about their conversation. We may never know."

A few entries later, Bushrod related the contents of a letter Martha Washington had received from her husband that inquired into the state of Mount Vernon's affairs and updated her on his progress in Philadelphia.

"This is incredible," Erika said. "A firsthand account of a letter from Washington to his wife."

"What's so incredible? I bet he wrote her hundreds of letters. It's not like they had phones."

"You're right, but after her husband died, Martha Washington burned all correspondence between George and herself to protect their privacy. Only a handful of letters between the couple exist today."

A cheesy grin crossed Parker's face. "Celebrities and George Washington have something in common. They both hate the paparazzi."

She narrowed her eyes. "Very funny. Look at this."

Erika pointed to several underlined words in the next entry.

"Washington apparently spent some time at the Pennsylvania State House in Philadelphia."

"Why would Joe underline that?" Parker asked. "Is it important?"

Erika didn't answer. "Here's another reference to a rising sun, but he uses the phrase in an analogy to describe the recently deceased Benjamin Franklin."

She stabbed her finger at the phrase several lines lower.

"Time does little to dim my fond memories of Mr. Franklin. Much as his presence illuminated all he touched like the rising sun, so too did the world dim when he passed. A bastion of knowledge, his light still shines and contains the greatest triumph."

The words *rising sun* and *contains the greatest triumph* were underlined.

"That's the second reference to a rising sun. And look." Parker removed the letter that had started his journey. "He also wrote about this greatest triumph before. Do either of those phrases mean anything to you, history dweeb?"

"Very funny."

Erika's fingers flashed over her keyboard. "Nothing on a greatest triumph of any kind. The phrase is too general. Let's see what Google has to say about rising sun."

A few more clicks and she sat back in her chair.

"*Rising Sun* is a movie with Sean Connery and Wesley Snipes. It's also a novel written by Michael Crichton, and the movie is based on the book."

She recalled reading the book, something about the Japanese buying up massive quantities of American real estate. Reading on, Erika let out a tiny gasp when she looked at the next hit.

"Did you find something?" Parker asked.

She pointed at the third link, and his eyes went wide.

Chapter 25

Philadelphia, Pennsylvania

There are few more beautiful places to watch a baseball game than Citizens Bank Park, home of the Philadelphia Phillies. Located a stone's throw from the Delaware River off I-95, the stadium had replaced the team's old home, Veterans Stadium, in part so the owners could build additional luxury boxes to generate greater revenue. Corporations from all over the Delaware Valley had lined up to purchase the sleek, ultra-modern suites.

Vogel Industries owned a box along the third base line, though Preston rarely attended a game. As a young man he had not been athletically inclined, his own lack of skill morphing into resentment of those who succeeded where he failed. He had little interest in sporting events, deeming the contests as beneath him, unworthy of his attention. In his mind, the owners of professional teams were far more deserving of admiration and attention than the athletes in their employ.

The reason for his presence at tonight's contest sat in a front row seat on the suite's porch, munching on a hot dog. Senator Clifford Hunter had been a catcher and team captain during his time at Yale, though his days were now spent in Washington where he currently served as chairman of the Senate Appropriations Committee.

Up for reelection, Senator Hunter was on the fundraising trail, which stopped tonight in Philadelphia. Preston had invited the senator to his suite to talk donations and for the opportunity to have a private conversation about Vogel Industries' proposed oil venture far from any prying eyes.

"I trust you're enjoying the game, Senator?"

The fate of his plan lay in the hands of elected officials such as this man. As such, Preston had to put up with these pompous windbags and make sure they agreed to play ball. It would only take one pissed-off Congressman to derail his entire plan.

"I'd be a lot happier if your damn pitchers would give my boys something to hit."

A lifelong Yankees fan, Senator Hunter had jumped at the chance to watch his beloved Bronx Bombers square off against the Phillies.

"We've only had two hits in the first four innings," Hunter said. "This could get ugly."

"I doubt the Phillies will be able to hold down all that high-priced talent for long."

He motioned for Brooke to close the open-air porch doors, ensuring their privacy.

"How is the reelection campaign shaping up, Senator? I'm looking forward to another six years of Cliff Hunter at the helm."

At the mention of the election, the senator's focus turned from the game on the field to the evening's new contest, which was to secure funding for his campaign. Cliff Hunter's family owned one of the largest scrap metal businesses on the east coast, and before he had gone off to Connecticut and acquainted himself with the other bluebloods, Hunter had spent his childhood learning the art of running a business from his entrepreneurial father. He knew how the political machine worked, that the grease for this giant engine was stored in a bank vault.

"Spectacularly well, Preston. If the voters deem me worthy, I would be honored to continue my service."

Cliff Hunter had to be aware that his reelection chances were anything but spectacular. Unemployment in his hometown state was at record levels, and polls had the race as dead even.

As leader of the largest committee in the Senate, Hunter's name was attached to virtually every piece of legislation involving spending, which put him squarely in the bull's-eye of all the deficit hawks who screamed to reduce expenditures.

"Excellent news. I can't imagine that anyone would stand a chance against a respected and established legislator such as yourself."

Preston sat down next to Hunter, though his eyes never left the field.

"Have you heard about my latest venture?" he asked. "I held a press conference this morning."

The Appropriations Committee was responsible for writing legislation to allocate federal funds to government agencies, departments, and organizations on an annual basis. If somebody wanted money, they had to get it from the Appropriations Committee, and as chairman of said committee, Hunter wielded enormous influence over who received their full request and who went home empty-handed. Basically, if you wanted to get something done in Washington, Clifford Hunter was the man who made it happen.

That's why Preston had invited the senator to his suite. While Preston might not have had the ability to craft legislature opening the Arctic Refuge to drilling, what he did have was a nearly limitless supply of money.

Senator Hunter, on the other hand, did not.

Even in the hallowed halls of Congress, the effects of the great recession had been felt. Campaign contributions were down across the board, and Hunter couldn't pass up this opportunity.

"Indeed I have, Preston. An ambitious goal to say the least. You do realize the Refuge is currently protected from drilling by federal law?"

"I do, Senator, and I believe it is only a matter of time until that antiquated restriction is eliminated. As I stated earlier today, the pristine natural beauty of Alaska would remain untouched while the oil we remove will go directly to the American people."

Hunter said nothing, his eyes on a pair of young women launching hot dogs into the crowd.

"But enough about my little idea," Preston said, showing his teeth. "I'm sure you have far more important issues to consider, and rightfully so. You must receive requests like mine every single day from your fellow senators. A heavy burden for any man."

The unspoken message was clear as day. Cliff Hunter controlled the purse strings and, by extension, how his colleagues voted. He was capable of gathering enough support for a bill to pass, including a bill to open a federally protected preserve for drilling.

Preston turned to leave but stopped short.

"Oh, I almost forgot. I received a call from an organization that claimed to be raising money for your campaign, something called *Americans for Freedom*. I get calls almost daily asking for money, so I wanted to make sure they're legitimate."

"Yes, that's my primary fundraising operation. I apologize for bothering you, Preston. Forget about it."

"Nonsense, Senator. I would be remiss in my duty if I were to ignore them. This country needs men like you in charge."

"Thank you, Preston. I appreciate your faith in me, and I have to say your idea regarding drilling in the Refuge is intriguing. Is it really true no harm would come to the wildlife?"

Vogel's smile could have dazzled a blind man. "It certainly is. In fact, the areas I propose to drill in are a minimum of five hundred miles from any land currently populated by an indigenous species. The animals wouldn't even know we were there."

Senator Hunter looked up at Vogel.

"If that's the case, then I think a review of the current restrictions may be in order. I'm sure my fellow senators would agree."

Preston's chest tightened a notch. With Hunter's support, legislation to open the Refuge for drilling was guaranteed to pass. Now all that remained was to pay the bill.

"That group was called the *Americans for Freedom*, correct?"

Americans for Freedom was a tax-exempt organization founded by several of Hunter's close friends to indirectly support his campaigns through advertisements and commercials. They had created the group to take advantage of the fact that, as they did not directly advocate the election or defeat of any candidate for federal elective office, the group was not subject to a maximum contribution limit from any individual or organization and there was no limit on how much they could spend.

Vogel could bypass any dollar restrictions on donations by contributing to this organization, thereby defeating the purpose of contribution limits and padding Hunter's war chest for the long slog of reelection.

The senator nodded. "That's the name."

"In that case, I'll have my assistant mail this to their headquarters."

Cliff Hunter glanced at Vogel's checkbook and nearly choked on his beer.

A fifteen-million-dollar check could do that to a man.

"Senator," Vogel said as he rose to leave. "It has been a pleasure. I look forward to voting for you in the fall, and to offering you a private tour of my upcoming drilling operation."

Cliff Hunter shook Vogel's hand and wished him well. When he sat down alone, however, he struggled to ignore the realization that every man had a price, and he'd just learned his.

Chapter 26

"The Rising Sun Armchair. Also called George Washington's chair. This can't be a coincidence."

Erika clicked on the link. Several photos of an antique mahogany chair appeared, hand-hewn wood supporting a padded leather seat underneath a carved sun. She pulled up the first one. Two eyes and a nose were visible on the circular face, with golden rays that flowed outward. Only half the face could be seen as the sun began its daily journey across the sky.

"Listen to this," Erika said. "George Washington used this chair for nearly three months of the Federal Convention's continuous sessions. Benjamin Franklin said, *I have often looked at that behind the president without being able to tell whether it was rising or setting. But now I know that it is a rising sun.'.*"

Her eyes danced as she spoke. "The chair was made in 1779 and used by Washington during the Constitutional Convention in Philadelphia in 1787. He sat in this chair while presiding over the creation of our constitution."

"Wait a second. I thought we had a constitution before the Revolution started. Didn't they draft one in 1776?"

Erika stared at him with a look she usually reserved for ditzy coeds.

"No, the Declaration of Independence was approved by the Continental Congress on July 4, 1776, to formally declare the thirteen American colonies were no longer a part of the British Empire. We had been at war with Great Britain for over a year at the time. The Constitution, ratified in 1787, created a new form of government that we still have today."

"That's what I was going to say before you cut me off. Anyway"—he ignored her sigh—"why would Joe care about a chair Washington had used over a decade before? Twelve years had passed by the time Washington returned to Philadelphia because President Adams asked him to."

While it was clear Parker's uncle was directing them to the chair used by Washington, why had he done so? Its historical significance was obvious, but for any connection to exist between a chair the nation's founder had used over two hundred years ago and the murder of Joseph Chase seemed impossible.

Parker flipped through the journal's few remaining pages in search of any other references to a rising sun but came up empty. The final excerpt detailed a visit to Mount Vernon in late 1799 during which Washington had organized his estate and discussed improvements to be addressed the following summer.

"We need to figure out what Joe got from the Library of Congress and look at it ourselves. Judging from how this journal just cuts off, he may not have had a chance to transcribe everything."

A sense of despair rose up inside of him. *Nothing else to find.* As he tried to close the book, however, what he'd assumed was the endpaper came loose in his hands.

"What the hell?"

He wasn't holding the final page of the journal at all. It was a loose sheet, actually a pair of them, which had been folded and tucked away inside the rear cover.

Erika nearly jumped over the desk. "What's that?"

"I don't know. It came out when I tried to close the book."

He laid two folded pieces of paper on her desk. Slightly darker than the journal's pages, they had been folded just right so they fit unseen inside the book.

Erika held up a hand. "Don't touch them."

She ran across the room and retrieved a pair of white cotton gloves that Parker knew were used to handle paper artifacts and protect them from oil on the handler's fingers.

"The outer piece appears to be modern brushed vellum stationary," she said, the paper in hand now. "No visible markings. The inside piece is clearly older, though I don't see any evidence of decay or damage."

The sheets separated in her hands.

"The inner, older piece has portions missing, and four numbers written in the upper corner."

Parker could now see the older piece had holes cut out of it. Across the top was a handwritten sequence of numbers that Erika recited.

"Seven, seven, nine, nine."

"Does that mean anything to you?" he asked.

"Nothing comes to mind. I honestly don't know what this is. It could refer to a date, but I don't recall seeing those numbers anywhere in this journal."

She double-checked, but there was no entry for July 7, 1799.

"It looks like those holes were intentionally cut," he said.

Neat rectangular patches of varying size had been cut out of the thick paper in horizontal rows.

"It kinda looks like Morse code with the different sizes."

"I agree," Erika said. "But my guess is this paper predates Samuel Morse's code by about fifty years."

"What makes you think that?"

"Morse code was invented in the mid-nineteenth century but didn't come into widespread use until the twentieth century. This parchment is made of linen, which was the primary source of paper until the Industrial Revolution. Each piece was made by hand from linen rags that were ground into a pulp, and then pressed into shape. If I'm right, this dates from around 1800."

"Then what are the holes for?"

"I don't know. I'll need to do some research first."

"Come on, Professor. Don't tell me you're stumped?"

Erika blushed slightly, a coy smile on her lips. "I am certainly not. What I am, however, is interested in the other sheet of paper you found, the newer one. What do you make of this?"

She opened the folded parchment to reveal a sketch of the rising sun chair.

Parker's jaw dropped. "You have to be kidding. Do you think my uncle made that?"

Erika removed a magnifying glass from her desk and peered at the drawing.

"It looks like the same type of ink was used to write the journal entries and to draw this picture. Now, I'm not a forensic document examiner, but

I'd say whoever wrote in this journal is the same person who made the drawing."

The hand-drawn chair nearly filled the page, the rising sun on the headrest inches from the top, chair legs extending nearly to the bottom of the paper. Composed of precise lines drawn in a strong, unwavering hand, the overall image was fairly basic. Parker's view of the drawing faced directly at the chair, as though he were standing in front of it to look at the carved sun. *Hold on a second.* Parker squinted. There was something different about this drawing and the computer images they'd seen.

"Pull up that picture of the chair again. Something isn't right with this sketch."

Erika complied, and in a few seconds, he was looking at a crisp digital image of the chair.

"What are you talking about? I don't see anything different." Erika studied the drawing in detail but failed to spot the slight change.

"Did you forget your glasses at home?"

"Very funny. In case you forgot, your uncle is dead and two men just tried to kill you."

"Look at the sun on this drawing. *It's upside down.*"

Instead of the face being in a normal position, the eyes were underneath the nose, and the rays that extended outward now pointed to the ground.

"That can't be a mistake," Erika said. "Everything else matches perfectly. If Joe sketched this picture, he wouldn't have made such a glaring error by accident."

Joe was trying to tell them something, and the answer was right there. A thought had been buzzing around Parker's brain for the past minute, teasing him like a voice just out of earshot.

Erika dropped her pen on the desk, and the buzzing thought became clear.

"He's telling us what to do."

"What are you talking about?" she asked.

"Joe's letter was a clue about where this journal was hidden. Granted, I only found the hidden compartment by accident, but still, I was right. Joe left this book for me to find and sent a letter with the location written so only I would understand."

"Maybe you're right. But what's Joe trying to tell us now?"

"Maybe the hidden book is meant to serve two purposes. One, to keep it away from whoever is trying to kill me. Two, and you made me think of this, he may have hidden the book to tell us the next step on his trail is also hidden."

"First of all, how did I make you think of this crazy idea?"

"When you dropped your pen, it reminded me of the pen on Joe's desk. The lever for his hidden drawer."

"You're welcome," Erika said. "Do you think he's sending us on some type of quest? If there really is something for us to find in this chair, and Joe knew about it, why wouldn't he go and check it out for himself?"

Parker shrugged, unable to answer.

"You seriously think *George Washington* used this chair as some kind of dead drop?" Erika asked.

He'd expected a healthy dose of skepticism, but not outright opposition. "In the past few days I've received a letter from my dead uncle, been interviewed by the police, found a hidden compartment in a desk, been *shot*, and now may have found a way to uncover who murdered Joe. If you don't want to help me, fine. I'll do it myself."

"I'm sorry," she said. "I realize you've been through a lot lately, but I'm having a hard time believing all this."

She studied the ceiling for a moment.

"Let's say I am willing to entertain your idea. What do you propose we do?"

"Where is the rising sun chair right now?"

Erika consulted her monitor. "The same place it has been for the last two hundred years. At Independence Hall on Chestnut Street, right here in Philadelphia."

"I assume the building is open to the public?"

Erika nodded. "If we want to go inside, we need a ticket for one of the free tours. I can reserve them online."

"Good. When do the tours start?"

"The first one is at nine, and the building closes at five."

"Get two tickets for tomorrow morning. You and I are going on that tour."

"Hold on a second. What exactly do you think we're going to do once we're inside?" Erika asked. "In case you weren't aware, we'll have to go through a security screening. That means federal officers who carry firearms."

"That's fine. I'm not worried about them."

Her unanswered question hung in the air. It remained that way because she wasn't going to like his plan, and he was making this up as he went.

"I'm still waiting for an answer."

"Joe drew the sun upside down. He mailed me a letter with the hidden location of this book"—Parker indicated the journal—"written in such a way that I'm the only person who could find it. I think he intentionally turned the sun on its head because that's what he wants us to do."

The excitement tingling inside him went well with the disbelief on her face.

"You think there's some kind of hidden compartment in this chair that will unlock by flipping the sun upside down?"

"Not only that," he continued, "but I suspect George Washington hid something in that chair, and whatever he put there is somehow related to his return to military service."

To his surprise, Erika appeared to consider the idea. "In his letter, Joe said he found the key to locating Washington's journal. If that journal still exists, you may be on to something."

She crossed both arms on her chest as she spoke. "Let's say I agree to go along with this hare-brained scheme of yours. How will we get close enough to the rising sun chair to test your theory? Visitors can only look at the display from a distance."

There was only one option, and she wasn't going to like it.

"You're going to have to trust me."

Chapter 27

Citizen's Bank Park hummed with energy, but Preston Vogel didn't notice as he headed to a waiting car, focused on his next move. The Guild required an update on the evening's progress.

Senator Hunter's cooperation guaranteed the Refuge would open for drilling, and Preston planned on having the only government permit. Preparations had already been underway for months, and now all that stood between Preston and his oil was the soon to be circumvented federal ban. All necessary equipment had been assembled and teams were on standby. They could expect to extract crude oil within three months and sell the black gold to refineries immediately.

Preston grinned. He knew one thing for certain. You could never have too much money.

Inside the diamond-black Rolls Royce Phantom that Preston used for daily travel were hand-stitched leather seats, and between them a combination humidor and cooler, perfect for every occasion. A button caused the storage compartment to slide noiselessly out from the floor well.

He took the Cuban Monte Cristo that came out but passed on the chilled bottle of Dom Perignon.

His cell phone vibrated as he lit the illegal cigar. Preston noted a familiar number on the screen and pressed the phone to his ear.

"The information should be available tomorrow. I was able to access the request records but couldn't tell what was delivered for review," said the voice.

"We need to know what Chase found and what information could have been passed to his nephew. Speaking of that, did you find him yet?" Preston asked.

"Not yet. Frank tagged his bank accounts and credit cards, but we haven't had any hits."

"He must be found."

Preston hung up and stared at the city skyline. Parker Chase was hidden among the glittering lights, in possession of a book capable of destroying The Guild. For over two centuries Vogel and his predecessors had operated in the shadows, expanding their influence and enriching each member.

He'd be damned if it all fell apart on his watch.

With a few puffs his cigar came back to life, the ember glowing crimson with a heat that left red spots on his vision. Parker Chase might have escaped this time, but he had no idea what he was up against now.

Chapter 28

Philadelphia, Pennsylvania

Sunlight filtered through open blinds, which, coupled with the sound of early morning traffic, was better than any alarm clock. Erika loved living in the city, one reason being she never slept in too late.

She padded lightly across the bamboo floor to her bedroom door and looked into the living room to find Parker slumbering on her couch, oblivious to the outside world.

They had come back to her apartment last night, exhausted. She'd dressed his wound as best she could, and fortunately it looked like he wouldn't need stitches for the shallow gash. Parker had been lucky. A few inches either way and he'd have been in the morgue.

Erika turned on the shower and jumped in, the hot water bringing her fully back to life. When she emerged from the bathroom wrapped in a towel, Parker rolled over and studied her lithe form through one eye.

"What about my other two wishes?"

"Unless one is for coffee, don't get your hopes up."

She fiddled with the coffee maker until aromatic dark liquid dripped into a pot. They would need to be sharp today, considering the litany of federal laws Parker planned to violate.

Accompanied by a chorus of pops and cracks, Parker sat up and stretched his arms overhead, yawning as he rose.

"How does your arm feel?" Erika asked.

He twisted it gingerly back and forth. "Not too bad, all things considered."

Erika handed him a steaming cup, black, just the way he liked it.

"Drink this. Our tour starts in a few hours."

The shower started running again as she changed.

Thank goodness. That boy needed to clean up. She didn't want to tell him how awful he looked.

He'd fallen onto her couch as soon as they got back last night, asleep in seconds. When she'd covered him with a blanket, it had been much harder than she expected to turn away and leave him alone, injured and certainly scared. Had it really been a year already?

She shook her head. This was no time to get emotional. People had tried to kill Parker yesterday, would likely try again. She was way out of her league, and all it took to remind her of that was the funeral card bearing Joe's name on her kitchen table.

Speaking of the kitchen, her stomach was rumbling, and it was a sure bet Parker's was too. She opened the refrigerator just as someone knocked on her front door.

Parker raced out of the bathroom with wide eyes.

Erika held a finger to her lips.

More banging, louder this time. And her door didn't have a peephole.

"Who is it?" she called out.

"Nicholas Dean, Central Intelligence Agency. I'm looking for Erika Carr."

Parker had vanished when she turned back around.

With no other choice, she took a deep breath and opened the door.

A man loomed outside. He was huge, his rumpled suit bulging with muscle. Dark bags hung beneath his eyes; yesterday's five o'clock shadow covered a granite chin.

"I'm Erika."

A polished silver badge appeared, and the mountain rumbled.

"Dr. Carr, I'm investigating the murder of Joseph Chase. May I come in?"

"Of course. Please excuse the mess. I wasn't planning on having any visitors."

"No need to apologize, Dr. Carr. You'll have to forgive me for showing up unannounced, but this can't wait. I'll only take a few minutes of your time."

His eyes swept over the kitchen, a modern, open design with new stainless-steel appliances and a granite counter that ran the length of the far wall. Erika sat at a high table with stools on each side and motioned for him to join her.

"Would you like something to drink?"

He declined with a shake of his head.

"Then what can I do for you, Agent Dean?"

Erika tried her best to look concerned. Maybe he wouldn't pick up on how her mind was racing, trying to recall what she should and shouldn't know about the past twenty-four hours.

"Do you have any idea where Parker Chase is right now?"

"No. I expected to see him yesterday. We'd planned to inventory Joe's office, but he never came. Why do you ask? Is he all right?"

Agent Dean's eyes never left hers. "I don't know." He ran a massive paw across his face. "What I'm about to tell you is part of an ongoing federal investigation. If you share this information with anyone, I could put you in jail until the case is resolved. Do I make myself clear?"

A wayward strand of blonde hair had fallen from her ponytail. She tucked it away, hoping that Dean couldn't hear how loudly her heart thudded.

"I understand."

Agent Dean proceeded to relay what had occurred since his interview with Parker, describing the gun battle in Joe's apartment that had killed Detective Nunez as Parker had risked his life to escape with a mysterious book.

As they talked, Erika tried to show distress at Nunez's murder and fear for Parker's safety, and the raw, honest emotions came forth easily.

"Are you certain he was shot?"

"We found blood that's likely his at the scene. My guess is he sustained a flesh wound and is scared out of his mind right now."

"How did you know Parker was in trouble? If you hadn't shown up when you did, he'd be dead right now."

He avoided the question. "You're right. I need to find him before they do kill him, which is why I'm here. In my experience, if someone wants you dead badly enough, they're going to keep trying."

Nick Dean stood and handed her a business card. "I appreciate your time, and if you hear from Parker, or have any idea where he might be, you need to call me."

One step toward the door, he turned on a dime.

"Do you mind if I use your restroom?"

Shit.

"Around the corner, first door on your left."

Agent Dean disappeared, and a moment later a door in her hallway clicked open.

It was not the bathroom door. Moments later, it clicked shut, and a different door, one that squeaked slightly, opened.

That was the door to her bathroom.

Each second felt like an hour, and Erika's entire body tensed, waiting for Agent Dean to come around the corner holding Parker by the neck.

Her heart thudded in her ears.

What was taking so long?

Just as she stood to check, the toilet flushed and Agent Dean reappeared.

"Sorry to bother you, Dr. Carr. Have a pleasant day."

"No bother at all. If I hear anything I'll call right away."

"Please do."

Only when the door closed did she start to shake.

Chapter 29

From inside the guest bedroom closet, the sound of the front door closing was soft as a whisper.

To Parker, it screamed freedom.

His legs burned from being stuck in one position for so long. Moments later, Erika flipped on the light, blinding in the dark space.

"He's gone."

Unable to see, Parker half-fell, half-crawled from his hiding spot, joints screaming at him as his knees popped like Rice Krispies.

"Thank God. I don't think I could have lasted much longer in here."

His back emitted a sharp crack as he stretched, the firework noises a testament to the countless devastating collisions his body had endured during his football career.

"So what did Agent Dean want? Did he ask you out on a date?"

"As a matter of fact he did, and I accepted."

That wiped the grin from his face.

"Very funny. What did he really want?"

As Erika relayed her conversation with Nick, one thing jumped out.

"Why would he avoid your question? I'm glad they turned up when they did, but how did it happen?"

"Maybe you're just lucky?"

"I'm always lucky," he replied with a wink.

"And your jokes are still lame. Do you think we should tell Agent Dean about what we found in Joe's journal?"

"No, not yet. If we bring him in on this, the entire government could be close behind. Who knows what they would do? I guarantee you we'd never see Washington's chair. Joe trusted me to find this book and unravel the clues, to finish what he started. I'm going to see this through."

There was no trace of fear on Erika's face, only a hard determination that mirrored his own.

"I agree. Agent Dean can wait a little longer. Let's see what we find at Independence Hall." She eyed the towel around his waist. "You need a new outfit."

"Where can I get some new gear? I don't really have time to run out and shop right now."

She turned and walked to her bedroom.

"You're in luck. Do you remember how I promised to send you a box of your things after we broke up?"

"I think so," he replied, not wanting to disclose his secret hope of Erika showing up at his doorstep with his stuff.

"Well, I don't want you to think I'm crazy, but when I packed your clothes, I couldn't bring myself to give them back."

Erika reappeared holding a box with his address written across the top.

"I guess I didn't want to lose the last part of you I had." A scarlet glow spread across her face and she stared at the floor, unable to meet his gaze. "I know I sound crazy."

"No, I don't think you're crazy. I know you are."

She actually laughed at that one. "I'm not the one who's in the middle of a Jason Bourne movie right now. You don't have much room to argue."

He opened the box to find several shirts, an old pair of jeans, and the long-lost pair of running shoes he'd searched for endlessly last summer.

"I've been looking for all this stuff. Do you have any idea how expensive shoes are?"

Erika giggled as she disappeared into her closet while he sorted through his treasure box.

"I put them up for sale on eBay, but you'd be surprised how few people wanted anything that belonged to a washed-up college football player."

As she spoke, Parker saw her black spandex shorts and white tank top fly through the air toward a laundry basket. Parker was still staring at the discarded pile when he realized she was talking.

"Did you hear me? There's food in the fridge if you want some. I don't know about you, but dodging that federal inquiry made me hungry."

Food was not what was occupying his thoughts at the moment.

She came back out, fully clothed. "Now that you've got a new outfit courtesy of your wonderful ex-girlfriend, would you mind telling me what your plan is?"

"I'm glad you asked," he said as he pulled on his old jeans. "Because you're probably not going to like it."

They padded into the kitchen, raided the refrigerator, assembled some sandwiches, and wolfed them down in silence, each lost in their thoughts. Only after his last bite disappeared did Parker resume talking.

"The guards wouldn't be thrilled if we walked in and started messing with the sun chair, so we'll take a subtler approach," Parker said. "What time is our tour?"

"It starts in an hour."

"Good. Last night at your office I took a virtual tour of the Hall."

Parker reached across the table, dragged her laptop over and flipped it open.

"What I'm interested in is right here." He indicated a picture on the screen.

"What are you showing me?"

"That, my dear Watson, happens to be the Assembly Room in Independence Hall, which is where the sun chair is located. What I'm most interested in," he said rather dramatically, "is the fire alarm on this wall."

"It's part of your plan?"

He could tell Erika's patience was wearing thin.

"I'm getting there."

He indicated a courtesy notice from the Park Service on-screen.

"A high-school field trip is part of the same tour we're taking. Eighty noisy kids will be more than enough to distract any guards while I pull the fire alarm. Everyone heads outside, and with all the noise and confusion, I have plenty of time to see if our theory is correct while you keep an eye out for any guards. It will only take a minute to see if the sun carving on the chair is, in reality, a well-disguised vault."

She stared at him as though he were an alien.

"Let me get this straight. You want to pull the fire alarm in a *federal building*, then have me keep watch while you desecrate a piece of our national heritage?"

"First of all, I won't be desecrating anything. If the sun carving doesn't move when I'm there, we walk out the front door. If I do find something, I grab it and we'll leave. Either way, we won't be inside long enough to attract any notice."

Her stare could have melted sand into glass. "What about the guards? What do I tell them when they come to check if anyone is still in the building? 'Wait a minute, Mr. Guard. You can't go in there just yet. My friend is busy *destroying George Washington's chair.*' And that's not even considering the fire department."

Erika had always been the rational thinker in their relationship, and Parker knew the only way to win with her was by using facts.

"The nearest fire station is just under a mile away. Even if they don't hit any traffic, I've got at least five minutes, which is about three more than I need. We should be able to walk out with the last of the other visitors and get lost in the crowd, so I'm not worried about the fire department catching us."

She still didn't seem convinced.

"As for the guards, I need you to hang out near the door and warn me when they're coming. Again, I only need a minute or two."

"What would you have me do if a guard tries to come in?"

"Act like a crazy woman and tell him people are stuck in a different room. If I hear you start yelling and screaming, I'll run over and join the show."

As he studied her face, Parker sensed that he was close.

"Do you have any idea what kind of trouble you'd be in if you get caught? The federal government may be slow, but they're slow like an eight-hundred-pound gorilla."

"I've got a federal agent looking for me right now. What's it matter if a few more join the hunt?"

"You realize I could lose my job over this."

"No way, babes. I'm the only one who's going to break any laws, and if Agent Dean accuses you of lying to him, I'll say I came here after he left."

She was on the edge. Time for his trump card.

"I'd love for you to be there with me, but if you don't want to find out if there's anything in Washington's sun chair, I understand."

That finally did it. No way would she pass up a chance not just to study history, but to actually live it.

"You know I'd never forgive myself if you found anything and I wasn't there to see it. Let's do it."

Located on Chestnut Street, between Fifth and Sixth, Independence Hall was the centerpiece of Independence National Historical Park. A registered World Heritage Site, it contained the Liberty Bell Center, in which visitors could view the famous artifact, along with over a dozen other historically significant buildings and landmarks. Built between 1732 and 1753, the Georgian-style red-brick Hall consisted of a central building with a bell tower and steeple, attached to two smaller wings via arcaded hyphens.

In 1775, when the building was known as the Pennsylvania State House, George Washington was nominated as commander of the Continental army inside the Assembly Room, which would later host separate conventions during which both the Declaration of Independence and the Constitution were drafted and signed. America had been born inside this building, conceived by men who had changed the world.

It was also where Parker and Erika were going to violate any number of laws while hopefully avoiding detection by armed National Park Service rangers.

They exited Erika's apartment via an alley that connected her building with a side street, and Erika drove to the Park, located in the historic Old City section of Philadelphia. She retrieved their reserved tickets from the visitor center on Market Street and walked toward the East Wing, where the guided tour was about to begin. A group of high school–age kids wandered about, loud and unruly, just as Parker hoped.

A chaperone's voice rose above the din. "Everybody, gather round, please. The tour is about to start."

Dozens of plaid blazer– and skirt-wearing students came more or less to attention, with Parker and Erika trailing behind as a park ranger led them into the building.

"That ranger is the only one on this tour," Parker whispered, though none of their fellow visitors paid them the slightest bit of attention. "There were only three others at the entrance." Judging from their bored expressions, none of the rangers appeared the least bit interested in patrolling the grounds; instead, they stood in a sullen clump near the entrance.

"With all these kids, we should have no problem getting lost in the group after I pull the alarm."

"Just remember they have guns," Erika said. "You've been shot at enough for one week."

"My main concern is security cameras," he said as he indicated a black device screwed to the ceiling. "That's the only one I've seen. With luck, only the entrances will be equipped. If that's not the case and there is one in the Assembly Room, I'm not worried about anyone identifying me. I'll keep my head down and my back toward wherever it's recording. No one checked my identification, so they won't ever know who I am."

"This is a terrible idea," Erika replied. "But if you're up for it, I'll help."

Shrill laughter mixed with the tour guide's booming voice as they crossed from the East Wing into the central portion of Independence Hall.

Expansive by eighteenth-century standards, the twenty-foot ceilings stretching far above the wooden pillars and finished with crown molding were still impressive. The mahogany walls were decorated with simple, efficient geometric designs, and the overall atmosphere was solemn enough to quiet even a modern teenager, if only momentarily.

"Welcome to the Assembly Room, ladies and gentlemen. Within these walls, America was born."

The guide launched into the litany of events that had taken place here, from meetings of the Second Continental Congress to the Revolutionary War, when it had variously served as a hospital, prison, or even barracks. It was also the room in which the Constitution had been adopted.

As the guide detailed the momentous events, Parker focused. He had a crime to commit.

The room was large, seventy feet wide and twice as long. No security cameras, though his baseball cap was pulled low just in case. The main problem was a waist-high wooden railing that separated all visitors from the display area where the aforementioned events had taken place.

Two semicircular rows of tables covered in green cloth faced a central, elevated platform, upon which stood a single table draped with a green sheet. A pair of fireplaces flanked the dais to provide heat and light during the dark winter months.

Behind the lone desk sat his goal: George Washington's sun chair. Although it was less than thirty feet from where he now stood, any attempt to access the cordoned-off area would be noticed instantly. The fire alarm was to his right, where the railing met a side wall. When he activated the alarm, a siren would sound and the fire department would be notified, though nothing would pour from above in the absence of excessive heat. A red synthetic liquid designed to boil at around one hundred eighty-five degrees prevented a pin from dropping to activate the flow of water. When only a wall alarm was pulled, no water accompanied the sirens.

Across the room, the group began moving toward the exit leading into the Hall's West Wing, where the tour was scheduled to conclude.

It was the best chance he'd get. Parker nodded to Erika, and she fell to the back of the group, then flashed a thumbs-up.

Now or never. The alarm's cover slip went up, and he flipped the switch and an instant later the ear-splitting siren ripped the air.

Chapter 30

Pandemonium reigned inside the security office of Vogel Industries.

Frank Keplar had stormed into the suite that morning and turned things upside down. Apparently, a young man and woman had infiltrated their encrypted server and stolen classified material. Keplar never disclosed what they had stolen, just that whoever located the pair of thieves would get a ten-thousand-dollar cash bonus.

Photos of Parker Chase and Erika Carr were on every desk. The Vogel security team had been going nonstop all morning, tracking their bank accounts, driver's licenses, credit cards, and cell phones.

It was completely illegal, but ten grand was ten grand.

Hours of work produced little result, but finally a real alert flashed across one screen and a technician shouted for Keplar.

"I've got something."

Head in a fog, Frank ran over. He felt like he hadn't slept in days, and probably looked like it too.

"Give me some good news," Frank said.

"We got a hit on an Erika Carr, here in the city. She made a reservation with the National Parks Service for a tour of Independence Hall."

"What's her involvement with Chase?"

The technician consulted a flow chart of Parker's known associates taped to the wall. "They attended college together, and she is currently employed at Penn."

"Send someone over there," Keplar said. "If they're spotted, call me immediately."

The tech sprinted away, dodging through the confusion.

Frank turned and headed for his only sanctuary in the crowded room, blinking again and again against the fatigue. He couldn't take much more of this.

"I'll be in my office," he said to the room at large. "Do not disturb me unless there is a direct hit on Mr. Chase."

Hopefully they can handle this for a few hours. I can hardly keep my eyes open. Frank closed his office door and fell into a plush leather couch. He was asleep in seconds.

His door thundered open thirty minutes later.

"We found Parker Chase."

Frank rubbed his eyes and groaned as he sat up. *The hell with this shit.* "Where is he?"

"At Independence Hall with Erika Carr. They're walking into the building as we speak."

"Get our man on my phone immediately."

The tech ran outside, and seconds later the phone on his desk rang.

This better not be a mistake.

Frank picked up the phone. "Do you have eyes on them?"

"Yes, sir. We've spotted Erika Carr on Fifth Street, outside Independence Hall. Parker Chase is with her. They are taking a tour that starts in ten minutes."

"Are you certain she's with Chase?"

"Positive, sir. It's him."

Old City was two miles away.

"Stay where you are. Do not follow them inside, but make certain they don't exit the building. If you see them leave, call me."

Frank called Vogel's cell. If he knew the man at all, things were about to get interesting.

Vogel picked up at once. "What."

"We've located Chase. He's in Old City."

"Take care of him," Vogel said. "Permanently."

The line went dead.

Frank walked to a keypad set into the wall in a corner of his office. He punched in five numbers, which caused the false wall beside him to swing open, revealing a doorway. This led to a second door constructed of blacked-out bulletproof glass. He leaned over and let a laser scan his retina, and then the final door slid open to reveal a room-sized safe.

A personal safe room, designed to the specifications of the UBS Bank in Zurich. Bulletproof Kevlar walls surrounded him on all four sides, with a concealed escape hatch hidden behind the rear wall.

A Heckler & Koch MSG90 sniper rifle hung on the wall in front of him. Dozens of other firearms lined the room, but he paid them no mind.

Frank had eyes for only one beauty today.

A militarized version of the standard H&K PSG1, the MSG90 offered a basic 3G barrel instead of the usual heavy barrel, which allowed for the attachment of a suppressor. A device built for one purpose only.

To kill.

Now appropriately armed, Frank grabbed his cell phone and dialed with a song in his heart.

"Yes, Mr. Keplar?"

"Bring the black truck to my garage elevator. I'll be there momentarily. We need to make a short trip to Old City."

The first level of the parking garage located underneath Vogel Industries' building was reserved for executive-level employees. He took an elevator down, stepped out and saw the black Cadillac Escalade with his deputy director of security behind the wheel.

"Go to Fifth and Market," he instructed as he climbed into the backseat.

The engine's throaty roar reverberated through the underground garage as six thousand pounds of Detroit steel shot onto JFK Boulevard and headed east. Sunlight reflected off skyscrapers as they passed through the busy downtown area. Pedestrians filled the sidewalks and bicyclists competed with all manner of vehicles for space on the crowded roadway. He looked out to find a young man pedaling furiously less than a foot from his tinted bulletproof window.

Independence Hall was normally a crowded, busy area of the city, popular with tourists and surrounded by office buildings. Today was no exception. Frank signaled for the driver to park at Sixth and Walnut, giving him a clear view of the exit doors of Independence Hall, and then he called the man who had spotted Chase.

"Are they still here?" Frank asked.

"Yes, sir. The tour started twenty-five minutes ago and is scheduled to last for another twenty."

"Are you certain they're still inside?"

"Affirmative. I've been circling the building on foot from the moment they walked in."

"Well done. Carry on until you hear from me."

An interesting feature of the luxury vehicle in which he rode was that not only did the windows roll up and down vertically, they were capable of being maneuvered horizontally as well. Frank had also ordered a supercharged engine to replace the standard model, installed blast-resistant armor on the undercarriage and bulletproof glass throughout the vehicle, as well as adding a second fuel tank.

His window slid open enough to allow the suppressor to poke out. From where they were parked, Frank had a direct shot at anyone who walked out of Independence Hall.

His phone buzzed.

"What is it?"

"Something's going on over here, sir. I think the fire alarm just went off."

"Get inside. Find Chase and don't let him out of your sight."

Frank peered through the rifle's scope to see his asset rebuffed by the Park Service guard. After the asset had made several futile attempts to enter, the armed guard gestured emphatically that not only was he capable of guiding tourists outside, he could also put someone under arrest for failing to obey his orders. The asset wisely decided to walk away, phone in hand.

"They wouldn't—"

"I saw. How many doors does that place have?"

"Only two, front and back."

"Go to the front door. I'll watch the main exit. Call me immediately if you spot Chase, and whatever you do, don't lose him."

Frank peered through the scope on his rifle, studying faces as people streamed outside.

Chapter 31

Inside the office of the late Detective Kristian Nunez, Nicholas Dean pounded away at the keyboard on the desk set up for him, a half-empty coffee pot at his side.

Parker Chase didn't know it, but a net had been cast, far and wide. Despite its inherent lumbering nature, the FBI excelled in electronic surveillance. Seeing as how it was virtually impossible to exist without creating a digital footprint, it was only a matter of time until Parker flashed on the FBI's radar.

However, to be on the safe side, Nick had added Erika Carr to his search parameters after he returned from her apartment.

An alert popped up. Erika had two tickets for a tour today.

A pair of tickets? Perhaps the professor wasn't as innocent as she claimed.

Nick had an hour to kill before her tour started. If he was going to tail her today, he needed food.

And in this city, that meant one thing.

Opened in 1966, Geno's was a Philadelphia institution, known throughout the world, along with their fiercest competitor, Pat's, as one of the best places to get a famous Philly cheesesteak. It was lunchtime, and the line stretched down the street. Orders were taken and paid for at the first window, hot food delivered at the next. Nick took his greasy, steaming, dripping sandwich back to the car and dug in.

His cell phone buzzed after one bite. *Of course.*

Molten cheese dripped as Nick fumbled to answer.

"Dean here."

"Agent Dean, this is Philadelphia Homicide Detective Weir."

A lifelong friend of Kristian's, Detective Weir had volunteered to aid Nick in his search after Nunez's murder.

"We just got notice of an active fire alarm at Independence Hall."

Now, that *was* interesting. "Thanks for the call, Detective."

Nick rang off and, with a glance at his half-eaten sandwich, put the cruiser in drive and took off.

Red lights swirled on his roof as he sped through traffic, and a minute later the tall, elegant red-brick structure came into view, the National Park buildings surrounded by a low wall and green grass. Right now it also contained several hundred visitors, all of them focused on the Hall, from which a stream of people emerged as an alarm blared.

The closer Nick got, the less effect his flashing light had on traffic. A block from his destination, Nick parked by a fire hydrant and hopped out.

Sunlight warmed blooming trees that lined the walkway, fresh buds swaying on a spring breeze. Nick pushed through the crowd as car horns blared behind him. Hundreds of people milled about the grassy square.

Nick towered above the crowd, scanning every face as he moved without finding either Parker or Erika. The crowds that had gathered around Independence Hall began to disperse as he approached, further crowding the grassy expanse.

They were here, somewhere in this mass of people.

But where?

Chapter 32

Philadelphia, Pennsylvania

Blinding white strobe lights flashed and a wailing siren split the air.

Within seconds, the tour guide began leading everyone to the closest exit. Erika made a show of assisting others, and in all the confusion, no one noticed Parker slip over the waist-high railing. He ducked down and ran to the sun chair, dropping to the floor behind it. In minutes the building would be filled with firefighters in search of a blaze.

The sun carving failed to budge when he tried to twist its smiling visage upside down. *Damn. I'd better not be wrong.* He twisted again, pushing until the wood threatened to fall off, when with a crack he broke the rust of centuries and the grinning orb pivoted to reveal a hollowed-out space within the backrest.

Joe had been right.

Everything else faded away as he gazed on the postcard-sized leather package, secured with a length of twine. He reached for the soft, supple pouch as chaos reigned all around him, and as he clutched the knotted string, a park ranger appeared from the main hall and quickly scanned the room.

"Everyone, please exit through these doors. This is not a drill."

Parker dropped to the ground and froze, his heart thundering.

"Over here!" Erika yelled, pointing to the door. "We need help."

Only once the ranger vanished did Parker stuff the pouch under his shirt, dart over the railing and scamper to her side.

"Well?" She glared at him.

He was silent as they hurried out, among the last to exit.

She smacked his arm, and Parker nodded curtly.

"We need to get out of here first," he said.

When they were safely outside, he pulled the package from beneath his shirt.

Erika's eyes widened in disbelief.

"So it's true…" she said.

"Let's see what's in here." He began to undo the twine.

"Be careful with it," Erika said. "Don't damage anything."

As Parker unwound the string, someone grabbed his arm in a vise-like hold.

He looked up into the unsmiling face of CIA Agent Nick Dean.

"Good afternoon, Mr. Chase."

How had he found them?

Dean turned to Erika. "Dr. Carr, do you understand that I could arrest you right now for obstructing a federal investigation?"

Erika didn't respond.

"If you have one brain cell in your head, you're going to tell me what the hell is going on."

Parker glanced at Erika, who shrugged. *Time to come clean.*

"Joe sent me a letter before he died," Parker said. "I didn't receive it until after his funeral."

"Did he tell you about the secret compartment in his desk?" Nick asked.

"Not specifically. He said his life was in danger, that someone was after him because of some research he was doing."

Nick said nothing, but he didn't arrest them either.

"He mentioned his desk in a way that made me suspect he'd hidden something in it. I didn't know for sure if there was anything to find when I came out here." Parker explained how he'd accidentally knocked a false pen over and revealed the hidden compartment.

"Why would your uncle hide his journal?" Nick asked.

Parker told Nick about the journal's contents, from how Joe had copied down a host of entries he believed were written by George Washington's nephew, to the sketches of the sun chair with an inverted face on the backrest and his theory that this had been purposeful, indicative of a hidden artifact.

"Were you right about the sun chair?"

Parker indicated the leather package.

"The carving moved when I pushed it, exactly like the picture indicated. I found this inside."

As Parker held out the leather case, a red-haired woman jogging through the crowd turned directly toward their group. Earbuds snaked from an iPod on her hip. He stood back to let her through.

When she passed between them, her head exploded.

Chapter 33

Philadelphia, Pennsylvania

Blue skies promised a warm spring day for the Delaware Valley, but on the top floor of his downtown skyscraper, Preston Vogel stormed around like a cyclone.

Senator Hunter was scheduled to update him this morning on his progress. A bill had been introduced to open the Arctic National Wildlife Refuge for exploratory drilling by a single entity. It was grouped with dozens of other proposals, and Congress had convened over the weekend to tackle the backlog of legislation. Preston could only wait to see if Cliff Hunter had drummed up sufficient support to pass the bill.

His desk phone chirped.

"Sir, Senator Hunter is on the phone."

Finally.

"Thank you, Brooke. Put him through."

"Preston, how are you?" Cliff Hunter's cheery voice boomed through Vogel's office.

"That depends on whether or not you got my votes."

"I trust this is a secure line?"

"It is."

"In that case, I'll get to the point. My colleagues in the Senate were easily convinced regarding the merits of your proposal. The House was slightly more resistant. More than a few members are concerned with violating such a pristine landscape."

Preston found that hard to believe, considering that the *Washington Times* had recently referred to the Refuge as 'a mosquito-infested swamp that is shrouded in frozen darkness for nearly half the year.'

"Fortunately, my aides tell me that as of twenty minutes ago, we have two hundred twenty votes in favor of the bill."

A simple majority of all voting members was required to pass a bill in both the House and Senate. With four hundred thirty-five members in the House of Representatives, two hundred eighteen votes was the threshold for passage if all members voted.

Two hundred twenty votes guaranteed his plan had passed.

Which meant Cliff Hunter had just made Preston an obscene amount of money.

"Senator, that is wonderful news. You are a true patriot."

"The real winner today is the American citizen. Following the official vote, I look forward to an announcement detailing exactly how many jobs will be created, and how much revenue will be generated by your operation. The American economy is in sore need of a shot in the arm right now. I trust Vogel Industries will provide just that."

As much as Preston despised the control men such as Hunter wielded, elected officials could be useful on occasion.

"You'll receive an advance copy prior to the announcement for your review."

Hunter cleared his throat. "Also, after the vote is completed, my office will announce the creation of an interagency task force to expedite all necessary approvals and ensure Vogel Industries is awarded the sole lease to drill."

Preston was only half-listening, his mind reeling with the thought of making so much easy money.

"I have it on good authority that an air pollution exception will be issued so that drilling operations may commence immediately."

It damn well better be.

"Thank you for the update, Senator. I'll be in touch."

Preston hung up and called Frank Keplar. They couldn't afford any negative publicity now, not with the vote at hand. Right now the only person who could thwart his plans was Parker Chase. The man had apparently unearthed an item left by his uncle, and Preston had a sinking suspicion about what it pertained to.

Joseph Chase had been killed for a simple, straightforward reason. His research had veered too close to The Guild's true origins. On the verge of the most lucrative venture they had ever undertaken, it was no time for loose ends. Unfortunately, Parker Chase was exactly that.

"Dammit, answer the phone."

His call rang through to voice mail. Strange, as Frank Keplar almost never missed a call from his superior.

The light on his desk phone flashed red.

"What is it?"

"You have a call, sir. On your private line."

"Put it through."

A velvety smooth voice sounded in his office.

"Preston, you're not going to believe this. Those kids are on the right track. They could actually find it. The University of Pennsylvania logs all incoming research material, and I found what Chase ordered from the Library of Congress."

Preston's hands clenched into fists.

"What was it?"

"The diary of a man named Bushrod Washington. Nephew of George."

The breath caught in Preston's throat.

"You realize what this means, don't you?"

"It certainly isn't good."

"Please tell me you have the journal," Preston said.

"I had to place a request, and it should arrive tomorrow. I'll review it immediately."

"Call me when you've finished. I don't have to tell you what could happen if this information is uncovered."

The line went dead. Preston sat motionless with dismay and disbelief. This could not have come at a worse time. On the verge of completing the deal of his life, he suddenly found himself faced with a ghost, a long-buried secret that could ruin it all.

Chapter 34

A bullet ruined the jogger's head.

Her corpse, all blood and sweat, barreled into Parker's chest, the literal dead weight enough to knock him down and save his life.

The next two bullets flew high. One hit a tourist standing beside Nick; the middle-aged woman crumpled to the ground with blood pouring from a mangled arm.

Hysteria erupted. People ran blindly, screaming incoherently, some falling to be trampled underfoot as the crowd raced for safety.

Parker lay pinned to the ground by the dead jogger's corpse.

Where was Erika?

He shoved the lifeless woman off his chest and began to scramble to his feet.

"Don't get up," Nick yelled from where he lay on the ground. Erika was beside him, unharmed.

Where had the shots come from? Parker searched the crowds as people ran frantically in every direction.

Nick pulled his pistol out and scurried to a brick wall encircling the yard, though the waist-high barrier seemed to offer little protection for his massive frame.

Ignoring his order, Parker leapt up and darted through the churning sea of tourists to join Nick, dragging Erika along with him.

"Stay low until I figure out where the shots are coming from," Nick said.

Erika's hand was trembling; Parker pulled her close as they crouched down behind the wall.

"Do you have your keys?"

Erika produced a set from her pocket.

His only plan was to get the hell out of there as fast as possible. Nick could figure this out on his own. Parker gave a jerk of his head, and then held tightly to her arm as he raced back out into the crowd. The last he saw of Nick, the CIA agent was peering over the short wall in search of a target.

Parker had been in the middle of one gunfight already this week. He was in no mood for a second.

The crowd provided enough cover for them that no more shots were fired, but Parker figured chances were good that whoever was shooting didn't care about hitting innocent people. The shooter had already hit a few bystanders, and if it hadn't been for the jogger darting in between them, Parker knew it would have been his own body lying on the sidewalk.

"Who shot at us?" Erika panted as they ran. "Was it the same person who tried to kill you earlier?"

"I didn't see—"

A man slammed into Parker, knocking him to the ground.

As he got back to his feet, Parker spotted the gun holstered inside the man's jacket at the same time as the guy punched him in the face. He rolled with the punch and let his Krav Maga training kick in.

Parker blocked the next shot aimed at his face while he used his other hand to rip the holstered weapon from inside his assailant's jacket and throw it.

The guy swung again, but Parker dodged the punch, grabbed the guy's arm and pulled him in close to land two kidney shots.

"Come on." Parker turned and reached for Erika, only to be pulled down again when the man grabbed his ankle and yanked back. As the ground rushed up to meet him, Parker threw a blind elbow that landed home.

Got you.

The man fell, but twisted his body to deliver a swift kick that swept Parker's legs from underneath him. The attacker jumped to his feet and held out a gleaming blade as Parker lay on his back, winded and fully exposed. Suddenly his eyes rolled back, and he went limp. The unconscious man fell heavily to reveal Erika standing behind him with a gun, her hands wrapped around the barrel as though it were a club.

"I grabbed it when you knocked it away," she said.

"Nice work."

The gun started to quiver in her hands.

"Parker, what's going on? Who are these people?"

He stood with difficulty, took the weapon from her and put one hand on her shoulder.

"I don't know."

In the confusion, only a few people had taken note of the fight. One woman stared at them with her mouth hanging open.

The gun.

"Follow me," Parker said. "That guy might have friends."

Parker shoved the pistol into his pocket as they ran. They pushed through the crush of people to Erika's car. She blipped the locks as they approached and they scrambled in.

"Where should we go?" Erika asked as she twisted the key in the ignition. The engine roared to life and she peeled away from the curb.

"I don't know," he said as she maneuvered through traffic. "Away from here."

"Do you still have it?"

Parker removed their prize from his pocket and handed it to her.

The size of a modern postcard, held together by a single length of fine rope, it resembled a small leather purse.

Erika stopped at a red light, unbound the rope and flipped the stolen satchel open.

"There are two letters burned into the leather. *G* and *W*."

The light turned green again and Erika turned her attention back to the road.

"We need to get back to my office," she said.

He knew better than to argue. He took the package back from her and stuffed it in his pocket.

They pulled into the turn lane so they could get onto I-76, the fastest way back to University City. Parker glanced in his side mirror and saw a motorcycle slipping between the rows of slower traffic, headed their way. The driver's helmet visor was open, revealing a familiar face.

"Oh, shit."

"What? What's oh shit?"

"You see that bike behind us? It's the guy who tried to kill me at Joe's apartment."

The bike was only three cars behind them now, and as soon as Erika swerved out of line toward the highway, the driver spotted her car.

He pulled a gun from beneath his jacket and aimed directly at them.

Chapter 35

The crosshairs on his scope settled on Parker's head. Safely ensconced within the oversized SUV, Frank breathed evenly and pulled the trigger.

Only for a jogger to come out of nowhere, directly into his line of fire. He could only curse when her head exploded instead of Parker's.

He ripped off two more shots, missing with both.

"Get out of here," he instructed his driver. "I'll meet you back at headquarters."

Frank jumped out, phone in hand.

"Find Chase and take him out," he shouted at the other operative outside Independence Hall. "No one will notice in this mess."

"Understood." The man disappeared into the commotion.

Pandemonium reigned on the picturesque square. People pressed against him from all sides, forcing Frank to shoulder his way through like a linebacker.

Slowly the sea of humans parted and the dead jogger appeared at his feet, looking like a dropped doll. Parker, Erika, and their companion had vanished.

Where would I go if I were them?

He glanced wildly around, his gaze lighting on the rows of cars lined up at the curb. *Yes.* Erika drove a dark blue Volkswagen.

Frank raced back to the street, but when he barreled through a shell-shocked group of elderly tourists, he nearly tripped over the agent he'd sent to take Chase out minutes ago. The man was flat on the ground with blood leaking from a broken nose.

Useless.

He looked up as a blue Volkswagen rolled past with a familiar face behind the wheel.

Erika Carr. And Parker Chase was in the passenger seat

As she halted at a stop light, Frank saw a red sport bike idling not ten feet away. Frank ran to the machine and shoved the driver off, flashing his gun in the guy's face when he started to argue. Ahead of him the blue sedan began to inch toward the expressway on-ramp. Frank leveled his gun as Parker locked eyes with him.

Erika floored the accelerator and shot through oncoming traffic, narrowly avoiding a head-on collision before she skidded down the on-ramp. The agile coupe hugged the ground as they barreled down the shoulder onto an eight-lane expressway, Frank goosing the motorcycle throttle and mirroring their path.

The Schuylkill Expressway connects the city of Philadelphia with its outlying suburbs, a sprawling yet congested region of scenic beauty home to millions of people. Although the expressway was normally a parking lot during rush hour, late morning traffic moved rapidly as Parker and Erika flew over the endless asphalt.

Erika accelerated around several vehicles, but the street bike followed her with ease.

"I can't outrun that thing," she said.

The Volkswagen's four-cylinder engine sounded like a plane straining to get airborne.

"Try to keep cars between us and him," Parker said. "If he's worried about maneuvering that thing, he won't be able to get a shot off."

A sharp crack ripped the air followed by a dull *thunk* from the rear. "Or maybe he will."

"What did he hit?" Erika asked. "Are you all right?" Keeping her focus on the road, she swerved between cars, every driver staring at the maniac passing them at nearly a hundred miles an hour.

She braked sharply to negotiate a sharp curve and sent Parker jolting against his seatbelt. The gun he'd grabbed minutes ago vanished into the footwell.

"Are you going to shoot back or what?"

Releasing the belt lock, he bent down, grabbed the firearm and twisted around, eyes on the speeding bike. The driver buzzed past another vehicle and leveled his gun.

"Hold on," Erika said.

She stomped on the brakes. The gunman swerved viciously mere feet from their rear bumper, narrowly avoiding the much sturdier sedan, his front tire wobbling as he passed.

She twisted the wheel and tried to smash the bike as it came level with them. At the last second, the bike's wheels gained purchase on the shoulder and shot forward. A storm of gravel bounced off Erika's windshield.

"Damn," Parker said. "Nice move though. Try and keep it steady."

The engine's roar was replaced with the shriek of wind as Parker rolled down his window. Erika's hair flapped, stinging her face like tiny cat's teeth.

Parker leaned out with one hand on the doorframe and took aim. Ahead of them, the biker had regained control and was looking around in search of his target.

Parker fired twice before the bike cut in front of a tractor trailer and disappeared.

"Try and catch him," Parker said. "I'd rather be shooting at his ass end than the other way around."

Erika pulled out and flew past the truck, but the tiny bike was nowhere to be found.

"Where did he go?" she shouted.

Parker craned his neck, peering amongst the other vehicles. No sign of him.

She gritted her teeth. She didn't have a gun, but her Volkswagen was a lot bigger than that bike. She would crush the bastard if she got a chance, bury him between two cars.

Suddenly Parker put the gun inches from her nose and fired.

Her ears stopped working. Shattered window glass nicked her face at the same time she spotted two bursts of fire coming from her left side. The biker was back and firing at them, sending a pair of bullets into the car. The radio dial exploded into a million fragments of glass and plastic.

A fog filled her head. The biker whipped past them again, flashing across several lanes before disappearing into traffic ahead. Her ears felt like they were filled with water. She saw Parker's mouth moving. *Take a deep breath.* Her chest felt tight and her hands shook on the wheel. *No time for this now*. She breathed in, out, in again, and held the car steady as they raced along.

Slowly, like a movie reel picking up speed, her hearing filtered back and Parker's voice came sharply into focus.

"Are you all right? Erika, answer me."

"Yes, yes, I'm fine."

"Sorry about that," he shouted. "He popped up out of nowhere."

They rounded a familiar curve in the road, a place she despised. "These four lanes turn into two up here and traffic always backs up," Erika said. "He'll be able to sneak through the stopped cars with no problem, and we'll be sitting ducks."

"Maybe not. You can crush his ass with this thing."

Erika squinted. Was that him up ahead? "There he is."

The biker rode alongside a bright yellow Hummer, both headed toward the merge point.

"He's trying to hide from us," Parker said. "Move up behind him so I can get a shot."

Erika looked in her rearview mirror and was shocked to see nothing but open road behind them. All of the drivers they'd passed must have stopped as their high-speed gunfight zipped past.

A quarter mile ahead, however, were two lines of slow-moving traffic.

Cold air roared through her shattered window as Erika redlined the already taxed engine, but the sport bike whipped around several larger vehicles and disappeared again.

Parker twisted in his seat and caught a glimpse of the motorcycle lurking behind a van, letting them get ahead before it shot forward once more to keep pace with the speeding Volkswagen.

"Go, go, go," Parker shouted. "We're dead if he gets any closer."

Cars boxed her in on either side, and her throat tightened. She had nowhere to go.

"I can't move," she said.

"Take the shoulder."

Erika whipped the steering wheel over and began tearing down the shoulder, traffic only inches from her broken window.

The bike doggedly followed suit.

Her mirror collided with the side of a pickup truck. Debris filled the car, shards of blue plastic covering them both.

"Stay straight and hold on," Parker said.

Warmth covered her forehead, and Erika reached up to find blood dripping from a fresh cut. Parker turned in his seat and pointed his gun out the side window.

She held the wheel in a death grip as a guardrail scraped the door.

"Careful," Parker shouted as he grabbed the doorframe.

She righted the vehicle's path, searching for an opening in traffic.

The rear window disintegrated an instant before Parker dove to avoid the bullet and slammed into her shoulder. Her arms crumpled under his weight. Sparks flew as they slammed into the truck on their left, bounced off and then hit the guardrail again, ripping the passenger mirror off. Parker righted himself and took aim, ducked as two more shots hit the trunk, and then popped back up to return fire.

"How do you like it?" he screamed, and was answered by a further volley of gunshots that shattered her rearview mirror and punched a hole in the car's roof.

Now she had no idea what was behind them.

"I can't see him anymore. Where did he go?"

"He's right behind us, coming up fast. Can't this thing go any faster?"

"It's already floored!" she screamed.

The panic came back in a wave, pushing aside any rational thought. This guy, this crazy biker, was going to drive up and pick them off. She couldn't dodge him or run away, not in this car. He'd pull up and shoot them like targets at a firing range. She sucked in her breath hard and saw a sign flash by. One she'd seen many times. *We can get off here.*

The wave of fear receded and her head cleared. An exit ramp loomed ahead, right where it had always been, ever since she'd moved here.

"We can take this exit," Erika said. "We'll lose him on the side streets."

"We're not going to make it," Parker said. "He's coming, and I'm out of bullets."

"Where is he?"

"Right behind you."

Perfect. Erika stepped on the brakes with both feet, her tires squealing as they dropped from eighty to zero in an instant.

With nowhere else to go, the bike's front tire landed on her trunk.

Engine screaming, the bike climbed up the car, vaulting onto the roof and shooting forward, invisible as it rumbled over them and then somersaulted through the air in front of them.

How did he do that? The guy should have slammed into her car and smashed into pieces. She watched, open-mouthed, as the bike crashed back onto the road and skidded forward, shedding hunks of metal and plastic as went.

She blinked and the driver bounced up, patting his pockets like he was searching for his wallet. Sometime during his impromptu flight, the man's gun had apparently disappeared.

Erika stood on the gas. Gravel spurted out behind her as she closed on him.

A split-second before impact, the biker dove over the guardrail and disappeared down the steep incline. Erika smashed into the motorcycle, sending it spinning like a toy.

She kept going, hurtling toward the exit ramp as Parker scanned the ravine for any sign of the biker.

"There are railroad tracks down there, but I didn't see him land."

Erika slowed for the exit ramp, moving on autopilot. Other than a few slack-jawed stares from drivers she passed on the shoulder, everything appeared almost normal.

The wind even made a pleasant whistling sound as it coursed through the bullet holes in her car.

Chapter 36

Ardmore, Pennsylvania

Preston Vogel owned many properties, but his favorite was the twenty-thousand-square-foot mansion in Ardmore, fifteen miles from his downtown office. Located on Philadelphia's historic Main Line, the sprawling estate provided an oasis of calm in which he could do as he pleased, free from scrutiny.

Tonight, Preston sat at a desk with enough surface area to host a dinner party, a pen in hand.

As tended to happen when he finally had a moment of peace, his phone rang.

Brooke appeared at his door.

"It's for you."

"What a surprise."

He'd been expecting a call regarding what Joseph Chase might have uncovered from studying Bushrod Washington's diary. Vogel needed to know if Chase had somehow stumbled onto a secret that had been buried for over two hundred years.

"What did you find?" Vogel asked when Brooke connected the call.

"I have to do some field research first," the caller said. "But I think Professor Chase may have been following a hidden path laid out by George Washington himself."

"What the hell are you talking about?"

"Bear with me. First, a little history. Washington never had any children.

Bushrod was his nephew and the closest person Washington ever had to a son. He actually inherited Mount Vernon when George died."

Preston's grip on the phone tightened. "Get to the point."

"Patience, my dear Preston. Washington's journal covers a wide range of subjects, from daily happenings on the estate to meetings he hosted with people like John Adams and Benjamin Franklin."

"What does this have to do with a hidden path?"

"I'm getting there. A few things caught my attention when I looked through the journal. One is that around the time Washington died, Bushrod drew a chair in his diary. It's the only sketch I found, and it isn't just any old chair. This one still exists."

"I assume this has a point?"

"The chair was used by George Washington while he presided over the drafting of the Constitution. It's currently on display at Independence Hall."

Preston didn't see the connection between a chair George Washington's ass had been on and their current problems.

"So what?"

A sigh wafted through the phone. "You have to realize, at this point I'm not certain of anything, but I think Washington may have hidden something in that chair."

"What would George Washington hide in a chair? More to the point, when can you search it?"

"As to what it may be, I don't want to speculate. I need to physically inspect the chair first, and doing so for research purposes should not be a problem, though I don't know how soon I would be able to obtain the necessary permits."

Preston had learned a long time ago that almost any problem would disappear if you threw enough money at it.

"Who's in charge of the place?"

"The National Park Service."

"I'll have my charity make a donation tomorrow. That will get the Park Service to give you permission to inspect the chair. For purely academic reasons, of course."

"Of course."

Preston hung up. This had better work. Given how smart the guy claimed to be, there'd be hell to pay if Preston had just wasted his money.

He tipped a glass of whiskey to his lips and cool fire rolled through his body. Time to focus on his upcoming speech. Somehow he had to convey sincere concern for whatever protected species inhabited the godforsaken wilderness of the Refuge.

Of course he wanted to ensure the continuity of the indigenous wildlife's daily existence. At least that's what he had to tell the public audience.

Fortunately, while a single person might be intelligent and rational, large groups of people were easily manipulated. And all the more easily if you promised them a few bucks in their pockets.

The phone rattled again. His direct line this time.

"Vogel."

"Preston, we have a problem." Frank Keplar didn't sound so good.

"What kind of problem?"

"I missed the shot."

"What shot?"

"At Independence Hall. A jogger ran in front of Parker when I pulled the trigger, got her head blown off."

Preston's jaw tightened as Frank detailed a sequence straight off the big screen. A high-speed shootout on the Schuylkill Expressway, and at the end the pair had still got away.

"Do you have any idea what will happen if my head of security is arrested for attempted murder? Where are you now?"

"One of my men picked me up. No one can trace anything to you or the company."

"You'd better pray that's true."

One hand ran through his well-coifed black hair, a nervous habit he'd failed to rid himself of.

"Go back to the office. I'll meet you there shortly."

For the first time in years, fear's cold fingers reached out and touched Preston Vogel.

Chapter 37

A taxi cruised down Kelly Drive, the scenic roadway following the Schuylkill River's curving east bank across from the more heavily traveled expressway. Parker and Erika sat in the back seat as their driver spoke rapidly in Hindi, his low voice alternately melodic and coarse as the man argued into his Bluetooth headset.

After Erika had laid waste to the motorcycle, she'd swerved onto the nearest exit ramp and ended up in the gentrified Manayunk neighborhood of the city, where their bullet-ridden car had understandably garnered unwanted attention.

Only once they were certain they'd lost the death-dealing motorcyclist had she ditched the battered car, removed the license plate, and headed with Parker toward Main Street. Within minutes they found a cab and were on their way back into the city.

Erika hadn't said a word since, and Parker worried she'd gone into shock.

"Are you all right?" He touched her shoulder as he spoke.

Erika jerked away.

"What?" She blinked rapidly. "No, I'm not all right. Did you miss the madman shooting at us?"

"You realize what this means. We found something other people don't want us to know about. I know you're upset, but the smart play is to keep moving. It's our best shot at getting out of this alive."

Her eyes narrowed. "Are you serious? You want to keep going?"

"Easy," Parker said and held a finger to his lips.

"We were just *shot* at." Erika made no attempt to keep her voice down. "I don't know about you, but it's a new experience for me. The only place I'm going is straight to a police station."

He really didn't want to do this. On one level, it wasn't fair. "If that's what you want to do, fine. We can give them this and let some government drones figure out what it is."

Parker removed the sun chair package from his pocket and held it out. She almost reached for it, then stopped herself.

"Parker, don't do this to me. You know I want to look at that, but you also know as well as I do that we're way out of our league here. Do you want to end up like your uncle? We're no good to him if we're dead."

"You're right, but I can't stop now."

She turned away and stared out the window, arms across her chest.

"Listen," Parker said. "Give me a day. If we don't know what it is by tomorrow, I'll call that CIA guy myself."

She turned to face him, keeping her mouth closed.

"Don't you want to see what George Washington left for us?"

Erika's fist shot out and punched his wounded arm.

"Fine," she said as he grimaced. "But know that right now I hate you. Mainly for appealing to my professional side. And if we don't figure out what the hell is going on by this time tomorrow, it's over."

"Take us to Thirty-Sixth and Walnut," Erika said to the driver.

Ten minutes later they stopped in front of Erika's office building. If they were going to properly study a document from Colonial America, there was no better place to do so than in the University of Pennsylvania, founded by Benjamin Franklin.

Erika cleared a spot on the desktop for their treasure. Hands covered in white cotton gloves and aided by a document magnification lamp, she began her inspection.

"The twine is proper for the period, and the leather appears to be of the correct age as well."

"That's fascinating, Professor. Why don't we look inside?"

She shot a wicked glare his way before untying the knot. The twine fell off, and Erika unfolded the leather container to reveal a folded sheet of thick parchment. Erika gently opened it, and Parker leaned forward to see a series of seemingly random letters and numbers.

19 18 11 18 7 4 23 17 19 7 10 7 26 26

LVIXCVIXCVIIIWCIIICXI

10 11 26 26 20 23 23 25 6 3 20 7 22 26 11 9 7

There were no other markings anywhere on the page.

"What is it?"

Erika said nothing, her eyes flashing back and forth over the text.

"Do you think it's a code of some kind?"

"Yes, Sherlock, I think it's a code. Thank goodness you're here."

"Hey, I'm just trying to help," he said.

"Then get me a pen and some paper."

Biting his tongue, Parker rifled through the top drawer of her desk and came up with what she needed. She motioned for him to set them beside the pouch.

"Now be quiet and learn something."

Parker sat across from her, watching as Erika disappeared and Dr. Carr came out.

"I'm going to work under the assumption this was left behind by George Washington. Ignoring the enormous historical importance of this document, I think I know what we have."

As she spoke, Erika wrote the alphabet on a sheet of paper.

"During the Revolution, a variety of codes and ciphers were utilized by both sides to convey sensitive information. There was no Secret Service, no CIA, or FBI. If people wanted to send secure messages, it had to be written and coded."

"How are we supposed to figure out what kind of codes George Washington used?"

Erika finished the alphabet and turned toward him.

"You may not believe this, but over the past two centuries, some people have managed to solve the ciphers that were common in those days. We don't rely solely on our brains anymore, you see. We have these things called computers, and they're pretty good at solving problems. In fact, your uncle taught a class that explored cryptography during the Revolution."

"I hope you kept your notes."

"One of the most popular types of encryption used in Washington's day was what's known as a substitution cipher. This means that each letter of the alphabet is assigned a specific number, so if you know what number is associated with each letter, the code is broken."

"How can we tell what letter goes with what number? Maybe they're in order?"

"It wouldn't be much of a code if number one was A, number two was B, and so on. Usually a random letter is chosen as the starting point, though even that isn't very hard to decipher."

"What about the letters in the middle?" He indicated the grouping of alphabetical characters. "They're all bunched together. Do you think they're some kind of inverse code, with letters substituted for numbers?"

"Not only do I think you're correct, but I bet you already know what numbers are hidden."

What was she talking about?

"Stop messing around. I clearly have no idea what those letters mean. You're the cryptographer here."

"Think for a second," Erika said. "Where have you seen those letters before? They're very important to your favorite sport."

What did this have to do with football? Just as he was about to yell at her, it hit him.

The Super Bowl.

"Roman numerals."

Erika was already typing on a keyboard. "Correct. I suspect these are Roman numerals strung together. We just have to figure out where the spaces should be."

She opened her laptop and tapped at the keyboard for a moment. A list of all the Roman numerals from one to one hundred appeared on the screen. She pressed a button.

"Here," she said as a printer began to hum. "Take this list and see what you can find. It's going to take some guesswork, but you should be able to figure out where the spaces belong between the letters."

Fifteen minutes later, his pen went down.

"I think I got most of it," he said to Erika, who hadn't moved from her seat as she worked on the numerical pieces to the puzzle. "There's one problem, though. The *W* doesn't fit at all."

Erika glanced up for the first time since he'd started writing.

"What have you got?" she asked.

"The trick is to stop at the *I*, which is a one. Almost every number ends with that character, so here's what I've got."

Taken as a string of Roman numerals broken down by his logic, the sequence of alphabetical characters revealed five numbers.

56 96 98 W 103 111

"As for the W, I have no idea."

"Not bad, Junior. I'm glad at least one of us is making progress. I've got to admit, I have no idea what these numbers are hiding, or even if they're a code."

Several sheets of crumpled paper littered the floor at her feet, and the smooth pieces atop her desk were covered with crossed-out numbers and letters.

"If this were simply a substitution cipher where one letter correlates with each number sequentially, the most logical solution is to associate the most common letter with the number that appears most often. For instance, twenty-six and seven both appear five times, more than any other number. Logically I would assume that one of them represents the most commonly occurring letter in the English language."

"Which is the letter E."

"Correct. Working backwards, the next most common letter is T, followed by A, O, and N."

"So how do we tell which one is E?"

"Normally I would say seven, because there are only a few letters that are grouped together, which is the case with twenty-six in two separate places. Unfortunately, E is also often found twice in a row, in words like *keep* or *deer*."

Parker studied the chart for a moment.

"If you assume seven is the code for E, eight is F, and so on, what do you have?"

Erika sifted through the crumpled papers and smoothed one out to reveal the answer.

QPIPEBUOQEHEXX

HIXXRUUWDARETXIGE

"A bunch of gibberish."

"What if you assume that twenty-six is the E?"

She grabbed a different crumpled ball and unfolded the answer.

XWPWLIBVXLOLEE

OPEEYBBDKHYLAEPNL

More nonsense.

"After this I tried a different cipher that has been found from that time period, the Caesar cipher."

"As in Julius Caesar?" Parker asked.

"The one and only. His cipher was used by men who had studied Roman texts on warfare, of which Washington was certainly one. The key is to replace each letter with the one that is three steps ahead in the alphabet. For example, A becomes D, B is E, and so on."

"Did you get anything from it?"

Erika pinched the bridge of her nose and began to massage her temples. "No. We may have to wait until tomorrow to figure this out."

"What makes you think we'll be able to solve this tomorrow when we can't do it now?"

"Because tomorrow I'll have access to Penn's proprietary code-breaking software. I don't have clearance to access it from my computer, but the network administrator is a friend of mine and will let me use his machine to run this code."

Parker took in the sequence of letters and numbers on the table once more. "I can't believe we're having so much trouble with a code this short. It's amazing how backward it seems—that we have all this technology and a simple puzzle like this is stumping us."

"What did you say?"

She sat rock still in her chair, eyes stretched wide open.

"Parker, that might be it. Oh, I can't believe I forgot."

"What? What are you talking about?" he asked.

She ignored him and began scribbling numbers across a clean sheet of paper.

"Would you please tell me what the hell you're talking about?"

"For a dumb jock you can be pretty insightful."

She had started to try a new line of numbers to go with each letter, beginning with their original attempt, which assumed that the number seven signified the letter E. However, now she had written the numbers *backwards* from that point, with the number eight above the letter D, nine above C, and so on.

"I never tried to go the opposite way. If you do it this way, K is associated with number one, and the numbers go backwards until you get back around to L, which is twenty-six."

Moments later, it appeared.

"Look at this," she shouted. "It's—"

"What could possibly be so exciting in this old building?" a silky-smooth voice called from the hallway outside.

"That's the department chair, Dr. Newlon," Erika whispered. "Go hide somewhere. I don't want to explain why you're here."

Parker dove behind a filing cabinet just as the thick wooden door creaked open. From his viewpoint at ground level, he saw a pair of patent leather wingtips click into the room. He peered out as far as he dared. It was the well-dressed man Erika had been speaking with when he barged into her office after the shootout at Joe's apartment.

"Dr. Newlon, how are you?"

"In need of the excitement and energy you possess in droves, Erika. What are you studying this fine afternoon?"

Parker lay still, heart thudding in his chest.

"I'll share a secret with you, but you've got to promise to keep it between us."

"I will take it to the grave, my dear."

"I lost the thumb drive that had all my research for the term paper we were discussing earlier and just found it now. You have no idea how worried I was that it was gone and I'd have to start from scratch."

"Now that is a frightening thought," Dr. Newlon said. "One that I've also experienced a time or two myself. Thank goodness you found it."

"Now I can spend some time working instead of tearing this place apart."

"Excellent news. How is everything else?"

The two made small talk for a minute, after which Professor Newlon excused himself. Erika double-checked that he was down the hallway before calling Parker out.

"I think that guy likes you," Parker said, dusting off the knees of his pants.

"Oh, shut up. He's a wonderful man, kind and caring. He's supervising my dissertation and has been a tremendous help."

"I never heard my uncle talk about him."

"Dr. Newlon is a very strong-willed man, much like Joe was," Erika said. "He's an accomplished academic in his own right, but I think Joe's success always bothered him. Newlon has a healthy ego of his own."

"Good for him. So what's the deal with my brilliant stroke of genius?

Did you figure out what the message says?"

He leaned over her desk again and paused while Erika shifted a pile of documents off the parchment as well as the paper she'd been working on.

"I didn't want Dr. Newlon to see this," she said. "He's not your uncle, but he's still pretty damn sharp. The last thing we need right now is someone else getting involved."

She pointed to the sheet of paper, where the centuries-old message was revealed.

STATEHOUSEBELL

56 96 98 W 103 111

BALLROOMFIREPLACE

Decoded, the separate words were clear.

"State House Bell? Ballroom Fireplace? What is that all about?"

Lips moving, Erika began muttering to herself.

"State House, State House, where have I heard ..."

Suddenly she broke for her keyboard and pounded away.

"I knew it. Look at this."

On the screen was a picture familiar to every American.

"The Liberty Bell," Parker said.

The iconic representation of freedom, complete with the famous crack, was known across the world as a symbol of everything America stood for. He didn't need the digital image to remember how it looked, because he'd seen it less than a day ago, outside of Independence Hall.

"The bell came to America in 1752 and was hung in the State House here in Philadelphia. It wasn't until 1835 that the name 'Liberty Bell' was used to describe it."

"So when this letter was written," Parker said, "no one had ever heard of the Liberty Bell."

His eyes fell to the last part of the decoded message.

"You don't happen to know of any patriotic fireplaces? Possibly in a ballroom?"

She ignored him and wrote out his interpretation of the Roman numerals.

56 96 98 W 103 111

"What do the numbers represent? Some kind of coordinates?"

"I'm not very good with latitude and longitude, but that could make sense. I would expect more cardinal directions than just west, though."

A search for coordinates matching those numbers revealed the problem.

"There would have to be either a north or south direction to go with it," Erika pointed out.

Parker thought for a moment.

"Try both of them for the first three numbers."

"North puts you in Saskatchewan, a province in Western Canada, close to the Arctic circle. South is in the South Pacific Ocean, West of Argentina."

Neither spoke for a moment.

"Parts of Saskatchewan were included in the Louisiana Purchase in 1803, but they were ceded to the United Kingdom in 1818," Erika offered.

"If we think this was written by George Washington," Parker said, "we've got a few problems. One, he died in 1799. Modern-day Canada wasn't owned by the United States for another four years, so the chances of Washington incorporating this into a message are next to zero. Two, unless there's an island in the middle of the Pacific that no one knows about anymore, those can't be accurate. Three, and most importantly, every single clue we've located so far has been here in Philadelphia. Whatever Washington was up to, he would have involved an area that was securely under American control."

"Good point. Until 1800 it was the country's capital," Erika said. "It doesn't get much more secure than that."

As she spoke, the Liberty Bell snapshot on the computer monitor caught his eye again.

He leaned over her desk and studied each word inscribed on the gigantic metal alarm clock.

PROCLAIM LIBERTY THROUGHOUT ALL THE LAND UNTO ALL THE INHABITANTS THEREOF LEV. XXV. V X.
BY ORDER OF THE ASSEMBLY OF THE PROVINCE OF PENSYLVANIA FOR THE STATE HOUSE IN PHILAD[A]
PASS AND STOW
PHILAD[A]
MDCCLIII

"What about those Roman numerals on the bell? What do they stand for?"

"MDCCLIII is the year it was cast: 1753."

That didn't work. Between the M and D of the year, the bell's crack snaked upward, a line that pointed toward the message inscribed above.

Erika opened her mouth to speak, but Parker held up a hand. There was something about this whole situation, the codes they were breaking, the Roman numerals. They had the pieces, but it didn't fit together. Not like it should.

What was he missing?

He peered again at the famous birthmark on the bell, and suddenly he got it.

"How many words are there on the Liberty Bell's inscription?"

"I don't know. What does it matter?"

He leaned across Erika and printed a close-up snapshot of the inscription.

"Write this down."

As he began to count the words, Erika stared at him like he'd asked her what flavor a clock was.

"What are you talking about?" she asked. "Don't ignore me."

He counted, beginning with the first letter inscribed on the bell's surface.

When he reached 56, the letter *S* was above his finger.

"Write down an S."

Erika scribbled it down, and suddenly her eyes went wide and a smile crept across her face.

Parker dictated the next five letters, which created a single word.

SPOWEL

"That can't be right," Parker muttered. "What the hell is a spowel?"

"It's not a word," Erika said. "It's an abbreviation."

"For what?"

"It's an abbreviation for a person, not a thing. Someone you'd recognize if you knew anything about the history of Philadelphia."

Erika tapped the keyboard and called up an old picture with a biography underneath.

"This is Samuel Powel, the first mayor of Philadelphia. His old home is only a few blocks from the Liberty Bell."

"Look at that," Parker pointed to the screen. "Martha and George Washington's twentieth wedding anniversary was celebrated in the Powel

House ballroom."

A few clicks revealed the interior of the ballroom, which was dominated by a fireplace set between two pillars, all surrounded by white and black marble.

"How late is that place open?" Parker asked. "We might as well go see what the fireplace looks like. I bet if we poked around in there for a few minutes we'd get an idea why Washington was so interested in it."

"Do you really think we can just walk in and 'poke around' a historical landmark?"

"If not, you can finally put your credentials to use and get in there to do some research. I can be your assistant and we'll have all day to look around."

"Parker, stop and think for a minute. Do you remember what just happened to us? Every minute we keep going down this path is another gamble with our lives."

Hard to argue with that. He really had no business doing this. He could justify foolhardy actions when it was just his life in the balance, but now that Erika was along for the ride it was a different story.

"You're right. This is dangerous."

He sat on her desktop, took in the fear on her face.

"But you know me, Erika. I can't quit now. Look how far we've come. Think about what we've discovered. I'd never be able to forgive myself if anything happened to you, and I'd never stop wondering what was out there if I gave up now."

"What do you mean *gave up*? Stop being so hardheaded. Do you think Joe would want you to get killed over this?"

She had a point. A few good ones, actually, but his mind was set.

"That's why I'm doing this alone. I can't risk you getting hurt."

She almost laughed. "Stop it with the chivalry act. You know if you find anything, you're really going to need me."

Erika grabbed her handbag and walked to the door with their findings in hand, pausing when she reached for the light switch. She turned and cocked an eyebrow at him.

"What, you thought I was going to beg to go with you?"

Sometimes he wanted to throw her out of a window.

"Come on," she said. "If we leave now we'll have at least an hour to look around. No sense in wasting time."

As he trotted down the hall beside her and out into the parking lot, a figure hidden in the bushes outside watched them run. After they were out of view, the man slipped quietly inside and walked toward Erika's vacant office.

Chapter 38

Scarcely controlled chaos descended on Independence Hall. City cops patrolled the area alongside park rangers while most of their superiors argued over jurisdiction.

One man who didn't let the semantics interfere with his investigation was Nick Dean, currently in the park rangers' office looking down on an unconscious man who might or might not have answers for him.

Beside Nick stood a recruit fresh out of the academy. Either the kid had perfect posture, or he was nervous as hell.

"Get me some smelling salts," Nick said. "I'm waking this guy up one way or another."

As the young cop ran off, Nick leaned back and rubbed his eyes. Damn, but they were dry as sandpaper.

He'd ended up covered in blood after trying to get information from this guy, a man they'd found unconscious on the ground at Independence Hall. Parker and Erika had vanished, and to top it all off, reports had filtered in of a high-speed shootout on the Schuylkill Expressway. How, or even if, it related to his dead jogger, he had no idea.

In short, he had nothing. An army of technicians were currently analyzing the sun chair Parker had mentioned, but Nick wasn't counting on it offering much.

He turned when the door banged open again to reveal Constable Baby-Face clutching a handful of smelling salt packages.

"The park rangers had some in their first aid kit. Is there anything else you need, Agent Dean?"

"No. Sit down and let's see if we can get this guy talking."

When bullets had started flying outside, Nick had searched for the shooter without luck, and by the time he turned around Parker and Erika had vanished. Dozens of officers had responded and were now interviewing witnesses and reviewing surveillance footage. Several people remembered seeing his unconscious guest struggle with another man who fit Parker's description, and the guy had a nasty cut on his head. It wasn't much, but it was the best lead he had right now.

Nick ripped open a packet of the powerful salts and wafted it under the guy's nose.

"Hey, buddy, wake up."

The man didn't flinch. Nick shoved the pungent crystals directly into a nostril, and the man's head thrashed back, tears streaming from both eyes.

"Whoa, stop! Get that shit away."

The guy sat up and attempted to shove Nick's hand aside. The salts didn't budge.

"Get that shit out of my nose."

As he protested, the guy looked up and eventually found Nick's face. It was a long journey.

"Who are you?" he asked. "What are you doing to me?"

The man's identification listed his age as thirty-four, with a local address.

"Relax, I'm here to help you. My name is Nicholas Dean. I'm an agent with the CIA." He flashed his badge.

"Where am I? What's going on here?"

"You're in a US park ranger office. We found you outside on the ground and saw the big gash on your head. That's a nasty cut."

The man's eyes shifted back and forth, taking in the small, sparse room.

"You said you were CIA. Why would a spook like you come to put a Band-Aid on my head? That don't make no sense."

"Listen, Mr.—what is it again? Breen. Mr. Breen, I'm here because a murder has occurred on federal grounds, and that kind of thing gets the government's attention very quickly."

By now Mr. Breen had risen to his feet and was gingerly probing the back of his skull.

"Who got shot? 'Cause I sure as hell didn't do it, if that's what you're gettin' at."

"We're not certain yet, mainly because most of her face is gone. And no, I don't think you did it, but I do find it interesting that several people swear they saw you struggling with a man immediately after the shooting. A man who we believe may have information about this murder."

"You talkin' about that guy with the piece? Hell yeah, I was struggling with him. I saw his gun and thought it was my civic duty to subdue him."

Nick cocked an eyebrow.

"You're telling me you tried to fight an armed man?"

"Black belt in ju-jitsu, and I'm trained in hand-to-hand combat. If somebody hadn't knocked me in the head, he would've been done for."

"May I ask where you learned to fight?"

"I'm in private security."

Apparently satisfied his head wound wasn't serious, Mr. Breen stood to leave. "You know, I appreciate your concern, but I've gotta go. Good luck finding the bad guy."

"I still have some questions for you."

"Too bad. If I'm not under arrest, I'm leaving. If I am, I want a lawyer."

There was more to be learned by following the mouthy punk than by detaining him, Dean decided. Where he went or who he talked to might prove very interesting.

"In that case, Mr. Breen, you are free to go."

The young officer stood and escorted their aggressive pugilist outside, but before the door could close, a second cop hurried in.

"Agent Dean, here's the background information you requested."

Nick grabbed the single page, a detailed biography of the man who had just left. It appeared Mr. Walter Breen was in his mid-thirties, single, and had been charged twice for assault and battery but never convicted.

"This guy got off two assault charges?"

"You'll see that with some security guard types like him, sir. Below his rap sheet you'll find an employment section."

"You know anything about this security outfit he works for?"

"Not offhand, but I figured you'd ask so I did a little digging. They cater to wealthy individuals and large corporations. Claim to offer the latest in personal and executive protection for the discerning client."

"I'm wondering if his employer had anything to do with those two assault charges he beat," Nick said. "No offense, but I doubt a South Philly tough like him has the resources to do that on his own."

"I'll see what I can dig up, Agent Dean."

"I'd appreciate it."

Outside, policemen moved around firefighters and park personnel. A steady stream of people shuttled in and out of the main door, dying sunlight casting a reddish light through the towering windows that fronted the hall. Until the techs finished processing the chair Parker had mentioned and compiled a report, Nick couldn't move forward with his investigation. He gritted his teeth. Each time it seemed he had caught a break, everything went to hell and he was back to square one. Parker had found some strange box containing a book they claimed was connected to George Washington, but how did that relate to the dead girl outside, or any of the other fresh corpses he'd seen in the past few days?

Unless the surveillance detail they'd put on Mr. Breen turned up any information, the only two people who could answer that question were Parker Chase and Erika Carr.

Both of whom were nowhere to be found.

Unfortunately, Nick didn't have any men to spare for a search, so unless they happened to walk into his office, he was out of luck.

And right now he was a mess. Every muscle ached, his eyes burned, and he was angry as hell. "I need some fresh air," he said to no one in particular.

Outside, a horse-drawn carriage waited for riders, the horseman decked out in full period regalia. Nick dodged an errant horse turd and turned south off Chestnut onto Third Street, where a green Starbucks sign promised a reprieve from the bitter government coffee he'd choked down earlier.

Steaming cup in hand, he pulled out his cell phone and was rewarded with a blank screen. The damn things were useful, but fragile. They weren't designed for urban warfare outside of a boardroom.

Upon further inspection, he realized that it wasn't broken, it was just dead. *Crap.* He seriously could not catch a break today. Sighing, he clamped a plastic lid down onto his coffee and trudged back to the park ranger office, where he found an outlet. He pulled out his charger and plugged the phone in, then nearly dropped it as it erupted in a frantic series of buzzes and the screen lit up like a Christmas tree.

Alerts from the tracking device he'd placed on Parker Chase's car. A whole bunch of them.

Chapter 39

Philadelphia, Pennsylvania

A glass of whiskey sat on Preston's expansive desk. Ventilation fans hummed in the background, covering any strains of afternoon traffic that drifted up from the jam-packed streets of downtown Philadelphia.

Preston gazed at the amber liquid, lost in thought. He looked up when Brooke walked through the door.

"Mr. Vogel, everyone is signed in for the conference."

Once the door closed behind her, his attention turned to the business at hand. Three other members of The Guild were waiting to begin an emergency video conference call. According to their organization's original charter, each member was required to make themselves immediately available for any emergency meeting requested by the president, regardless of time or place.

The high-definition wall monitor flashed to life, displaying three faces in a circle around the view his camera transmitted, which occupied the center spot. One area of the screen was blank, held open for the final man who would be joining shortly.

Each member was connected via a multi-layered conferencing system that utilized a SSL/TLS connection and was constantly monitored for any intrusion attempts. Routed through the most extensive firewall on the market, each member could speak freely, secure in the knowledge that what they said would not be heard by any outsiders. Such stringent standards were necessary, given that if the federal government knew about their activities, every single person on this call would be in jail for the rest of their natural lives.

"Gentlemen, thank you for joining me. We have a serious matter to discuss, one that none of us have dealt with in our lifetimes. Parker Chase, nephew of Dr. Joseph Chase, has surfaced here in Philadelphia. It appears he is on the same trail his uncle was."

Chesterton Rupp's voice boomed through the room.

"Have you taken care of him?"

"Mr. Chase has so far proven more resourceful than expected."

"Does he have military training?"

Preston gritted his teeth.

"He's a financial planner."

"A *banker* is giving you trouble?" Rupp scoffed.

"Believe me when I say that Mr. Chase's luck has run out."

"I hope you can handle this," Mr. Graves said.

The arrogant prick. What had Graves done to solve their problem? Not a damn thing, that's what.

As Preston opened his mouth to remind the insolent buffoon who was in charge, their final member joined the call, his face flashing on-screen.

Silver hair pulled into a ponytail and impeccably dressed, Alexander Newlon cut a stylish figure.

In addition to serving as the history department chair at the University of Pennsylvania, Dr. Alexander Newlon was also their organization's bookkeeper and chief policy strategist. Intimately involved with every aspect of The Guild's existence, Newlon had been the one to uncover Joseph Chase's research into Washington's journal, a line of inquiry that had struck at the very heart of their group's origins.

For the first time in over two centuries, The Guild's existence was threatened not by competition or law enforcement, but by a dark secret, thought to have been buried long ago.

"Good afternoon, gentlemen. Pardon my late arrival."

Newlon shuffled some papers on his desk, his angular features taut. "Early this morning I reviewed a document authored by one Bushrod Washington, nephew of George, first president of the United States," he said. "Based on the contents, it's my belief that President Washington constructed an elaborate puzzle he intended for his nephew to uncover and ultimately deduce the solution. Unfortunately, Bushrod wasn't up to the task, and Washington's path remained hidden. Until now. Within the past month, as you know, a former colleague of mine, Dr. Joseph Chase, managed to decipher the hidden message contained within the document.

"A few hours ago, I spoke with Dr. Carr in her office. After she left the building, I inspected the contents of her room and found information pointing to a historical mansion here in Philadelphia, a building known as the Powel House."

"Several of my men were dispatched to intercept the pair," Vogel said. "I expect to hear from them shortly. Dr. Carr was accompanied by Parker Chase when she departed. Gentlemen, I don't have to tell you what is at stake here."

Each member was aware that this organization had been founded upon a dark truth. Its full extent was closely guarded by the current leader and the historian, but the other members were keenly aware that should the full extent of their founding father's actions come to light, all would be lost.

"Are you talking about the same book Joseph Chase was reviewing before he died?" Chesterton Rupp asked.

"Yes. This is the first opportunity I had to review the document."

"Will you be able to follow the trail Washington left once those two are eliminated?"

"Mr. Rupp, I am one of the world's preeminent scholars on our nation's history," Newlon replied. "If whatever Washington secreted away is still there, I will find it."

Preston decided to cut off the squabbling.

"And on that note, why don't we move on? I received word today that Vogel Industries will receive the lone permit for exploratory drilling in the Arctic National Refuge."

The last thing he needed was to have his own men fighting with each other, and fortunately the distraction worked. News of his success in Congress made everyone forget about Parker Chase. After discussing the inevitable financial windfall and what profits were expected from the venture, Preston ended the call.

All but one of the video screens went dark. Preston stood in front of a floor-to-ceiling window, the city beneath him. Alexander Newlon waited in silence.

"Alex, what do you think would make George Washington go to such great lengths to hide something? He was the president, the most powerful man in the country. Why go to all this trouble?"

Newlon ran a hand through his silver mane. "I've considered that, and the truth is I'm not sure. I'd guess Washington had something highly volatile and extremely valuable. Now, is it valuable like a diamond? Maybe. However, we may not be talking about a tangible object. It could also be information. If this is the case, what was valuable two centuries ago may not be so today."

"Do you think …?" Preston left the question unfinished.

"I don't know. Is it possible? Yes. Likely? No. As you're well aware, there was never any evidence found of this plan. Your ancestor believed it to be, but couldn't prove it."

As The Guild's historian, Alexander Newlon was responsible for a singular task, ill-defined and without expiration, based on suspicion and rumor. Newlon, like his father and grandfather, and all the men in their line before them, was forever searching for something that might or might not exist. For two centuries a succession of Newlons had toiled, ears open for any signs of what they sought, with nary a word or page to be found. And that was exactly what Alexander had wanted. If nothing was ever found, The Guild was safe, as it had been since its founding. Over time, Newlon had come to suspect his efforts were an exercise in futility, and Preston agreed with him.

Now he wasn't so sure.

"Frankly, I don't give a damn whether he was right or not," Preston said. "If proof does exist, it needs to stay buried. I can't afford the type of negative publicity that would come from such a discovery. Public opinion is a powerful thing, Alex. It could derail the project."

Preston poised a finger over the "end conference" button.

"I'll inform you when Chase is no longer a threat. I look forward to hearing about what you uncover."

When Newlon's image vanished, Preston called Frank Keplar.

"What's your status?"

"Chase is in the museum with a female. Our man is moving in to eliminate him as we speak. What should we do about the girl?"

"Kill her as well."

Chapter 40

Heavy traffic filled the streets bisecting Penn's campus. Plenty of yellow taxicabs zipped about, and Parker stepped up to the curb, hand raised. A cab drew to a halt alongside them and Parker opened the rear door, ushering Erika in first.

["Rittenhouse Square," he told the cabbie.]

Five minutes later, Parker and Erika spotted his SUV parked near Joe's apartment, miraculously ticket-free. Parker paid the cabbie and he and Erika climbed into his car. He figured there was a decent chance that the apartment was being watched by one of the people who were after them, so he looped around back and took a scenic route to Old City, with two quick stops, first at a fast food joint for burgers, and next at a sporting goods store for more bullets. Parker had hunted his whole life, knew exactly what he needed, and was in and out with fresh ammo in minutes.

Luck was with them, because just as they arrived, a spot opened right in front of the Powel House Museum.

Both he and Erika sat and chewed silently, staring at the museum as they ate.

"So, Professor Carr, what's the plan?"

"This was your hare-brained scheme," she reminded him. "You figure it out. I'm here for my expertise."

The recent carnage only a few blocks away at Independence Hall hadn't kept people at home. Pedestrians of all ages walked around them, many admiring the historic buildings that lined the sidewalk. Despite the rapidly setting sun, it was still warm outside, an opportunity for people to escape their homes after a long winter.

"We can go in and take a look around," Parker said. "My guess is that the place will be empty, but even if some tourists are inside, it won't be like Independence Hall. This is a privately run museum, not part of the national parks system."

"You're probably right," she said. "First, though, let me be clear: this time we're not going to destroy anything. Some of the stuff in there is priceless. Think about it. Our nation's first president used to walk on these floors."

Parker saw nothing wrong with a little destruction if it helped him learn who'd killed his uncle.

He also saw no reason to share this with her.

"Understood."

The three-story museum was the end unit of a series of row homes. White shutters framed an abundance of windows, and a solid black oak door flanked by white columns sat underneath the fluttering American flag.

A large gated garden abutted the property, with a black metal fence about his height. For an important historical landmark, the protection was almost farcical.

"Check out this placard," Erika said. "You might learn something."

A sign in front of the property told passerby about the history of the Powel House. George Washington's name featured several times.

"Let's get inside," Parker said. "This is neat and all, but I doubt we'll find anything out here."

"You never know what you'll find until you look," she said. "Patience was never one of your virtues."

The front door opened to reveal a narrow hallway with sky-blue walls beneath cloud-white ceilings. A red and blue diamond pattern stretched out on the floor in front of them, imprinted on the wooden floorboards. Several period paintings paired with antique furniture gave the impression that they'd stepped back in time. Parker half-expected a butler to appear.

"How beautiful," Erika said. "The colors are so vivid."

A mahogany balustrade led up a stairway in front of them. As they passed a portrait of Samuel Powel, someone called out.

"Welcome to the Powel House."

Parker glanced around and saw no one.

"May I offer any assistance?"

The source walked around a corner. Instead of the blue-haired old woman he expected, Parker found a handsome young man, stylishly dressed in a designer T-shirt and jeans. He was about Parker's age, with black hair and a two-day beard.

"Hi," Erika said, offering a winning smile. "We're looking for the ballroom fireplace."

"Follow those stairs to the second floor, and the ballroom will be to your rear. It overlooks the sidewalk."

"Thanks for the help."

Upstairs, a tall entranceway framed the ballroom; a large landscape painting hung over the fireplace.

A creamy blend of black and white marble surrounded two golden posts that supported the iron grate inside. Blackened bricks composed the interior, free of any logs or coal.

"I didn't see anyone else in the house," Parker said as he moved to join Erika, who was already studying the antique heating system. "See any hidden doors?"

Parker crouched, pulled out a flashlight and scanned the interior.

"If there is something here, and that's a big if, it had to be hidden well enough that normal cleaning or maintenance wouldn't uncover the hiding spot. Here, pass me your flashlight."

Parker handed it over, and Erika leaned further into the framework of the fireplace, disappearing into the chimney.

"Keep a lookout for anyone coming upstairs."

Parker kept one eye on the door and his ears open, but the only thing he heard was the faint sound of Erika poking around.

Tapping noises came from inside the fireplace. Several quick knocks in a row, then silence, followed by more taps.

"What are you doing in there?"

Her reply was all muffled nonsense, so he got down on his knees and looked inside.

"What?"

"I said I'm looking for any hollow bricks. If I wanted to hide something in a fireplace, I'd pull out two layers of brick to create a small storage area. Put whatever you want to hide in there, cover it back up with the first layer of brick, and you've got yourself a nice hiding spot."

"So if any of those bricks sound funny when you tap on them, it could be the hiding spot."

"You know, you're not as dumb as you look."

"Less talk, more search in there."

As he spoke, he heard the sound of voices approaching the room.

"Wait a second, I hear something."

He crept over to the door and leaned out, where he could hear the guide detailing the house's long and colorful history to a new visitor. False alarm. He walked back to the fireplace.

"It's just another tourist," he whispered to Erika, who was standing innocently to one side examining her phone. "Keep searching."

Erika ducked down again and went back to her knocks and taps, and he had little to do but watch. After a while, he couldn't hear the guide anymore and no one walked up the staircase. The other guest must have left.

By now Erika had searched nearly every brick on the inside and was working around the grate. After a minute spent twisting and straining, she crawled out and sat down. Streaks of soot covered her face.

"I hit every brick on the floor and the walls and didn't find a damn thing. They're all solid."

She swiped at a bead of sweat dripping down her face. "There's nothing else inside there. The message specifically pointed to the fireplace in this room."

For once, she looked to him for answers. "What am I missing? Everything we've found so far has proven to be correct, even two centuries later. Unless we're completely wrong about the coded message, there's no other place that makes sense."

"Let me get in there and have a look."

She handed him the flashlight and scooted aside.

"Knock yourself out. There's not much room in there for people our size, so be careful you don't smack your head. It might knock some sense into you."

He bent down and crawled into the fireplace. She wasn't kidding. His shoulders nearly scraped each side of the chimney. From outside, the fireplace appeared large and inviting, big enough to warm the entire ballroom. Inside, however, was a different matter. He couldn't imagine being a chimney sweep. No wonder every picture he'd ever seen of the craft depicted a miserable child with soot-streaked clothes.

He shined the light upward. Above him, blackened bricks rose toward the sky, but no sunlight was visible. Based on how clean the interior portion was, he doubted the fireplace had been used in decades.

"Did you check the whole way up the chimney?"

Erika's head appeared below the marble frame. "I reached as far as I could but didn't find anything. I don't think anyone would hide something that far out of the way. Washington wouldn't have put it somewhere where his nephew needed help to retrieve it. I'm sure Samuel Powel would have asked questions if Bushrod Washington had wanted to take apart his fireplace."

That made sense. He craned his neck once more, then stood on his tiptoes and reached as far up as he could with the light. There was a chinking sound and a cloud of black ash rained down onto his head.

"Ah, dammit. This is just perfect."

He flung an arm across his face to muffle a barrage of sneezes and stumbled out of the fireplace.

"Do you have a tissue? I got coal dust in my eyes."

"Coal dust?"

Suddenly Erika reached for the flashlight.

"Where did that much dust come from?"

She shoved him aside and forced her way into the chimney.

"If all that dust fell on you, there must be something above I didn't notice that has never been cleaned."

She pushed her arm as far up the wall as it would go, twisting her neck to follow the flashlight beam.

"There's a ledge up here that I can barely reach." She ducked out of the fireplace and handed Parker the flashlight again. "Stretch up there and see if you can feel it."

Wiping his nose on his sleeve, he took the light and stepped back into the tiny space. Sure enough, a few feet above them he felt a small shelf where one row of bricks stuck out. His fingers scraped the wall behind them.

"It feels like an extra row of bricks up there, a shelf that sticks out maybe six inches."

"Get out of my way. I need you to boost me up." She tugged at his shirt.

Parker stumbled out of the now sooty interior, bringing a cloud of black dust with him.

"Put your leg in here so I can stand on it. And keep your eyes open in case anyone walks by."

He knelt down on one knee and leaned his other leg in so Erika could stand on it. As she wobbled around, he squinted toward the door, but neither saw nor heard anything.

"We're good. What's up there?"

Only her legs were visible. Neither one moved.

"What's going on? Did you find something?"

A scraping noise echoed from inside and a single brick crashed down, inches from his foot.

"Are you all right? That thing is falling apart. You should—"

"I found it."

Parker's chest seized tightly.

They'd been right.

Erika stepped back down and they backed out of the fireplace. She held a metal container about the size of a cigar box; rust covered the outer surface.

"Where was it?"

"The mortar around one brick had crumbled. The brick behind it was loose, and I was able to wiggle it out. This was hidden where the next row should have been."

Parker ducked inside the fireplace again and grabbed the protruding ledge, pulling himself up. The structure of the chimney was such that it was four rows of bricks deep, but like Erika had said, someone had removed the two interior rows from this particular level. He could just see it dimly now with the light filtering up from the room. The metal box had been hidden inside, and when the two outer bricks had been replaced, the alteration was virtually invisible.

The squeak of rusty hinges called him back outside. Erika had forced the container open, and nestled inside was a book, about the size of a modern paperback. The cover was made of cracked leather, worn and slightly peeled.

Two black letters had been scorched into it.

G. W.

Parker whistled softly. "I guess we were right about who left the clues.".

He reached to flip open the cover, but Erika blocked his hand.

"We can't open it here. Do you have any idea how important this book is? An undiscovered piece of our nation's past?"

Her knowledge and experience were a big reason they had come this far. He respected her opinion, but only to a point.

"I appreciate your input, and I'm going to completely ignore it. We've almost been killed over this. I'm looking inside."

She clenched her jaw, but only for a moment.

"I'll handle it. I've done this before, so you get to hold the container and watch."

Erika removed a pair of white gloves from her back pocket. A small section of the back cover hung loosely as she lifted the book, only to set it gently back into the box.

"Put it on the mantel. I don't want you to drop the box and lose any fragments."

As Parker turned to comply, a high-pitched voice shattered his concentration.

"Put that box on the ground."

Chapter 41

Philadelphia, Pennsylvania

A vehicle turned onto South Third Street, moving toward the red-brick rowhomes.

"Understood."

Charlie Brewer clicked off his mobile. The boss, Mr. Keplar, needed his help. Two kids were in a museum in Old City, and they had something he wanted.

A freelancer, Charlie took whatever work he could find and didn't ask questions. If Keplar wanted these two kids dead, Charlie would get it done. He collected a cash payment and followed orders.

Brewer parked his car outside the Powel House and pulled up the two photos Keplar had sent to his phone. A man and a woman. Easy stuff. He strode into the museum wearing his best "I'm just a tourist" face and entered an empty hallway, long and painted a shade of blue that reminded him of Easter eggs.

A young man greeted him, all smiles. "Good afternoon. Welcome to the Powel House. May I help you with anything?"

"Yeah, I'm looking for my cousin and his girl. I'm supposed to meet them here. She's tall, blonde hair."

"They're upstairs. They just got here a few minutes ago."

Dollar signs flashed across Brewer's vision.

"Thanks. Would you mind telling me a little bit about that beautiful painting behind you?"

As the man turned around, Charlie craned his neck and glanced up the staircase. Several doors were visible, but there was no sign of anyone. Satisfied, he pulled out a metal police baton and whacked the guide's head in mid-sentence.

He dropped like a rock, but Charlie was ready and caught him. He laid the guy behind a desk, out of sight of anyone who might walk inside.

He took the stairs to the second floor, picking up a pair of indistinct voices coming from the upper level. With a boxer's light step, Charlie crept up the final few polished wooden stairs. Into his coat pocket went the police baton; out came a handgun. He also removed a thin, black suppressor which, when screwed onto the gun's barrel, reduced the sound of a gunshot to nothing more than a whisper.

Two different people were inside a room ahead of him, one male and one female. Outside the open door, he peered around the thick, carved frame.

It was his target.

The girl's voice was hard to hear, almost like she was in a closet. The guy was holding some kind of box. With both of them distracted, Charlie walked in.

Chapter 42

Nick snatched the phone and found himself looking at a map of Philadelphia.

A solid red dot represented the tracking device's current location. A chart detailed each time it had been activated by movement, and the most recent entry told Nick that Parker's car had moved a short while ago from its original location near Joseph Chase's apartment.

Now it was parked less than four blocks away.

Nick ran out the door, his still-steaming coffee left untouched.

He bolted down the crowded sidewalk. Passersby tumbled aside as the big man cruised past; heartfelt curses followed in his wake.

Parker's SUV was parked on the street in front of a three-story red-brick townhouse. He felt under the rear bumper; the tracking device was still firmly in place.

Some sort of flag hung from the colonial manor behind him. At first glance it appeared to be the stars and stripes. Then a sharp breeze blew the material up, and he realized the stars weren't right. In fact, most were missing, the remaining ones arranged in a circle. It was an original version of the flag, from when America had only thirteen colonies.

Nick peered through the front windows. The bottom floor was empty.

He twisted the thick doorknob and pushed; the door swung open on quiet, well-oiled hinges. A few steps in, and Nick knew something was very, very wrong.

The first clue was the pair of designer shoes sticking out from behind a large desk, which it turned out belonged to a slender young man who was currently prone on the floor, breathing but unconscious.

A bloody gash on his head indicated this guy wasn't suffering from narcolepsy.

Before he could help the young man, his second clue arrived.

Two gunshots from upstairs, followed by the unmistakable thud of a body hitting the ground.

Chapter 43

Parker whirled around to see a squat, wide man inside the ballroom door. His flat tweed cap covered a shaved head, and a black leather jacket shielded him from the coming nighttime chill.

In one hand was a sinister metallic pistol—aimed at Parker's chest.

How did these guys keep finding them?

"I'm not gonna say it again, kid. Put the box down."

He did, gently and slowly. As he did so, his arm brushed the heavy bulk of the handgun in his pocket, confiscated during their earlier escape from Independence Hall.

A loaded gun.

"What's inside that rust bucket?" The guy jerked his weapon in the direction of the box and then trained it back on Parker.

"No idea," Parker said.

Curiosity spread across the man's squat features. Footsteps clicked on the wood floor as he strode to the container near Parker's feet.

"Back up."

His gun barrel jerked twice, sending Parker and Erika scurrying away.

The man knelt down and flipped the rusty lid open. Ancient hinges squealed in protest.

When the guy looked down, Parker fired two shots and sent the man down in a heap.

"Oh no." Erika's shaking hands covered her mouth. "What did you do?"

"He was going to kill us," Parker said matter-of-factly. He reached down and grabbed the metal container.

"What are we going to do?" Erika asked. She leaned against the wall, hardly able to stand. "I can't handle this, Parker. I just can't deal with this."

He stood and enveloped her shaking frame in his arms. She was on the verge of losing it when they could least afford the distraction.

"You're right. We can figure out what's next after we get out of here. Somebody might have heard those shots and called the cops."

After a moment, she took his proffered arm and followed as he led her out to the stairs.

"Put the gun down, Parker." A massive, bulky figure blocked their path.

Erika's fingers pressed painfully into his bicep. Parker looked into the hard eyes of CIA Agent Nick Dean.

"I said put the gun down."

Dean's own gun was out, pointing at the ground.

Parker's handgun rattled when it landed. "He was going to kill us, Agent Dean."

Dean glanced around Parker, noted the body. "Who is he?"

"I've never seen him before, but he said his boss wanted this."

Parker held out the metal box.

"What is that?" Dean asked.

Erika spoke up. "It's what George Washington left for his nephew to find. We solved the code Bushrod left in his journal."

"A metal cigar box?"

Parker opened the lid. "Right after we found this, that guy came in. I have no idea what it is."

"Where'd you get that?" Dean asked, pointing at the gun Parker had dropped.

Parker hesitated.

"You don't want to tell me? Fine."

A pair of cuffs appeared from Dean's pocket.

"I took it from the guy at Independence Hall," Parker said hurriedly. "Erika knocked him out with it."

"Does anyone know you're here?"

"I didn't think so until that guy showed up. Now you're here. Guess I was wrong."

Dean pocketed his gun. "We have to move. Come on."

Dean turned and walked downstairs without another word, heading for the front door.

"What do you think? Can we trust him?" Erika's gaze shifted between Parker and Dean in rapid succession.

"He's the only person who hasn't tried to kill us today. I don't think we have much choice."

She tugged at her hair. "Do you have any idea how much trouble we could be in?"

Strangely, what he'd done didn't bother him at all. When that guy had pointed his gun at Erika, the decision had been easy.

"There was no way I was going to let him hurt you."

She leaned her head into his shoulder and drew her free hand across her face.

"It's going to be all right," he told her. "I promise."

She nodded against his chest, stepped back and squared her shoulders, her mouth a grim line.

"We better not keep him waiting."

Parker retrieved his pistol and they hurried downstairs to find Agent Dean waiting outside.

"Follow me, and put that box away." Dean plunged headlong into the crowded sidewalk.

Parker tucked the metal box inside his coat and they followed Agent Dean, Erika in the lead. Parker scrutinized every face they passed and kept looking nervously over his shoulder, certain they were being followed. Erika must have felt the same way; her head swiveled back and forth as she walked. More than once she ran into Dean's back, which earned her a scowl.

When they approached a small grassy park wedged between two buildings and a metal fence, Dean walked through the gate and found an unoccupied bench.

"Sit down," he said, in a voice that left no room for argument. "No one can sneak up on us in here."

They did as he ordered.

"Now, I want you to tell me exactly what happened from the moment I last saw you at Independence Hall. Leave anything out, and you're going to the station on murder charges."

Parker swallowed. The last time he'd tried to tell Dean what was going on, they'd been shot at.

"This didn't work out so well last time, Agent Dean," Parker said. "Shouldn't we go somewhere more secure?"

"No one followed us here, and I'm the only person who knows where you are. The one thing you need to worry about right now is me."

"How did you know we were in that house?" Parker asked.

Dean said nothing.

"How did you find us? Have you been following us all day?"

"I placed a tracking device on your vehicle in Pittsburgh. That's how I followed you to Philadelphia, but it didn't do me any good when you weren't driving."

"When I got back in the car and drove here today, you knew?"

Dean nodded.

Parker sat still for a beat. The federal government was tracking him? Maybe those conspiracy theorists weren't so crazy.

"Isn't that illegal? I mean, you can't just put anything you want on someone's car."

"You don't like it? Call the police."

Parker started to protest, but thought better of it. The guy had saved his life.

"After that jogger got her head blown off at Independence Hall, we ran. Did you ever figure out who shot her, or why they did it?"

"I'm asking the questions, Mr. Chase. I'll explain what's been happening when you're finished answering them."

"A man attacked me when Erika and I ran away from Independence Hall."

"What did this man look like?" Dean asked.

Parker thought back to the blur of his struggle.

"Dark hair, solid, Caucasian. I didn't get a great look at him. I was too busy looking at the gun and the knife he had."

Dean nodded toward Parker's pocket. "Is that his gun?"

"Yes. I actually pulled it away from him and tossed it while we were fighting. When he pulled out a knife, Erika whacked him on the head with it."

"Did you injure him badly?" Dean asked.

"He was bleeding all over the place," Erika said. "I thought he might be dead."

Dean whipped out his cell phone and displayed a photo.

"Was this the man who attacked you?"

"That's him," Parker said. "How did you get his picture? Do you know who he is?"

Dean ignored them and dialed a number.

"I can't believe this," he muttered. "Hello? Listen, that guy we brought in earlier, the one with the head wound? You need to bring him back in. I've got a witness who saw him carrying a firearm."

"Did you actually talk to this guy?" Parker asked.

Dean ignored him again, turning his body away. "I don't care what his lawyer says, just do it. I'll be back soon." He hung up and looked at Parker. "Yes, we talked to him. Now finish your story."

"After she hit him, we ran to her car and tried to get as far away as possible. Before we could leave, some guy on a motorcycle came after us. He chased us on the highway, shooting the whole time. He eventually crashed and we got away."

"I figured it was you two out there."

"Agent Dean," Erika said, "what were we supposed to do? Those two guys were trying to kill us."

"I don't blame you for what happened. I would have done the same thing."

Erika raised her eyebrows and scrutinized Dean more closely. "Okay," she said, mollified.

"After we lost the motorcycle guy," Parker went on, "we went back to Erika's office to study what we found."

"In Washington's sun chair."

Neither of them responded, and Dean frowned.

"Listen. If you work with me, I'm not going to ask about the fire alarm that went off. Emergency responders never located anything burning. I was told a wall alarm activated the warning system. In case you're wondering, falsely activating that alarm would be a federal offense."

Parker glanced at Erika, who widened her eyes in mock innocence.

"I found a leather pouch behind the sun carving," Parker said. "It had a single sheet of parchment inside."

Parker and Erika alternately detailed the pouch's contents, the mysterious mix of letters and numbers written inside, and the process they had used that had ultimately broken the code.

"How did you know where to look in the fireplace?"

"We didn't," Erika responded. "But there are only so many places you can hide something in it. We hit every brick with a flashlight until we found a hollow one. I pried it out and found this."

She indicated the metal box.

Dean gave a low whistle. "Not bad for a banker and a teacher. What's in the box?"

"A book of some type," Erika said. "I'm not sure what's written inside, if anything, but I can tell you right now there's no way we can look at it here, exposed to the elements. We have to go to my office or an appropriate facility to inspect it. There's no telling what kind of damage we could do without the proper equipment."

As she spoke, a pair of old women tottered into the park and sat down on the bench beside them.

"I suppose you're right, Dr. Carr. Besides, there are some things we need to talk about. Come with me."

Dean stood and walked away, not even looking back at them. With no place else to go, Parker turned to Erika.

"It's not like we have a better choice," he said.

Dean was a CIA agent. If anyone could protect them, he could.

They got to their feet and hurried after him. Several minutes later, they arrived at his car, but Dean made no move to get inside.

"We're taking your car," Dean said. "The government can track mine."

Parker didn't argue. Dean grabbed a few things from inside his sedan, and they hopped into Parker's red SUV after Dean pulled the tracking bug off and crunched it to pieces on the sidewalk.

They walked into Erika's office twenty minutes later.

Only once they were inside her office did Parker speak up. "Have you been able to figure out who might be after us?"

"The short answer to your question is no," Dean said. "This case came across my desk less than a week ago, and so far, all I've got are dead bodies, two kids with a crazy story about George Washington, and an entire pissed-off police department that thinks I got one of their detectives killed."

Dean's haggard face spoke volumes.

"I don't know what the hell is going on here or why this is happening, but I'm hoping you two can help bring whoever orchestrated your uncle's murder to justice. Seeing as how someone was about to shoot you over this"— Dean's head tilted toward the metal box resting on Erika's desk— "I'm guessing we might find something in there."

With a sharp creak, the lid opened under her touch. The leather book they had seen earlier, with the initials *G. W.* burned into the cover, stared out at them once more.

Erika donned her cotton gloves and opened the cover, and her eyes went wide.

Chapter 44

Preston Vogel paced back and forth in his office, clenching and unclenching his fists with each turn. The city slowly came to life far below him, stretching for miles until downtown Philadelphia merged with the suburbs. An untouched meal sat on his desk. With the impending announcement that Vogel Industries was to begin drilling, he'd been on edge all day, terrorizing any of his staff who dared to cross his path. Right now, his team's lead geologist was learning Vogel's definition of preparedness.

"I want everyone ready to mobilize within twenty-four hours of my call."

Preston Vogel had spent the day ensuring his advance drilling team was prepared to commence operations at a moment's notice. After their license to drill was officially approved by the government, his men would be on site within forty-eight hours. Time was money, and he wasn't going to waste either.

The small light on his desk phone blinked.

"Yes, Brooke?"

"Mr. Keplar is on the line, sir."

"Put him through. Frank, I trust you have good news."

Keplar didn't mince words.

"Parker Chase evaded our attempt. Given the police activity on Penn's campus, we believe it unwise to station men at that location, though after recent events I doubt they'll return there anytime soon. His whereabouts are currently unknown, and we assume he is still with Dr. Carr."

"What happened?" Preston asked, icicles on both words.

"My asset was found with two bullet wounds. Chase and the girl were gone."

"He was *shot?*" Preston's voice rose to a squeak. He cleared his throat. "Where did Chase get a gun?"

"I have no idea," Frank said. "Multiple firearms are registered in his name, but we had no evidence he carries any on his person."

Fury rose slowly, white-hot and unstoppable. Preston couldn't afford any slip-ups now, and for the threat to come from *a banker?*

"Listen very carefully. I don't care what you have to do or how you do it, but this charade ends now. Find Chase and Dr. Carr. Kill them."

"What about the items we suspect are in their possession?"

"If you can locate and obtain them, do so. If not, their deaths will suffice. Have I made myself clear?"

"Yes, sir."

"For your sake, I hope so."

He hung up before Frank could respond. If this went on much longer, Preston would take matters into his own hands. Even the appearance of weakness would deal his authority an immense blow. For decades he had run The Guild with an iron fist. He led by example, and if Parker Chase continued to dodge every bullet sent his way, Preston was more than willing to start pulling the trigger himself.

He poured a large measure of bourbon, and as the ice popped and crackled, he had an idea. A way to kill two birds with one stone.

As it stood, he had a problem. Parker Chase had knowledge Preston wanted. He wanted to know what Chase had found and what else he knew. If Chase were killed, then Preston's problems were likely solved. And recovering whatever it was that Parker and Erika had located might help him uncover the truth behind one of The Guild's greatest mysteries, one that dated to their founding.

A topic about which Preston hadn't spoken in years.

He picked up the phone. Alexander Newlon answered on the first ring.

"Dr. Newlon, we are faced with a unique opportunity."

"What opportunity would that be?"

"A chance to uncover the truth behind our past."

Even the good professor had nothing to say to that.

"You will receive a delivery within the hour. Inside the package will be a container of clear plastic stickers. Each is a combination digital microphone and GPS locator that transmits sound and location to a receiver, which will also be in your delivery."

"Did your man find Chase yet?"

The story of Chase's most recent escape left Newlon silent.

"As you can see," Preston concluded, "it's time we upped the pressure on our young adversary. Contact Erika Carr and arrange an informal meeting with her, preferably in her office. Attach as many of these transmitters to items in her possession as you can. Make sure you get one on her phone."

"Preston, you realize that as a respected member of the academic community I could lose my job and go to jail if I'm caught."

"Would you rather face the authorities, or me?" Preston said pointedly and hung up.

He sat back in his chair and took another sip of bourbon, deep in thought once more. Perhaps the most recent failure to eliminate the pair would prove fortuitous after all. If they were indeed following a trail laid by President Washington, there was the chance Vogel could tie up two loose ends: one regarding the present, and the other rooted in the past. Once Preston learned what Professor Chase had known, and once whatever it was that Parker Chase and Dr. Carr had found had been confiscated, the two would no longer be needed. Their deaths would cement his security during the upcoming expansion of Vogel Industries' energy division in Alaska, and might provide a glimpse into the events that had shaped The Guild's existence.

Chapter 45

Nick Dean looked from the book to Erika and back again. "Does that mean what I think it does?"

"I think so, but I'll need to inspect the book further before I can be certain."

Erika opened the cover with practiced care. Old paper, musty and brittle, crackled in protest. Each page had begun to fray at the edges, the passage of time forever leaving an imprint.

Elegant script looped across the top of the first page.

"'Mount Vernon, Virginia, 25 April 1797,'" Erika read. "That's one month after Washington retired from the presidency."

She turned to the computer and began typing. The printer whirred to life, producing several sheets of paper while Erika grabbed a magnifying glass from inside her desk.

"These are some of Washington's papers at the Library of Congress," Erika said. "I'm not a forensic document examiner, but we should be able to tell if this book's style is consistent with verified examples of his writing."

The oversized lens hovered over each document as she whipped back and forth, muttering under her breath.

Finally, she looked up at Nick. "This looks authentic. Of course, the paper has to be analyzed, but I'd wager George Washington wrote this."

"That's great," Nick said. "But remember why we're here. There are people out there right now who are trying to kill you, the same men who murdered Parker's uncle. I need to know if this book contains a clue as to their identities or motive."

Erika tossed a notepad into Parker's lap.

"Make yourself useful and take notes."

Parker wasn't sure, but he swore Nick *almost* cracked a smile.

"This first page talks about his distillery," she began. "The estate is producing whiskey, and Washington expects to turn a tidy profit."

Parker squinted, trying to read upside down as he wrote.

"Listen to this," she continued. "Washington is making plans for his nephew Bushrod's career. He's going to see if his friend James Wilson, who signed the Declaration of Independence, will recommend his appointment to the Supreme Court."

"Can you pick up the pace?" Nick asked. "We're sitting ducks in here if anyone shows up."

Parker's pen moved rapidly in time with Erika's voice as George Washington's thoughts and feelings came to life, over two centuries after the author had died.

Soon an hour had passed, and they were no closer to understanding why Washington had gone to such great lengths to conceal his personal journal. Erika was only halfway through the volume and Parker was getting antsy.

Suddenly Erika drew in a breath. "Look at this."

"What? Look at what?" Both Parker and Nick jumped out of their chairs.

"Washington received a personal visit from John Adams in the summer of 1798. Now, remember that in 1798 Washington was appointed as the senior officer of the US Armies by President Adams. He was essentially the commander-in-chief of our armed forces again. This happened because war with France seemed imminent, and Adams was a lawyer and smart enough to realize that Washington was a far better choice to lead a war."

"What does this have to do with anything?" Nick said.

"Maybe nothing, maybe everything," Erika said. "Listen to what happens next."

She turned the page.

"Basically, this says that when Adams came to recruit Washington back into service, they discussed more than just the impending war with France. According to these notes, Washington and Adams talked at length about slavery, and Washington had some fairly strong thoughts on the subject."

Erika pointed to a line of text.

"I can only say that there is not a man living who wishes more sincerely than I do to see a plan adopted for the abolition of slavery."

"Strong words from a man who measured each one. At the time, Washington was the most popular and influential man in the country. It would have been disastrous for him to publicly air his disdain for slavery. He spent the better part of his adult life fighting for and organizing a new nation, and I'm sure he realized a few ill-timed words could tear it all down."

"Why would it be so bad for him to say he didn't agree with having slaves?" Nick asked.

"Think about it. Many wealthy Americans, men who had supported and funded Washington during the war, made their money primarily through the free labor slaves provided. Most white Americans vehemently opposed abolition, especially in the South."

"We all know how that turned out," Parker said. "I realize there would be no way for Washington to forecast it, but if the Civil War was going to happen no matter what, why not get it over with six decades earlier?"

"For one, he couldn't see the future. Two, America was young and growing, still searching for an identity on the world stage. To be blunt, there were more pressing concerns at the time. If Washington had chosen to fight this battle during his lifetime, our nation would have torn itself apart at the seams and never risen from the ashes. It's terrible, but in some ways we're lucky he didn't speak out."

"What else does it say in there?" Nick asked.

"It seems that Adams visited him several times a month up until July, when Washington finally accepted the post."

She fell silent for several minutes. Vents buzzed to life when the heating system kicked on. Her office clock ticked interminably and Nick fidgeted in his seat. He and Parker shared a look, and Parker could only shrug.

What can you do?

"Nick, you're an investigator," Erika finally said. "Tell me what you think." She turned to face Agent Dean. "Washington has been writing more and more about his dislike for slavery and the inherent opposition between Revolutionary goals and the slave trade's existence. He writes about his intention to free every slave at Mount Vernon upon his death."

Parker scribbled with abandon, trying to keep up.

"While he's contemplating all of this, Adams is entreating his old boss to come back and lead America against the French. Washington isn't sure, doesn't know if he wants to give up the life of a gentleman farmer, until all of a sudden in July 1798, he agrees. No indication that he was leaning toward accepting the position of senior officer of the army."

"Maybe he had a change of heart?" Nick offered.

"I would be inclined to agree with you if it weren't for this."

She flipped the book around so they both could read the journal.

Today completed agreement to end the injustice within our borders."

"Talk about a cryptic statement," Parker said.

Nick leaned back and said, "That sounds like he made some kind of deal. The question is, with whom? Obviously the first suspect is John Adams, but why wouldn't he spell it out? Is there any other mention of an agreement of some kind?"

"That's the thing. There's nothing. Why allude to this mysterious agreement, which just happens to come right before he accepts John Adams's offer, and then not elaborate?"

"You may be reading into this too much," Nick said. "This is a journal, and what are journals for? To express your thoughts and feelings, things that you can't or won't say out loud. This was the only private medium for someone like Washington to express himself. Maybe it was just a note, a reminder about some issue completely separate from what he and Adams were discussing."

"You're right, but that doesn't fit," Erika said. "Washington wasn't given to random actions or outbursts; he was a man of purpose. He was conscious of the effect his words had on others and took measure of what he said."

"Which would make sense if this were a speech," Nick countered. "This is from his private journal, which was hidden inside a chimney. He certainly didn't expect the whole world to read it."

"You know what's strange?" Parker asked, his eyes on the text.

They stopped in mid-sentence.

"After Washington mentions this agreement," Parker said, "he doesn't say a single thing about slavery anymore. Not one word."

"You do realize slaves weren't emancipated until 1863? I don't think anyone in power seriously discussed the issue before the Civil War," Nick said. "Erika?"

"Look, it's as good an idea as any, but that's a stretch," Erika told him. "There's got to be a logical explanation for this."

"The lack of proof could be taken either way," Parker said.

"Parker, it's a decent idea, and we'll keep it in mind. I need to read everything in this book before we move forward." Her hand rested lightly on his, asking for patience.

Erika's phone broke the silence. She looked to Nick, who motioned for her to answer.

"Erika Carr."

A man's muffled voice was audible through the headset, but Parker couldn't make out anything.

"Good afternoon, Professor ... Yes, I remember that ... Right now? I suppose that would work. Can you give me ten minutes? Great. See you soon."

"That was Professor Newlon," Erika said. "He needs me to review a dissertation. It shouldn't take long, maybe a half hour, but I figured you guys wouldn't want to be here when he shows up. I also need to reserve one of our department vehicles to use. You never know when we might need another car."

"Good call," Nick told her. "I need to tell my men how to handle the mess you left behind, and the fewer people who see us, the better. Hide that book until we get back, and call me if you run into any trouble."

Nick and Parker stood to leave, but before they walked out Erika grabbed Parker's arm.

No words came out, but none were needed. Her face was pale, her mouth a tight line.

Parker placed a hand over hers and squeezed.

"Don't worry. We'll be close by."

She gripped his arm more tightly. Nick stepped outside and scanned the hallway, which gave them a moment alone.

"I can't tell you how much it means to me that you're here," she whispered.

"I know, babes. I wouldn't want to be anywhere else. Besides, I'm just a dumb jock. I need a nerd like you to figure this out."

She leaned into him, still holding on. It was like old times, before their paths had diverged.

"All right," he said, giving her hand a last squeeze. "Get this taken care of and we'll get back to the grind."

As he turned to leave, she put her hand on his face, turned it toward her and kissed him lightly on the lips. Startled, he kissed her back, and then she stepped back to her desk, all business once more.

"Let's go, Chase." Nick's tone carried some urgency.

Parker hustled into the hallway.

Outside, the brisk spring air had turned colder and snapped Parker back into focus.

"I don't know about you, but I'm starving." Nick pointed toward a sandwich shop across the street.

Parker's stomach rumbled in agreement. He hadn't eaten in hours.

"Good call. I'll grab her something too and we can be back here in no time."

After the traffic light ahead of them turned green, Parker and Nick crossed the street. As they crossed, a black Cadillac Escalade pulled into Erika's parking lot. It stopped at the front door, and a silver-haired man jumped out. The rumbling vehicle pulled away again and parked close by, and its driver got out and scanned the area before following his passenger inside. The building didn't have metal detectors, so he didn't have to worry about the handgun tucked into his waistband.

Chapter 46

Conversation drifted into the hallway from Dr. Newlon's office. Inside, he and Dr. Erika Carr discussed the merits of a dissertation.

Just down the hall, Frank Keplar slipped into Dr. Carr's vacant office.

The first tracking device stuck to the back of her flat-screen monitor.

Erika's coat hung on the antique wooden rack just inside the door. Keplar attached the second transparent plastic tracking button to the underside of her collar. Fastened to the black material, the GPS-equipped receiver became invisible.

Frank lifted her desk phone from the hook and tucked a third tracking button on the underside, next to the speaker. He glanced at his watch.

Less than two minutes had elapsed.

Frank slid open each of her desk drawers, but found only student papers. On her desk he shifted through a newspaper, several stacks of papers, a notebook with scribbled writing, and a metal box. The box squeaked loudly when opened it to reveal an old book.

Voices sounded outside the door. A small group walked past without stopping, but it was enough. If he were caught in Erika's office, it would ruin any chance of covertly intercepting information. A last circuit of the room ensured nothing had been disturbed.

Keplar strode down the hallway and out toward his vehicle. A few minutes later, Newlon appeared from within, joined him inside the rumbling Escalade, and they headed back across town toward Vogel's building.

Chapter 47

A chill hung on the evening air. Parker zipped his coat as he and Nick walked, hands stuffed into pockets. The streets were alive as they passed coeds sipping cold beer in any number of bars.

College life. How he missed those days.

"Let's try that one," Nick said before heading into a sandwich shop. Neither man said much as they ate. Parker couldn't get a read on the government agent; the big man's silence was almost gloomy.

"Are you from around here?" Parker eventually asked.

"No."

Tough crowd.

"How long have you been with the CIA?"

Nick's stony expression would have made rocks jealous, but after a few seconds he answered.

"Fifteen years. I went to Langley straight out of school, was transferred to Montana, and now I'm here."

"Montana? I didn't know there were enough people out there to warrant a CIA office."

"You'd be surprised what goes on when no one's around to see it."

Parker wasn't sure, but it looked like Nick smiled. Just for a second. He blinked, and it was gone.

"Where'd you go to school?"

"Columbia."

"What'd you study?"

A sidelong glance indicated the conversation was over.

Nick polished off his food and got up, leaving Parker to trail behind. When they returned to Erika's office, she was at her desk, the cracked leather book open beneath her nose.

"Did you find anything else?" Nick asked.

"Nothing yet."

For the next hour Erika pored over the manuscript, dictating notes to Parker while Nick fidgeted in a chair.

"This is the last page," she said. "It's dated July 7, 1799. That's only five months before Washington's death."

"Anything interesting?" Nick asked.

"Not that I can see. According to the text, Washington is about to leave Philadelphia, where he had been planning strategy in the event of a French attack. He talks about Mount Vernon and some other items, but nothing that helps us."

She finally looked at each of them.

"This was the last time Washington was in Philadelphia, so unless he had someone else hide this book for him, I'd guess it's been hidden in that chimney since July of 1799."

The final few pages were all blank.

"We had to have missed something," Parker said. "Why would Washington hide this book if it didn't contain the next step on his path?"

"I agree, but there's simply nothing that correlates with what we've found," Erika said. "If Washington didn't spell it out in plain English, which he didn't, we have to consider that he used a code or phrase of some kind that could only be recognized by the intended recipient. It's possible Washington and his nephew would recognize the hidden meaning of a word or sentence in here that no one else could."

Nick got up and peered over her shoulder at the book. "How the hell are we going to find a hidden meaning in this thing? It's impossible."

Hidden meaning.

A thought bobbed, just out of reach. Try as he might to focus, it remained fuzzy.

"Let's start at the beginning," Nick said. "Maybe we'll pick up on something you missed."

"Give me a second," Erika said as she rubbed her eyes. "My brain needs a break."

Parker stood and stretched, bringing forth the usual musical accompaniment of cracking vertebrae and joints. His shirt was torn from the wrestling match at Independence Hall.

A tear. Something that was torn.

Then it clicked. "I know what we're missing," Parker said.

"What are you talking about?" Nick asked.

"Where's the journal from my uncle's desk?"

"In my filing cabinet," Erika said.

She removed Joe's book and laid it on her desk.

"What are you thinking?"

Parker flipped pages with a fury.

Got it.

With a triumphant flourish, he held out the piece of partially destroyed parchment that he and Erika had found earlier.

"What the hell is that?" Nick asked.

"It's how we're going to learn what Washington was really trying to say. If we put this sheet on top of the correct page," Parker unfolded the paper as he spoke, "the cut-out areas should reveal a hidden message."

Erika's face lit up. "I even know what page we need," she said.

She grabbed his wrist and pulled him around so she could see it as well.

7799.

Written in the upper corner, the directions had been right in front of them the whole time.

"It's a date," he explained. "July 7th, 1799. That's the page we have to look at."

"Well," Nick said, "what are you waiting for?"

Erika turned to that page. What they saw now appeared to be nothing more than an account of Washington's strategic planning and more mundane issues.

Received word that Britain may be sympathetic to French cause. We must avoid this alliance at all costs. Our military feels the strain of defense now. Recommended to move diplomatic endeavors with King George from rear of import to front. Information on possible alliance taken from intercept of May 20 letter.

Time continues to chase all those of dubious character and suspicious intent from this former haunt of soldiers and spies. All around find fellow citizens engaged in the pursuit of Liberty.

William Lee acquired new piping for distillery, which we will deliver as per purchase accord upon return to Virginia.

A. Hamilton and J. Jay to attend estate in two weeks' time.

When Erika slid the sheet of paper taken from Joe's journal on top, a completely different message was revealed.

Sympathetic strain rear of May 20 letter chase is suspicious spies all around deliver accord to A. Hamilton and J. Jay

Each word fit perfectly into one of the holes. There was no doubt the cover was in fact a device for revealing the hidden missive.

"Not bad, Chase." Nick clapped a massive hand on his back. "But Alexander Hamilton and J. Jay? Who's the second guy?"

"That has to be John Jay," Erika said. "He was the first chief justice of the Supreme Court. Washington nominated him."

"What do they have to do with anything? And what's a sympathetic strain?"

"One step at a time. John Jay was the first chief justice of the Supreme Court, but I believe that at the time this was written, in 1799, he was the governor of New York."

A few taps at the keyboard confirmed it. "Yes, he was in office from 1795 through 1801."

"Was he the boss when Bushrod was on the court?" Parker asked.

"Good thought, but no. Bushrod wasn't appointed until 1798, three years after Jay left. As you can imagine," she continued, "Jay was a close confidant of Washington's for years. In 1794, we were on the verge of war with Britain again, this time because of issues with fair trade and the fact that Britain basically ignored part of the Treaty of Paris, which was signed to end the Revolution. Jay was sent by Washington to negotiate a resolution, and he ultimately signed what became known as the Jay Treaty. At the time the public viewed it as a massive failure."

"So Jay got swindled?" Parker asked.

"Not really. While the backlash it created did contribute heavily to the formation of what became the two-party system, in hindsight it was a shrewd piece of bargaining on Jay's part. He realized that the American economy was heavily dependent on trade with England and guessed, correctly I might add, that England would dominate European commerce for the next century. It also gave America time to grow as a nation so that we could actually finance and win a war with one of the world's superpowers. Had he not done so, we likely would have lost the War of 1812 outright. Instead, we basically fought England to a draw."

"Okay," Nick said. "He was no dummy. And Jay was close with Washington. What about Hamilton? I don't really know much about the guy."

"Hamilton was Washington's secretary of the treasury. During the Revolution he was one of his most trusted advisors, and it was well known that both men had similar belief systems. Basically, if Hamilton was on your side, you could count on Washington's support."

"Is there any connection between Hamilton and Jay?" Parker asked. "I know they were both tight with Washington, but did they have a relationship?"

"Both men were leaders of America's first political party, the Federalists. And before you ask, Washington was not a member. He was an independent, but his views closely aligned with those of the Federalists."

Nick stood up and began pacing again. "We've established that Washington was close with both Jay and Hamilton. As to what he would want his nephew to deliver to them, any ideas what *accord* refers to?"

Parker spotted a dictionary on the shelf and opened it. "If we take the word at face value, it would be an agreement of some kind."

"That's what I thought as well, but an agreement about what?" Nick asked him.

"I assume Hamilton and Jay would have been able to answer that question." Parker turned to Erika. "Did they have any common ideas or goals? I'm sure after the war ended, everyone who'd fought for independence had a different idea of what it should be. Maybe these three guys were all looking for the same thing."

"Let me see," she said, typing away.

"It looks like both Hamilton and Jay served as president of something called the New York Manumission Society. It was a group of white men who promoted the abolition of slavery in New York, and in 1799 they succeeded."

Parker thought back to what they'd discussed earlier.

"How does that tie in with Washington? I thought he owned slaves."

"He did, though it's well documented that over time his attitude toward the practice evolved. He was a lifelong slave owner, but his will stipulated that every slave he owned was to be emancipated after his wife died. A prevailing theory is that he didn't address the issue more directly in his lifetime because he realized how divisive it would be. As I explained earlier, there were enough obstacles for Washington to deal with at the time, so he avoided this issue publicly."

"I don't think we're going to figure out what was in this accord right now. We can look into it later, after we determine what the first part of this message means."

Nick was right. They needed to keep moving.

Parker started with the obvious question. "Any idea what *sympathetic strain rear of May 20 letter* means?"

Erika stared at the words. "I can't say I've ever heard that phrase in my life."

Since he'd received Joe's letter, Parker had been subjected to one misdirection after another. The secret compartment in Joe's desk, a hidden scroll in Washington's chair, and now this book stowed in a fireplace. Everything beneath a shroud of secrecy.

"Do you think he's talking about an actual letter, a message written on a piece of paper?" Parker asked.

Erika shrugged. "Barring any evidence to the contrary, it's the assumption I'd make."

"Then why would Washington refer to the *'rear'* of a letter?"

"Maybe the back portion contains a hidden message just like his journal did," Nick said. "Which would leave us shit out of luck, unless you have another decoding page handy."

"We don't, so we can't worry about it." Parker turned to Erika. "Was Washington involved with espionage of any kind?"

"As the commander of the army, I'm sure he had some type of intelligence-gathering network," Erika said. "Let me check."

Parker fleshed out his idea while she researched.

"So far this whole thing has been a scavenger hunt. We find one clue, and it leads us to the next. There has to be a finish line, and I doubt it's on the back of some letter. Whatever we're after has got to be bigger than—"

Erika gasped.

"It's not strain, it's *stain*. Sympathetic stain was a chemical reaction developed by a physician named James Jay. It was used for secret writing during the Revolutionary War."

"James Jay? Any relation to John?"

"They were brothers, and Jay gave some of the stuff to George Washington for use during the Revolution."

"That sounds credible to me," Nick said. "What do you mean by chemical reaction?"

"There were two different chemicals involved in the process: one used to write a message, the second to develop it. The first chemical was called the agent, which was invisible ink for writing the message. The second chemical was called the reagent, which, when applied to the paper, made the hidden words visible."

Across her desk, Parker added this to the translation. "There must be a hidden message on the back of a letter Washington wrote to Bushrod on May 20."

Nick frowned. "If you're right, what are the odds this letter still exists? It would be over two hundred years old."

Erika's chair rumbled as she pushed back from her desk. "Well, Nick, that's actually not all bad. What we're talking about would be a letter from Washington to his nephew. Unlike Washington's wife Martha, his nephew didn't burn all of their correspondence when Washington died. Give me some time and I'll see what I can learn about Bushrod's estate. You never know, we might catch a break."

As Erika dove into her search again, Parker's eyes began to water. The words he'd written mixed together, and a fog crept into his head. "Erika, do you by any chance belong to a gym around here? If I don't get out of this room and stretch my legs, I'm going to go crazy."

"You're in luck. My gym just renovated their branch here in University City. It's open twenty-four hours a day."

A plastic keycard twirled through the air and landed in his outstretched hand.

"Don't take too long," she said. "I have a good feeling about this."

His workout clothes were in his car. With luck, the place would have a heavy bag that he could kick the shit out of. There was no better way to beat stress than that.

"Thanks. I'll be back in an hour. Nick, you interested?"

"No, thanks. Listen, keep your eyes open out there," Nick said. "You can't trust anyone right now."

"I'll be back before you know it."

Parker went outside, grabbed his bag and walked toward the fitness club. People filled the bars all around him, though the sidewalks were nearly empty as the thermometer fell. A deep lungful of the crisp night air invigorated his spirits, and he could already feel the fatigue washing away.

Inside the confines of Erika's office, none of them had any idea that every word they spoke was being relayed to an office across town, where two men listened with care.

Chapter 48

Vogel and Newlon almost banged heads as they leaned over the receiver on Preston's desk.

"Do you think they'll make the connection?" Newlon asked.

Preston exploded. "What do you think? That damn girl is sharper than you, Newlon. In one week they've uncovered more information and gotten closer than we have in two hundred years. At this rate, they'll figure it out by tomorrow night."

As primary guardians of The Guild, they were the only two living men privy to the complete story behind their group's origins. Passed down from an outgoing leader to his successor, the director and the historian forever guarded the truth of what had transpired on a wintry night in Virginia two centuries ago.

The seeds for The Guild's birth had been planted much earlier, in 1765. British Parliament had just passed the Stamp Act, which required colonial printed materials to be produced on paper manufactured exclusively in London. The crown required funds to pay for British troops stationed in North America, and King George wouldn't spend his own money when the colonists' would suffice.

These taxes produced an instantaneous response. The colonists believed that only colonial legislatures should have the power to levy taxes. Under the banner "No Taxation Without Representation," a citizens' group known as the Sons of Liberty was formed. Demonstrations often turned violent and destructive as membership swelled. Such was the outcry that less than one year later the Stamp Act was repealed.

One Sons of Liberty founder was a member of the Maryland General Assembly named Samuel Chase. Chase would later become an associate justice on the US Supreme Court, appointed in 1796 by George Washington.

Chase also served in the Continental Congress from 1774 through 1778, though this period of service was marred by his participation in one of America's first cases of insider trading. Chase attempted to corner the flour market using information gained via his position in Congress, and when this came to light, his reputation was sullied to such an extent that he wasn't reappointed.

As far as the history books went, this was the extent of his public indiscretion, and he avoided further conflict while serving quietly on the Supreme Court. In truth, Chase continued his illicit activities with wildly successful results. Chase died in 1811 as one of the richest and most powerful men in America, at the center of an invisible network whose influence extended across the free market.

This position of hidden power, an ability to orchestrate and control the movement of goods at an international level, had been achieved through a series of meetings in taverns in New York, Philadelphia, and Washington. After his failed attempt to manipulate the national flour market for personal gain, Chase had taken a subtler approach. He identified four other men, each a successful and fiercely independent businessman with experience in differing commodities. One by one, he convinced each that if he would work in concert with the others, their individual fortunes would grow exponentially.

Armed with Chase's government contacts and the combined knowledge and influence of the new associates, their group had been able to predict changes in supply and demand for goods. By acting before the competition, they ensured that their profits soared, and their enterprise came to be known internally as The Guild.

In 1798, however, they came under attack.

Samuel Chase learned of an impending situation that would decimate their profits. Normally, Chase would either buy the person behind the idea or intimidate them into abandoning their plans, but this time he couldn't. The man who had conceived of the idea that would end their dominance was the most beloved man in the country, if not the world.

George Washington.

So, faced with an unprecedented choice, Samuel Chase decided to murder the father of America. With Washington insulated from society on his estate at Mount Vernon, Chase plotted. When word came that Washington had fallen ill, Chase grabbed the opportunity.

One of Washington's personal physicians was known to frequent the local gaming parlors, and Chase had purchased all the man's debt. After an extended streak of bad luck, the physician was indebted to Chase to such an extent that he could never cover his losses.

Chase paid a visit to the indigent physician and told him all his debts would be forgiven if he would perform a service. Chase also explained that if he declined his proposition, debtors' prison awaited the good doctor, as well as a swift death for his wife and children. Faced with these terms, the physician had little choice.

The next night, when the doctor visited Washington's estate to check on his health, a dose of crushed hemlock and its juice were mixed with his normal medicinal cup. Within an hour George Washington was dead, poisoned by his own physician.

The next night, Chase himself silenced his unwilling assassin, the body tossed in the Potomac River.

For the next two hundred years, the descendants of Samuel Chase had kept the truth of their success a secret, shared only with the current historian. Passed from father to son, no more than four men on earth ever knew the true story of how their country's first president died. This information was never shared with other members of The Guild.

However, Samuel Chase had not been a fool. His sources inside Mount Vernon had passed along whispers of suspicion, bits of overheard conversation that proved nothing, but suggested Washington may have known his life was in danger. Chase knew that if the truth behind Washington's demise ever came to light, those responsible, or their descendants, would be vilified at best, or more likely hung for treason.

As such, the position of historian had been created. Tasked with rooting out any mention of or references to Chase's plot involving the physician, the incumbent was also responsible for tracking down any record of the proposed plan that would have decimated The Guild's profits.

For two centuries historians had searched without result. In the early nineteenth century it was determined that the search would best be conducted under the cover of academic research, and as such, each successive young man who was to assume the duties upon the death of his predecessor had been directed into a life of study. The guise of academia provided sufficient cover for any inquiries, and with a healthy stipend from Guild reserves, the current historian was free to search for incriminating evidence unburdened by the necessity of actual academic work.

Early historians had conducted their own research into Washington's death, and all had maintained detailed records stored in Guild archives to this day. Combined with all the research and investigations conducted since their inception, the archives constituted an impressive collection of historical research and discovery in their own right.

"Did you have a chance to review our private collection yet?" Preston asked.

"Of course I did," Newlon said. "We have nothing. As you're well aware."

Vogel knew it, but still. Decades of fruitless searching had lowered their guard, and over time, the threat of exposure had appeared diminished.

Until today.

Previously unknown information surfaced every hour, and it appeared Washington had left a trail. Vogel didn't have to guess where it led. The Guild was under attack once more. If their secrets were exposed, the revelations would shake America's economy to its foundations.

"I won't let some damn girl destroy everything we've built."

For the first time, Vogel had the upper hand. He could follow his three antagonists in real time and strike when he was ready.

"We need to get Keplar in on this," Alexander said. "He can take them out right now."

"And ruin our chance to follow Dr. Carr's lead? No, Alex, we don't need Frank right now. What we need is a competent historian to follow this trail."

Newlon scowled, though he remained silent.

"I have some pressing business to which I must attend. I'll be back within an hour. If you're hungry, call my chef and have him fix you something to eat. If Dr. Carr makes any further progress, call me immediately."

Maybe an hour spent listening to a successful historian would encourage Alex Newlon to greater heights.

As Vogel stood and left his office, a thought struck him.

"Then again, Alex, you may be on to something." He pulled out his phone and punched in a number.

Frank Keplar answered on the first ring. "Sir?"

"Parker Chase is en route from Dr. Carr's office to a fitness club in University City. I expect him to be there no longer than one hour. Take one of the men and wait for him to leave."

"And then what, Mr. Vogel?"

"Make sure Mr. Chase never returns home."

Chapter 49

A brisk wind had picked up outside the gym. Frigid tendrils slid down Parker's back like icy fingers and set his teeth chattering.

Hair still wet from the shower, he pulled his jacket collar up and moved faster, hunched against the chill.

Parker felt like a new man after the workout. Amazing what a good sweat did for you, and it was with a clear mind and renewed energy that he hurried back towards Erika's office.

Hopefully she and Nick had found a letter from May of 1799 with a hidden message, and they could finally figure out who wanted them dead.

Wind whistled and few cars moved on the streets as he walked. Ahead of him a pair of drunks leaned against a mailbox, one shielding the other's hands as a cigarette lighter sparked ineffectually.

He moved to pass them, shifting away from the street and toward the mouth of a dark alley. As he did so, the lighter sparked, and something caught his eye.

There was no cigarette in the man's mouth.

Before he could react, they were on him.

The lighter-wielding drunk punched Parker and sent him stumbling into the alley, unable to see in the darkened corridor. He kept his footing until one of them rammed into his back.

Parker's martial arts training kicked in. His arm slid behind the man's neck and twisted as he fell, driving the man's face into the pavement with a sharp crack.

When he looked up the second guy was airborne. He dove on top of

Parker, knocking the wind from his lungs. Blows rained down on his skull, and Parker kept his head from hitting the pavement when he went down, but the heavy shots blurred his vision.

He couldn't make out who he was fighting in the darkness. One man's lay beside him, his leaking blood, while the other loomed over top, backlit by a street lamp, nothing more than dark eyes glaring down.

The dead weight next to him made noise, a guttural moaning from a broken face. He was waking up.

Parker reasoned that if he couldn't see well, neither could his attackers. They were men, just like him.

And men could be killed.

Parker twisted, the incoming punch skimming off a cheek and connecting with the asphalt beneath with a satisfying crunch.

Before the man could recoil, Parker grabbed the guy's elbow with both hands and wrenched him forward into a head-butt.

Blood spurted onto the ground. Parker knew from experience that tears would fill his eyes and the man would reach for his damaged face.

Which was exactly what happened.

Parker shot up and ducked under his assailant's armpit, twisting his arm around until the man screamed and fell to the ground, howls of pain bouncing off brick walls as Parker turned to find the first attacker.

A boot flashed out and smashed off Parker's chin. He spun into a brick wall and bounced off, pain lancing through his jaw.

Streetlights glinted on steel as the first attacker held out a butterfly knife, like a greaser from the sixties. Blood trickled from his nose as he slashed.

Parker's foot shot out, connected with a kneecap. It was enough to send the blade whizzing past his face, missing by inches.

The man fell to one knee, and Parker backed away, deeper into the alley. The knife-wielding assailant helped his partner stand up, though his damaged arm hung loosely to one side.

Even injured, two were greater than one. Parker turned and sprinted into the darkness.

The escape nearly ended right then as a Dumpster loomed out of nowhere. He spun on one foot and dodged the heavy metal box. Scant beams of moonlight offered faint illumination as he came to a crossroads where impossibly narrow alleyways extended into the darkness on either side and ahead of him.

Footsteps sounded from behind. Parker turned right, broken glass crunching as he ran.

Fortunately, he'd kept his running shoes on, and brick walls flashed past on either side as he accelerated. The only thing he carried resembling a weapon were the keys in his bag and his cell phone. His gun was in Erika's office.

Unfortunately, said bag with keys inside was lying on the street, dropped when he'd been jumped.

Two sets of heavy footfalls echoed off the walls of the alley. A glance behind him confirmed that both men were still coming.

Erika's office lay somewhere ahead, he knew, though without landmarks, he was lost. An intersection appeared in the gloom, again a narrow alleyway that veered to either side.

He turned right, hopeful it would lead to a larger, well-lit street.

One step down the new path, and his left foot caught. Parker slammed into the ground, sliding as shards of glass cut his hands.

He'd tripped on a wooden box.

He stood as his pursuers rounded the corner, and the breath caught in his chest when one of them raised a gun.

Parker dove before the shot went off. There was a blinding flash and the bullet whizzed past. A chunk of brick exploded. Brick shards peppered him as he crashed into a wall and landed on his feet.

He looked up to find both men blinking fiercely. They must have looked at the muzzle flash.

Two steps and he was on them.

With both hands, Parker grabbed the arm of the man he'd injured and twisted with all his strength, sending the gun clattering to the ground as the shooter went down, whimpering in pain.

The other guy bull-rushed him, but Parker slapped the man's outstretched arms aside with one hand while his other flashed out and connected solidly with a chin.

The man's head snapped back, his body flying past Parker to careen into the wall beside them.

Behind him, the one-armed man moaned, trying to rise.

Not so fast. Parker reared back and kicked him in the head, putting an end to that idea.

His lungs worked overtime. A street fight ending with two unconscious thugs and a hell of a lot of noise along the way, all near one of Penn's busier streets. The kind of thing that attracted attention. *Where were the police?*

He needed to be long gone when they showed up. Parker retraced his steps, found his dropped bag, and ran back to Erika's office.

Sirens hovered at the edge of hearing as his footsteps faded into the night.

Chapter 50

Erika's building was nearly barren as Parker barged through the front door. A janitor stared as he passed, the mop suddenly motionless.

Parker found Nick and Erika in her office staring intently at a computer screen.

"How was your workout, big guy?" Erika said not looking up.

He fell onto a chair without answering.

Erika glanced up and caught sight of him. "Oh, my goodness. What happened to you?"

Their eyes took in the gash on his chin where he'd been punched, the cuts on his hands from falling, the torn pants and shirt. What Erika seemed to find most distressing was the copious amount of blood that covered his torso, face, and hands. She leapt from her chair and crouched in front of him.

Nick got to his feet, one hand checking his gun. "Where are they?"

"In an alley near the gym. Both unconscious."

Erika's hand hovered near Parker's face, trembling. "Are you hurt?"

"Not badly," he said. "My jaw hurts, and these cuts aren't serious."

For the first time, Parker took stock of his injuries. His jaw felt as though the teeth weren't properly aligned, though his probing tongue revealed none missing.

Nick poked his head out of the office and looked down the hallway. "Are you certain you weren't followed?"

"Yes. They were the only two around, and they're probably still in that alley."

"We need to go back there."

Erika's reply was thunderous. "You're not taking him anywhere near that place."

"What exactly happened?" Nick asked.

Parker related the story, step-by-step, of how he'd been jumped on his way home, fought them off in the alley, and eventually escaped.

"I'm impressed," Nick said when he finished. "Getting out of that alive wouldn't be easy."

"How can you say that?" Erika snapped. "They were trying to kill him, and you're *impressed* because they didn't? What kind of person are you?"

"The kind who knows this won't be the last time this happens," Nick replied. "Also, think about this. Those two guys are our only link to whoever is behind this. We figure out who they are, we might learn who's after you two, who murdered his uncle."

She couldn't argue with logic. "Fine. But I'm coming with you."

"You and Parker follow me," Nick told them. "And take this." Nick handed Parker the gun he'd used in the Powel House. "Be careful with this."

Parker nodded. He had been handling guns since childhood, though most had been rifles. He checked the safety, pulled out the magazine to verify it was still full, and slid the gun into his coat pocket.

"Let's go," he said.

Outside the building, once Nick had verified that they were not being observed, Parker led the way, and minutes later they stood next to the mailbox where he'd first seen the two thugs.

"They were standing here. I walked past, and they jumped me."

Parker pointed into the alleyway. Nick switched on a flashlight and walked in, gun drawn. Black liquid on the ground sparkled red under the beam.

There was blood everywhere.

"We fought here," Parker told him. "That's mostly their blood."

Nick's eyes followed his outstretched finger.

"I ran this way, and then cut down here."

Nick's flashlight led the way as they crept down the alley. Parker shuddered involuntarily as they walked. This gritty path could easily have been where he took his final breath.

Nick stopped them at the intersection, peering around the corner for any sign of the men. "Keep your heads down." He put his flashlight on top of his gun as they moved.

It was only a short distance to the next intersection, and Parker grabbed Nick's shoulder, whispered in his ear. "If they're still here, they should be just around this wall to the right."

Nick held up a hand. "You two stay back."

Erika pressed against Parker's back as they both leaned against the wall. Parker pulled out his gun.

Nick slid the flashlight ahead of him, around the corner.

For a second, no one moved. Then Nick turned around. "Are you certain this is the place?"

"Of course I'm certain," Parker said as he brushed past Nick and turned the corner.

The ground was barren.

"What the hell? There should be two guys right here." A splintered wooden box was strewn on the ground. "I tripped over that box. This has to be the place."

Nick aimed the white beam at Parker's feet. Reddish tinted puddles gleamed on the asphalt.

"I believe you. How badly were these guys injured?"

"I didn't think they'd be getting up any time soon."

Nick's eyes never left the ground. "Looks like you were wrong. Check everywhere."

They made a quick circuit of the area, but found nothing. Even the gun Parker had seen fall to the ground was gone.

"Whoever they were, those guys knew enough to get out of here before the cops came. These weren't amateurs."

Nick led the way out, and a few moments later they were back on the main road back to Erika's office. A few police cars drove slowly down the streets, but if they'd been called due to Parker's encounter, they had nothing to show for it and likely no idea where to look.

Once they made it back to Erika's building Parker cleaned himself up as best he could in the men's washroom, changing into an old pair of jeans and a sweatshirt from his car.

When he returned to Erika's office, she and Nick were hard at work once more.

"We made some progress while you were gone," Erika said.

"What kind of progress?"

"First, sympathetic stain is basically invisible ink, and we figured out how to reveal a hidden message. All you need is something acidic. The message is written with a base, and when you put the acidic chemical on it, the paper fibers that have the base chemical on them turn brownish and reveal the message."

"What about the letter?" Parker asked. "It won't do us any good if we can't find that letter Washington talked about."

"We may have found something." Nick read from his laptop. "When Washington died, Bushrod inherited Mount Vernon. His uncle had organized all of his personal paperwork, and most of this enormous collection eventually made its way to the Library of Congress."

"Which is why Joe ordered that journal from there," Parker said.

"Correct," Nick said. "Now, I say *most of* his paperwork is stored there. A small portion is kept at Mount Vernon, mainly documents with a connection to the estate. Fortunately for us, the on-site collection has been digitized and can be viewed online."

Parker walked over to find Nick had the papers in question on display. He looked over their shoulders.

"Notice anything about this one?" Erika asked.

"Well, it's addressed to Bushrod. It looks like ..."

Holy shit.

It was from George Washington, dated May 20, 1799.

"Do you think this is it?" Parker asked. "Is this the letter he's talking about?"

"We don't know, but it fits the message," Erika said, reaching back and slipping an arm around his waist. "It's unlikely Washington would write him two letters on the same day."

On the screen was a mundane missive, mostly detailing renovations that were to be done on the estate, and an update on the growing distillery. Nothing that indicated the letter was worth killing for.

"Nice work," Parker said. His heart rate picked up, bringing his spirits along with it. Maybe they weren't out of this race yet.

"Don't get too excited," Erika said. "We can't just waltz in there and dump chemicals all over their exhibit."

Nick was watching a video tour of the estate. "The letter is here, in a museum a few hundred yards northwest of the mansion."

A virtual tour of the building played out, from the arched entranceway through the pillared classical rooms. The manuscript gallery flashed on-screen and soon showed the letter in question, stored inside a glass container and illuminated by an overhead floodlight.

"How are we supposed to get into that case?"

Nick stopped the video. "I don't see any surveillance cameras in that room. I'd guess those display cases aren't bulletproof, just wired. If we can get inside without setting off any internal alarms, I can get us to the letter."

Erika's head whipped around. "Are you suggesting we break into that museum?"

"I am," Nick said. "As you said earlier, there's no way we'd be allowed to walk in and dump chemicals on that letter. We need to access the building at night, with no interruptions, and test your theory. If we find anything, we act on it. If we're wrong and there's no message, we leave."

Her jaw dropped. "Are you out of your mind? First of all, how the hell do you propose we do this? We have zero total experience breaking into buildings, Nick. Second, what if we get caught? Are you going to use your CIA badge to get us out of jail?"

"You two did a nice job evading security at Independence Hall earlier. With my help, this won't be a problem."

Parker couldn't help but grin. It was nice that *someone* appreciated their work.

"Unless of course you don't want to do it," Nick continued. "I can go back to Langley, make a few calls, and get access to the letter. But that will take time. Too much time, in my opinion. I'm offering this to you as a favor for what you've done and been through. Parker's uncle is dead. You could be next. I suggest you think about my offer before you answer."

Parker turned to Erika and saw that Nick's words had hit home. Her brow was furrowed and she stared at the floor as if weighing her options. Parker had known her long enough to know that she was nervous but also enthralled with the chase, the chance to discover a true piece of history that had been hidden for centuries.

He took her hand, and the touch seemed to galvanize her.

"Fine," she said, her voice firm. "Let's say I agree to do this. I'm not a secret agent, so you tell me how we can do all this spy stuff. How do you plan to break into that building?"

"Piece of cake," Nick said, and motioned them to sit down and listen.

Thirty minutes of detailed explanation later, Nick sat back and watched them consider his plan. They talked in low voices for a moment, and then Parker and Erika turned to face him.

"Let's do it," Erika said.

Nick gave her a wink. "I thought you'd say that."

Clanging came from outside as church bells tolled the hour.

"Erika, you and I are going to get your chemicals and a few other things I need," Nick said. "Parker, wait here for my call. If it turns out surveillance has been called off her apartment, you go there and bring back some clothes. Erika and I will be back here within a few hours. We leave for Virginia tomorrow morning."

He stood and walked out the door. Erika turned to face him, and despite the exhaustion that Parker knew she was feeling, she grabbed him in a bear hug, her arms squeezing him so tightly it was tough to breathe.

"We're going to solve this," she said. "I know we are, and I can't believe I'm doing it with you."

"What's that supposed to mean? I would make a badass secret agent."

"Of course you would," she said. "I'm just excited that you're here."

As she leaned in to kiss him, Nick poked his head back through the door. "Any day now."

"Okay, okay, I'm coming." Erika kissed Parker's cheek before she headed out the door. "See you soon. And Parker, please be careful. I couldn't handle it if you ..."

Her voice trailed off, unable to finish the thought.

A gust of cold air blew down the hallway as they walked outside, though Parker barely felt it. His stomach was tight with an anticipation he hadn't felt in some time. Tomorrow night they would find the message George Washington had left, and Joe would have justice, one way or another.

Chapter 51

Alex Newlon raced out of the conference room and shouted at Vogel's secretary.

"Go get Vogel."

She merely looked at him, a nail file in hand and one shapely leg propped on a chair. Newlon's face reddened dangerously, and Brooke leaned forward and pushed the call button.

"Mr. Vogel, Dr. Newlon would like to see you."

Without so much as a second glance at him, her attention shifted back to the impromptu manicure.

Preston walked out of his office door to find Alex Newlon glaring at an uninterested Brooke.

"In the conference room, Alex."

Securely ensconced in the massive room, Newlon dropped his bomb. "Parker survived the attack."

Vogel's chest went rigid.

How could Keplar have failed?

"What happened?"

Newlon's voice was different, Vogel noted with interest. He sounded nervous. "He thoroughly beat both men who attacked him."

This banker had now taken down Keplar and one of his men?

"It gets worse," Newlon continued. "That guy they're with, that Nick fellow, is a CIA agent."

Preston Vogel had lived long enough that very little surprised him any longer, but those three letters made his jaw drop.

"You can't be serious."

"I listened the whole time. This guy is a CIA agent, and he's dead set on helping them solve this."

That changed everything. It was one thing to kill college professors, but messing with a government spook? That guaranteed trouble.

Unfortunately, Preston didn't have any other options.

"Brooke," he shouted toward the door. "Get Frank on the line now."

As he waited for her to track down his chief of security, Preston considered the news from every angle. No part of it seemed positive.

"Do you have any idea why he's involved?" Vogel asked.

"None whatsoever," Newlon replied. "The man hasn't said much, just talked about how the three of them could infiltrate Mount Vernon."

"What?"

"Oh, I forgot to mention that part." Alex cleared his throat. "Erika thinks she found the letter mentioned in Washington's message. It's on display at Mount Vernon."

Shit. Vogel sat back in his chair. If they located the letter—and if there actually was a hidden message in it—Vogel Industries could be in serious trouble. The thought of them getting their hands on that paper and seeing what might be written on it sent a chill through Preston's body.

"You do realize what could happen?" he said. "What we stand to lose if any record of our actions exists?"

"Yes, of course. I understand that this could pose a problem for—"

"A *problem*?" Preston said. "If you call undermining the largest and most profitable venture of my lifetime a problem, then yes, that's all we have. Do you have any idea how volatile this is, Newlon? Samuel Chase, of whom I am a direct descendant, murdered George Washington. He orchestrated the assassination of the most beloved man in American history. What do you think that would do for business?"

Newlon hung his head.

"Perception is reality. You know that," Preston said. "The public would turn on me in a second, regardless of the fact this happened two centuries ago. Not only could my permit to drill be revoked, every other operation I have a stake in would come under fire. And do you think it would stop there?"

As he spoke, a slow fire consumed him until Preston grabbed a crystal whiskey glass from the table and raised his arm as if to hurl it at the wall behind Newlon's head. At the last moment, he drew in a breath and lowered the glass to his desk with a controlled thump.

"Start the recording," Vogel said evenly. "I want to hear everything."

Newlon [pressed a button on the laptop he held] and Erika's voice filled the room. Preston listened intently to a half hour of conversation. As she spoke, his anger passed like a summer squall, the sky all dark thunderclouds one minute, breezy sunshine the next.

An opportunity had presented itself.

"That's it," he said, pressing pause. "That's how we handle this."

"What is?" Newlon asked.

"Listen again," Vogel said, rewinding. Agent Dean's voice sounded.

"Parker, wait here for my call. If it turns out surveillance has been called off her apartment, you go there and bring back some clothes."

"Chase is alone, either at Dr. Carr's apartment or in her office," Preston said. "And exhausted. Without his government guardian angel, he's ripe for the picking. If we get rid of him, I don't think the other two will be in a hurry to continue searching."

The phone on Preston's conference table lit up. It was Keplar.

"What just happened?" Preston asked.

"I'm en route, sir. I'll be there in five minutes to explain everything."

Preston clicked off. Things were bad, but all was not yet lost.

As he leaned back in the polished leather chair, Preston took a cigar from atop his desk and clipped the end.

"I have some good news, Alex," he said, deftly changing the subject. "All of my teams are en route to Anchorage as we speak. From there, they can access the Refuge within hours of receiving formal authorization to commence drilling."

"Has Senator Hunter indicated when that may be?"

"A vote is scheduled in three days' time. By next week, we will break ground at a half-dozen sites."

Visions of black gold filled his mind. Once he gained access to the untapped reserves, they would be printing money.

"Mr. Vogel." Frank Keplar appeared in his office doorway.

Newlon and Vogel both gaped. Keplar's face, or what remained of it, was a complete mess. Normal noses didn't swerve violently in the middle. Blood caked his hair. His shirt was ripped in several places and covered with dirt. Both hands were grimy and bleeding.

"Explain yourself," Preston demanded.

Keplar delivered a succinct summation of the botched attempt.

"And the other man?"

"Recuperating with a friendly physician," Keplar said.

"What a mess. Get cleaned up and take a seat. We have an opportunity to fix the mess you and your men made earlier today."

Preston resumed listening to the recording, and it confirmed his suspicions.

"...spoke with the Philadelphia PD, and they don't have my apartment under surveillance anymore."

"That's good news. I'll head over..."

The police no longer had Erika Carr's apartment under surveillance.

"Parker Chase will be here within the hour." Vogel slid Keplar a scrap of paper across which was scrawled Erika's address.

"I suggest you send someone more capable to take care of him."

"Understood." Keplar grabbed the address and left.

"I'm famished, Professor Newlon. Would you care to join me for dinner?"

Newlon said he would

"I'll have the kitchen prepare something for us to eat while Dr. Carr and her friend tell us exactly what we must do to ensure this message remains hidden for another two hundred years."

After Vogel ordered their meal, he lit his cigar and puffed contentedly while they listened to Erika explaining in detail how to reveal Washington's secret message, unaware of the bug on her coat transmitting every word to Vogel's ear.

Chapter 52

A buzzing cell phone jerked Parker awake. He'd fallen asleep in Erika's office.

He glanced at the screen. Erika.

He pressed Answer. "Yeah?"

"Nick spoke with the Philadelphia PD, and they don't have my apartment under surveillance anymore."

"That's good news," he said, clearing his throat. His head felt like boulders had bounced off it. "I'll head over there now."

"Don't forget to bring the two red notebooks from the shelf over my desk. They're research notes that might help us."

"I won't," Parker said. Except with this headache, he might. "Are all my old clothes in that one box in your room?"

"Yes. Oh, and my running gear is under the bed in a gym bag. Grab it too."

"Will do. When will you guys be back?"

"We shouldn't be more than a few hours. We'll probably be back at my office before you are."

"I'll see you then."

"Parker." She blurted his name out before he could hang up.

"What's up?"

Silence for a few beats, then, "Be careful."

"I will," he told her. "Erika—"

"What?" Her voice was softer now.

"I..." He cleared his throat again. He could hear her breathing.

"Nothing. See you soon."

He rang off and stared glumly at the phone in his hand. They had been so busy dodging bullets that there hadn't been any opportunity to talk about them, about their current status, about any of it. He could read her like a book. The same was true for her, though.

So why bother keeping his feelings hidden?

Car keys in hand, he shrugged on a coat and walked out into the crisp night. Stars dotted a clear sky, and the muffled symphony of city life filled his ears—car horns, a siren in the distance. Somewhere a dog barked. Shadows crept along the ground alongside his own, dark patches of earth and concrete contrasting with the glare from headlights and street lamps. His fingers brushed the cool metal handgun in his coat pocket. He loved being out at night, but now, suddenly uneasily aware that he was on his own, the stolen .45 provided a sense of reassurance. Growing up in western Pennsylvania, Parker had hunted since he was a boy and knew his way around guns. Before yesterday, the animals had never shot back, but he was still confident he could handle himself in a tight spot.

Nick and Erika had taken a cab, so his SUV was still where he'd left it. He bleeped the locks open with the key fob and glanced around the interior, partly out of habit and partly out of a newfound sense of caution. Satisfied, he climbed behind the wheel, turned on a classic rock station, and set off.

Traffic was lighter than normal, given the hour, and Parker was able to zip through downtown without any trouble. He turned down Erika's street and had just spotted a parking space when something told him to keep moving. Taking a page out of Nick's book, he accelerated gently and circled around Erika's place. No lights were on inside, and the street seemed deserted. So far, so good.

Just to be safe, he parked several blocks away and walked back to her door, checking over his shoulder from time to time as he walked. Sodium streetlights gave the sidewalk a sickly yellow tint. He passed a man in an Adidas sweat suit out walking his dog. Windows were open in several of the houses, and he could hear the muffled babble of television shows and conversations floating outside. Erika's neighborhood had undergone a period of gentrification over the previous decade, morphing from an industrial wasteland of empty buildings and pawn shops into a trendy neighborhood complete with organic coffee bars and doggy daycares. Not a place where he was likely to get mugged.

At Erika's front door, he paused on the stoop and looked around one last time. Nothing unusual. He clicked the deadbolt open, and a flip of the light switch warned him before he tripped over a pair of sandals. He kicked them aside, locking the door behind him.

There were two red notebooks on a shelf above her computer, just like she'd said. He took them down and set them on the desk, then glanced at his watch. Ten thirty. Erika and Nick wouldn't be back at her office for at least a half hour. Just enough time for a quick shower to wash off the dirt and muck of the past few hours. He ripped off his ruined clothes and dumped them in a heap on the floor, then cut through her kitchen to the bathroom, wearing just his boxers. He turned the shower on full blast and then opened the linen closet. *Dammit.* The shelf where the towels should have been was empty.

She must have left them with the clean laundry in her room. He scurried back through the kitchen to her room, found his box of old clothes, and rummaged through it to cobble together an outfit of jeans and a black thermal shirt. Satisfied he wouldn't look like a displaced frat boy, he dug through the clean laundry for a towel.

A heavy thud came from outside her door.

Parker straightened, his body rigid. He strained his ears, listening, but the dull roar of his hammering heart made it all but impossible to hear anything. Above the sound of running water, he heard a muffled curse.

Someone was here.

A shadow fell through the open bedroom door, and then disappeared. The intruder went into the kitchen and headed toward the bathroom.

Parker crept to the open bedroom door. Between the doorframe and a hinge, he spotted a man in a tan coat and dark blue jeans, his blond hair buzzed tight. The intruder carried a serrated hunting knife by his waist. A set of brass knuckles was clipped beside it. Weak light fell through a window and glinted on the blade as the man headed toward the open bathroom door and the sounds of a shower going full blast

Parker grabbed the .45 from his jacket. He flicked the safety off and racked the slide. The sharp metallic click seemed as loud as a gunshot in the stillness.

Shit.

He stood rock still, straining to catch any sound, but the noisy shower drowned everything else out. After a moment he crept across the carpeted floor and glanced between the door and its frame.

The lanky man had vanished.

Without knowing the knife-wielding intruder's location, Parker was effectively trapped. The blond man could be lying in wait, or he could be in the bathroom. Staying put in the bedroom might backfire, giving Blondie ample time to call in backup and trap Parker there.

A drop of sweat slid down his face. Nothing moved in the kitchen, but that didn't mean the threat wasn't there, hidden and waiting. Or perhaps coming for him right now. Parker jumped away from the door, out of sight.

He forced himself to take a deep breath.

Think. Don't panic.

If he stayed put, the guy might conveniently walk in and get shot—or call a buddy and overwhelm Parker.

Fifty-fifty odds at best. Not what he was looking for with his life on the line.

There was a second option. Take the fight to him. Parker might not get the drop on him, but he'd rather bring a gun to a knife fight than wait for the odds to turn.

He peered towards the kitchen but only found darkness. He squinted into the gloom at a shadow moving toward him. Parker blinked, and it came closer.

He dove as a glistening knife flashed above his head. He rolled into a crouch, bouncing up and jumping back. *Where did he go?* The darkness was like a thick cloud Parker leapt, fists clenched together to drop a hammer blow on the man, but when it landed wood splintered. He'd gotten the drop on one of Erika's kitchen chairs.

The table in front of him shuddered. Parker looked up just as the blond man leapt, knife raised overhead. He grabbed the man's knife arm with both hands, but dropped his .45, which disappeared across the floor and out of sight. Pain erupted in his ribs as the blond man punched once, twice, but Parker twisted the blond man's arm and rolled over top of him. They thudded into a wall, jarring the man's arm free. The attacker leapt to his feet and slashed again at Parker, who kicked out and hit a kneecap, sending the slash astray.

The blond man tumbled ass over elbows, landing with his full weight on Parker, and suddenly Parker couldn't breathe. *Gotta move.* He gasped, but no air came. The guy was crushing him, and the knife had to be coming, must be ready to strike. Twisting and turning, Parker kicked the wall with both feet and squirmed from underneath the man. Cool, sweet air filled his lungs, and Parker kept rolling, right over a speed bump that gouged his back like a steel punch.

His .45.

He reached out, grabbed it, and turned to see the man coming for him. The gun came up and fired in one smooth motion. Two shots in a row, both landing home. The guy stopped in mid-lunge, brandishing the knife as he looked to his chest. He looked back to Parker, and then collapsed in a heap. When he landed, his fingers slowly unwound from the knife handle, then went still.

Damn, but that had been close. Too close. Then the adrenaline hit, and everything about him got shaky. Arms, legs, hands. It all shook for a minute. Then it ended, and Parker got unsteadily to his feet.

The questions came thick and fast as he stood over the blond man's corpse. Who was this guy? How had he found him? Parker's chest seized up. *What about Erika?*

He grabbed his phone and dialed her number, and it rang on and on. No one answered.

Chapter 53

"Thanks. I owe you one."

Nick hung up the phone and tossed a pair of duffel bags in Erika's car, each filled with the kind of equipment that only federal agents with connections could get at a moment's notice. An old friend had come through for him, working his magic to get these bags of toys for an old friend, all of it on unofficial loan from the Philadelphia PD.

Nick and Erika ran through their checklist one final time as they cruised back to her office.

"We have all the right chemicals to make this stain appear?" Nick asked.

Erika tapped the collection of bottles they'd purchased at a grocery store. "Check."

"I have the mission equipment. Parker's getting your research materials, and then we'll have everything."

Erika's phone vibrated in her pocket. "Parker's calling." She pulled the phone out and saw she'd missed a call from him moments ago. Her stomach tightened a tiny bit. "Hello?" She put the phone on speaker and Nick leaned in.

The knot morphed into a massive boulder as Parker told her about a blond man who had broken into her apartment and nearly killed him. Nick merely frowned.

"Are you sure the guy is dead?" he asked.

"Two shots in the chest," Parker said tersely. "He's not getting up."

211

"Get out of there right now," Nick said. "Meet us at Erika's office."

Nick ended the call before Parker could ask questions. Erika barely noticed when he handed her the phone, as the world seemed to have slowed down and everything was a tad out of focus. "How could this happen?" she asked. "Nobody knew he was going to my apartment." She shook her head, and things got closer to normal. "No one knows where we are except you."

Nick's frown had morphed to a definite scowl by now. "Trust me, I'm thinking about it."

She didn't say anything else until they parked outside of her building. "This isn't the first time this has happened," she said as they walked to her office. "How do these people know where we are all the time? It seems like they just appear out of nowhere. If they were following us, I think we'd be dead by now. Don't–"

Nick put a finger on his lips, and then leaned close to her ear. "That's a good question, and I may have the answer in here," he whispered." Nick hefted one of the black bags they'd recently acquired. "I'll explain when Parker gets back."

Back in her office, Erika sat twisting hair through her hands again and again. She glanced at the paper on her desk, where Nick had scribbled the ominous words.

ACT NORMAL.

Beneath that, he'd scribbled *BUGGED.*

Nick walked around the room, using some kind of electronic gadget to search her office. A clock on the wall ticked loud enough to wake the dead, but Nick didn't seem to notice. Erika's chest froze when a long shadow preceded footsteps coming down the hall, and when Parker walked in she leapt up and wrapped her arms around him, tears welling in her eyes.

"I'm so glad you're okay," she said.

"Same here, babes." He hugged her back. "Same here."

She stepped back and wrinkled her nose. "You smell *clean.* Did you take a shower?"

"Yes. I needed to."

Nick grabbed Parker's arm and steered him to the note. Parker's eyebrows went up, but he stayed silent.

Nick pushed a few buttons on his gadget, and the device crackled. They both turned to watch as Nick moved around the room, holding the electronic gadget at arm's length and waving it over anything and everything in the room. When he passed it over the coat on Erika's coat rack, the thing started blinking like mad.

"What the—"

He held a finger to her lips, silencing her question, and then lifted the collar of her coat. Her heart dropped when he removed a small, circular piece of clear plastic.

Nick scribbled another line on the notepad.

PLAY ALONG.

"Do you know where we can get some coffee around here?" Nick asked. "I need to wake up."

Erika's stomach dropped. They had put a bug on her coat. But when? With the warm weather, she'd left the jacket in her office lately.

That meant someone had been in here. Recently.

"There's a place across the street," Parker told Nick.

"Why don't you guys grab some? I'll stay here."

Erika blinked twice and pushed her questions aside. "That sounds great," she said brightly. "We'll be right back."

She and Parker stepped into the hallway while Nick continued his search.

"Do you realize what this means?" Erika whispered. "They, whoever the hell *they* are, were in my office."

Before Parker could respond, Nick came out and closed the door closed behind him. "I think I found them all. There was another one on your desk phone and a third on your computer monitor."

"This is terrible. They know exactly what we're doing, and what we plan to do next. There's no way to get the letter now."

Heat grew behind her eyes. They'd worked so hard, and for nothing.

"Not true," Nick said. "We can use this to our advantage."

Parker snapped his fingers. "We can send them off to chase shadows."

"Parker's right," Nick said. "If we feed them bogus intel, that will buy us time to do what we have to. Afterwards, when we're ready, I can set them up to take a fall."

"What should we do?" Erika asked. If he knew how to turn the tables on these guys, she was all for it.

"I don't want any interference when we're in Virginia," Nick said. "I'm not going there on official Agency business, so the fewer people I have to involve, the better."

"Why don't we send them in the opposite direction, toward New York?" Parker asked. "That way they'll have twice as far to go if they ever figure out what we're really up to."

"Good idea, but the problem is when they figure out we're screwing with them. Right now, whoever is listening to us thinks we have no idea we're under surveillance. If we can keep them on the hook, we can buy some time and grab these bastards when we're done."

Nick fell silent as a lone janitor rumbled past, pushing a garbage can. "We have to assume that everything we've said so far has been overheard," he said once the man moved on. "Which means we're going to push back our trip to Virginia by a day. Erika, make up a reason about needing to do some more research, or say that you have to fact-check everything with an outside expert before we go. Parker, you and I will play along."

Parker agreed. "It's been there for this long. What's one more day going to matter?"

"Exactly," Nick said. "After we set the bait, we'll grab a few hours' sleep at my hotel and head down in the morning. Erika, leave your coat here when we go."

The darkness in her mind vanished, as though the wind had picked up and blown it away, bringing with it a new day. Now they could take the fight to these guys. If whoever was listening in bought their act, by tomorrow they should know what these men were after, and why it was worth killing for.

Chapter 54

At her desk outside of Vogel's office, Brooke's eyebrows raised slightly at the sound of glass breaking and a metal tray bouncing off something hard.

Time to order another set of rocks glasses.

She put her head round the door. Vogel was thundering around the office, waving his arms like a toddler and kicking the remains of dinner into the carpet.

"Everything all right, sir?" Brooke said mildly.

"Get Keplar in here now!" Vogel roared.

"Right away, sir," said Brooke, and shut the door.

"This damn Parker kid should have died three times by now," bellowed Vogel. "Three times he lives. What the hell is going on?"

Vogel reached for his whiskey glass but found only air. He took a deep breath, but it didn't help. He really needed to stop wasting such good booze.

"How the hell does this happen? What kind of imbeciles is Frank sending after this guy?"

Newlon shrugged, sipped his drink.

Preston contemplated launching a second crystal missile, but at that moment Frank Keplar darkened his door. Their surveillance bugs had captured Parker detailing his battle with the blond assassin. Pressed as to why his man had failed, Keplar was at a loss.

"Perhaps there is more to Mr. Chase than meets the eye, sir."

As much as Preston didn't want to believe it, Frank Keplar had a point.

"Before we move forward, I need to know who you plan to use now," Preston said. "Parker Chase is clearly more resourceful than we gave him credit for. We cannot leave dead bodies at crime scenes, unless it's Mr. Chase and company."

"I'm going to handle it now," Frank said.

"Glad to hear it. I hope you don't end up like the others."

Preston turned to Newlon, who was still sitting quietly, sipping his drink. "Alex will go with you."

Hundred-year-old whiskey shot from Newlon's mouth. "What?"

"You heard their plans," Preston said. "Dr. Carr has work to complete around here for another day before they head down to Mount Vernon. Chase and the CIA man will be with her. If we need to distract Erika, you are the perfect diversion. She'd never suspect anything if Alexander Newlon called and asked her to meet. Now you can dictate the terms by which Parker Chase will be dispatched."

Newlon scrambled for a way out. "Preston, this is crazy. I have no experience in this type of situation."

"This isn't up for debate. You're going. We cannot afford any more bullshit. Vogel Industries' board of directors meets in three days, by which time I expect to announce that drilling operations have begun."

Frank turned to leave. Newlon remained rooted to his chair, knuckles white on the arms.

"Is there a problem, Alex?" Preston asked.

The professor wilted under Vogel's withering glare. "Are you going to inform the others about this?"

"The others? The last thing I want to do is get anyone else involved, and, as you're well aware, I don't need their permission to do anything."

A receiver for the listening devices Newlon had planted landed in his lap.

"Now, I suggest you take this and do exactly as Frank says. As you so accurately stated, you are an inexperienced liability. Don't end up dead like the others."

Those words hung in the air as Newlon threw back the rest of his drink and followed Keplar out the door.

Chapter 55

Frank led Dr. Newlon into his office. Behind Frank's desk was a steel door, and when he leaned in to the retina scanner, the eight-foot slab slid into the wall. Alex gaped at what was inside.

Row upon row of firepower. Automatic weapons hanging above boxes of ammunition, bulletproof vests next to stacks of ordnance. There was an arsenal in the room, enough to conduct a small war.

"My goodness. Is this legal?"

"Depends on what country you're in. Hold this."

Newlon caught the canvas backpack Frank threw at him. Several small blocks of a white, clay-like substance went inside, along with several sets of wires and blasting caps.

"Is this stuff stable?"

"Military-grade C-4. You can kick it, throw it, or stomp on it and nothing will happen. Attach a blasting cap and give it a jolt of electricity, that's when the fireworks start."

Handguns and automatic weapons followed, along with boxes of ammunition.

"Do you have the surveillance receiver?" Frank asked. Newlon said he did. "Good. Now follow me." Keplar grabbed the green bag with one hand and slung it over his shoulder. "We're going to Dr. Carr's office. Once she's alone, you're going to occupy her while I plant a little present on her vehicle."

Newlon looked unhappy about it but said nothing.

A private elevator whisked them to the parking garage, where Keplar jumped behind the wheel of another black Cadillac Escalade. With the tinted windows and a night sky overhead, it was impossible for anyone to see inside the vehicle.

"How many people are in the building at this time of night?"

Newlon considered the question. "Not many. Maybe the occasional student or professor, but no classes are scheduled this late, so for the most part the place should be empty."

"Any type of security in place?"

"The university police patrol both the building and the grounds."

"Then a personal attack is out. I can't risk anyone spotting me walking around that building."

Their bugs indicated that Parker and Nick had left some time ago, and it sounded like Erika was in her office with a television on.

Frank drove in silence for a few minutes. "All right, Mr. Newlon," he said at last, "we have a new plan. You'll stay outside with me and keep watch. While you stand guard, I'm going to attach a bomb to her vehicle. It should only take me a few minutes."

They pulled into the parking lot outside Newlon's office; few cars were parked and even fewer people were outside.

"Apparently her car is in the shop being repaired," Newlon said. "Erika was recently assigned one of our staff cars, which would be—" he craned his neck and then pointed "—that white sedan."

Frank parked next to Erika's vehicle. No one was in sight.

"Stand in front of the car," Frank said. "Keep your eyes open and tell me if anyone gets close."

Newlon did as instructed, so when Keplar popped the hood open, anyone who cared to look at them would see a man inspecting the engine and another man looking on.

Frank grabbed a small block of C-4, about the size of his palm. A blasting cap and several wires came next, and Frank slid onto the ground and rolled underneath Erika's vehicle with a penlight between his teeth. Gravel bit into his back as he worked.

In under a minute he secured the charge to her undercarriage, wired to explode when the ignition turned over. The electrical current generated by the starter supplied the necessary charge for detonation. Anyone inside the car would be instantly killed, with additional fatalities a possibility at up to twenty feet. With luck, Parker and their mysterious CIA agent would be within that perimeter and their problem would be solved.

Back on his feet, Frank leaned over the engine, standing next to Newlon.

"See anyone?"

"Nobody," Newlon said. "I haven't heard anything on the receiver other than her television."

"Is it unusual for her to spend the night?"

"Not at all. Assistant professors routinely work through the night to supplement their instructing responsibilities."

"Good. Get in the car," Frank said.

Across the street, a railway station parking lot provided an unobstructed view of Erika's car. With trains arriving and departing throughout the night, no one would question two men sitting in a car.

"What are we doing here?" Newlon kept glancing around, unable to sit still.

"Waiting."

"I don't want to be anywhere near this place when her car blows up," Newlon said.

"I do, so we stay." Frank leaned back in his seat. "Soon this problem will be taken care of, and you can get back to your studies, Professor Newlon. Until then, we wait."

Chapter 56

Inside a hotel room on Fourth and Chestnut, several miles from Erika's office, Nick rechecked each of his firearms. Parker and Erika sprawled on one of the suite's luxurious beds.

"Do you think they'll take the bait?" Erika asked, her voice muffled. She was lying face down on the bed, her head buried in a mammoth pillow.

"I don't see why not," Parker said. "They've sure as hell been listening to everything else we say."

"I hope your acting wasn't so bad they saw right through it," she told him.

With a loud *click*, the slide of the pistol in Nick's hands snapped shut. "You two were fine. While they're sitting around waiting for us to leave, we'll be in Mount Vernon verifying your theory. There's a chance we get back before they know we ever left."

Parker yawned as Nick stowed the gun in a black bag, filled to capacity with artillery and other implements of destruction.

"Wake-up call in five hours. We leave at oh-six-hundred sharp."

Parker yawned again and closed his eyes before Nick finished speaking. Sleep overtook him within seconds.

"Wake up."

Is it morning already? Fog clouded Parker's head, and blinding light assaulted his eyes.

"Come on, sleeping beauty. Get up." Erika's curvaceous form hovered over him like a guardian angel. Except this angel shook him without mercy.

"All right, I'm up."

Nick was already fully dressed, and Erika wasn't far behind.

Parker hopped out of bed and into the shower. Within fifteen minutes they were on the road, traveling south to Virginia.

Eight lanes of interstate highway were wide open at this hour of the morning as they cruised toward the home of America's first president, sixteen miles south of Washington. The drive passed in silence, each of them lost in thought.

The drone of tractor trailers disappeared as they exited the highway and concrete medians gave way to luscious green trees, rolling hills morphing into smooth terrain as they approached the Potomac River. Down a paved, two-lane roadway lined with towering foliage just beginning to bloom, they entered Mount Vernon. A wooden fence that looked like it had been hewn yesterday guided them down the twisting paved road until the trees disappeared. One moment they were shrouded in the shadows of a hundred tall oaks, and the next sunlight lit up an expansive estate, a collection of period buildings, each looking as new as the day it was built.

Public parking lots branched off to each side, and they pulled into a spot away from the other cars, several hundred yards from the building housing Washington's letter.

"The estate opened a few minutes ago, including the Books and Manuscripts Gallery," Erika said. "We each need an all-day pass. How do you want to do this?"

She directed the question at Nick, who was taking in their surroundings.

"Sometimes the best place to hide is in plain sight," he said. "We buy tickets like every other person here and walk right into that museum. At this hour most of the tourists are going to be at the mansion, which will make our lives easier. I need some privacy while I check out their security system."

Parker didn't need any further encouragement to get out and stretch. His stomach was rumbling. "I don't know about you, but I'm hungry. Keep your eyes peeled for a snack bar."

Morning dew sparkled on the freshly mowed lawns, while a cool breeze off the river brought the promise of warmer weather. Signs in several languages directed them to the ticket office, and snippets of conversation in each of them could be heard on the air.

He and Erika waited outside the ticket office for Nick, who returned with three passes. Walking past a growing line that led to the mansion's enormous front doors, the trio headed to the manuscript gallery.

The single-story colonial structure contained an extensive exhibit of manuscripts, maps, prints, and books from Washington's life. A thick chestnut door slid open when Parker walked through the arched entrance into a spacious room, artifacts displayed within polished wooden cases, all under protective glass covers. Single letters alongside entire books were presented for viewing, and recessed floor-to-ceiling displays of period globes and other furniture swept a visitor back to when the author of these texts lived next door in his stately mansion.

"Welcome to the Gilder Lehrman Gallery of books and manuscripts."

A short, wiry man with a shirt bearing the silhouette of Mount Vernon greeted them. The shock of red hair atop his freckled face made him look like he'd stuck his finger in an electric socket.

"Thank you for joining us today. My name is Ron."

Parker said hello, and then ignored Ron's encouraging smile.

Erika's coy voice drifted past. "Thanks, Ron. I'll be sure to yell if I need any help."

A wave of red washed over Ron's pale face. Parker could relate to the guy. He'd had the same reaction when he first laid eyes on this beautiful woman.

"I think Ron likes you," Parker whispered in her ear as they surveyed the room, feigning interest in each display.

"I like that strawberry hair he's got. Do you think he's single?"

Nick shouldered between them. "If you two are done joking around, can we get down to business? Good. Now, do you see any surveillance?"

Parker studied the room. No cameras, motion detectors, or guards.

"I don't see anything."

"Neither do I," Erika said. "What about the artifact cases? There's no way they would leave those unprotected. Some of the pieces are priceless."

On the rear side of a display case, red lights flashed above a numerical keypad. A stainless-steel lock was latched where the glass top met the wooden stand.

"It looks like this is wired to some kind of centralized system," Nick said as he leaned in and scrutinized the keypad. "You need a code to open the case."

Erika shielded her eyes. "This is reinforced glass. It's used for climate-controlled environments. Makes sense, because these documents would rot away if moisture or excessive light were allowed inside the case."

Parker wasn't familiar with document preservation procedures. "You're saying we can't just cut a hole in the glass?"

"Diamond-tipped blades might do the trick, but that produces two major issues. If Ron is deaf and somehow doesn't hear the drill, the letter could be damaged from broken glass, or ignited by heat produced from cutting. Either way, I wouldn't recommend it."

"Which means we need the code to this lock," Nick said.

Parker rubbed his eyes. "Great. What can we do now—have Erika flirt with the head of security and get the codes?"

"Watch what you ask for. I could do it."

"That won't be necessary." Nick bent over to tie his shoe, putting his face level with the alarm. "I can take care of a lock like this in a few minutes. What we need to know is how they protect the entrance doors."

"How are you going to take care of it?" Erika asked.

"It's a fairly simple mechanism," was all he said.

Nick rose and headed into an adjoining room, but the letter to Bushrod was nowhere to be found. Into a third room; same result.

"Are you sure this letter is here?" Nick asked.

"According to the website it is," Erika said. "I don't know how often they rotate them, but that letter should be here."

"Chill out, guys. It's over here."

Parker stood in front of the first display in a room to their left, which happened to be the center room in the building's square layout. In front of him, without a doubt, was the artifact they sought. A brass placard summarized the letter's contents.

Letter from George Washington to his nephew Bushrod Washington discussing renovations to Mt. Vernon, one of which can still be seen today on second-floor parlor of mansion.

"Told you," Erika said. "Still, can you imagine the odds?"

Parker thought about the past few days, and the word 'lucky' wasn't how he would describe them. "It's about time we caught a break. Don't jinx us, or the next thing you know a whole team of commandos will be in here with guns blazing."

They'd found the letter. Now came the hard part.

"How are we going to get inside this case?" Parker asked.

Erika glared at him and Parker realized this was a time for inside voices.

Nick moved back from looking through a nearby doorway. "There are two options, as long as the guard didn't hear you just now," he said. "One, we create a diversion somewhere else and hope Ron runs off for a while so we can break into this case and test the letter."

"Why don't we just take the letter and test it in Erika's office?" Parker asked.

"If you can explain to the federal government why I'm helping you desecrate a national monument, I'm all for it," Nick said. "However, stealing it is a bad idea. You have no idea how fast the feds will come down on your ass if they really want to. It's hard to get the government to do anything, but once you make them mad, watch out."

"The best crimes are the ones you've never heard of," Erika said.

"I knew you were the smart one," Nick said. "She's right, Parker. We need to do this quietly. As I was saying, we have a second option. This building's security is pathetic. The doors are alarmed, but it's basically a home system that anyone can buy. The front door has two sensors: one on the door itself, one on the top frame. When the alarm is set, a current moves between the two sensors. Breaking the current triggers the alarm. I can take care of that in under a minute. Once you're inside, there are no motion detectors, so you shut the door and walk anywhere you like."

"That's only half the problem," Erika said.

Nick dipped his granite chin. "Yes. Once we're inside, we have to deal with the display case security measures. The keypad here is actually more difficult to bypass than the door. Assuming a five-digit sequence, zero through nine for each, we have one hundred thousand possible combinations."

"That's a lot of options," Parker said.

"Sounds scary, but I can get it open. The only real problem we have is time. Once we access the stand, none of us knows how long we'll need to properly evaluate this letter."

"I should be able to tell within ten minutes if our hypothesis is correct," Erika said. "But there's no way I can test the letter without causing some measure of damage. Even if there's nothing to find, the chemicals will damage paper as old as this."

"That's a risk we have to take." Nick's tone left no room for discussion.

Parker had been running through their plan while Nick and Erika plotted. "You can get us into this building, and get into this display case, right?"

Nick said he could.

"I doubt any guards patrol this area all night. Like you said, this is a system anyone could buy, so it's reasonable to assume this operates like the one you have at home. If an alarm goes off, a guard notifies the police, who come and check it out." He needed to look at this situation like a criminal. "Why don't we come here at night after this place closes? We'd have the estate to ourselves, and as long as we don't set off any alarms, all night to work with."

"Not bad, Mr. Chase. Not bad at all. You took the words right out of my mouth." Such praise was sparse from Nick. Parker bumped Erika's shoulder and gave her a cocky grin.

"Oh, stop it," she told him. "Nick's the one who can get us in here. You just stole his idea."

"Great minds think alike," he said. "Try to keep up next time."

Sharp chatter in a foreign language came through the door. A group of Chinese tourists descended on the room, cameras flashing.

Nick grabbed a shoulder in each hand and hustled Erika and Parker out of the room. "We don't need to be in any of those pictures. A smart cop would find these tourists and ask for their cameras after a break-in."

None of the other rooms contained surveillance equipment. Outside, the crowds had grown and the walkways were getting crowded. Warmer air blew through the trees.

Nick grabbed a map from a passing tour guide. Unfolded, a bird's-eye view of the estate depicted the location of every building.

"These little squares are staff buildings, off-limits to the public. They're over here." He pointed down the paved walkway toward one of the single-story structures. "Let's take a walk. I need to know where security is headquartered."

Tourists walked in and out of each building they passed, surrounded by manicured lawns and hedges. They passed a working distillery and the path to Washington's tomb, brick walls guiding visitors down the somber trail.

"These two buildings aren't marked on this map," Nick said.

Two structures, both painted the obligatory white and red, sat side by side in front of them, flanked on both sides by wooden sheds in which employees in period dress described what life was like on the estate two hundred years ago.

A pair of men stood outside of the house on the right, talking quietly. One held the front door open as they spoke, and inside Parker spotted an array of electronic equipment. There were more than a dozen video screens, live shots of various estate locations on each.

Erika took a few steps toward the building and craned her neck. "All those cameras show outside areas except for the bottom four. It looks like they're inside the main mansion."

Nick stared at her. "How the hell do you know that?"

"I've got good eyes. And I recognize the mansion's interior from the website."

"There's a camera pole over there." Nick said, indicating a slender metal beam that reached several stories into the sky. "And a second one down there. If someone was to stay along the tree line, they could avoid being spotted."

"If we come here at night, how would we get onto the estate grounds?" Erika asked. "We can't just drive up to the front gate and hop over."

"You're right. This morning, I saw woodlands on the edge of the property that aren't fenced in. It's thick enough to hide a vehicle in, even if it's close to the road."

"What about all the surveillance around here?" she asked. "Those cameras aren't going to shut off at night."

"If we come in through the woods and keep to the tree line, the only time we come within view of one is entering the gallery where Bushrod's letter is stored. We aren't going to damage anything to break in, so unless the guards review all the evening footage, no one will know we've been there."

"I still have to dump chemicals on the letter to check it."

"We'll be long gone by the time anyone figures out what happened," Nick said. "Even then, this place is run by a non-profit. They don't have the time or resources to figure out who we are. Trust me on this. Everyday felony investigations are given short shrift by overworked and understaffed police departments. A couple of crooks who didn't even steal anything won't merit serious attention."

Nick meandered toward the security house, map held open as though he were lost. "Follow me. We need to get an idea of the layout."

Past the small security building, they found themselves along the edge of Mount Vernon's maintained property. Even back here several groups of tourists admired the landscape, posing for pictures with the scenic backdrop. No one paid their group any attention.

"The unfenced area is a quarter mile from here, past the entrance," Nick said.

He rubbed on his chin, eyes flitting about like fireflies. "We park in the woods, make our way over here and stay in the shadows. Get inside that gallery in under a minute, check your theory, and get out. Ten minutes later we're back in the car headed to Philadelphia."

"Why don't we check out the mansion?" Erika asked. "I've never been here before."

Nick shrugged. "Reconnaissance is always a good idea. Make certain you get a handle on the layout of this place while we're here. You never know what might happen tonight."

Chapter 57

When Preston returned from a meeting with the board of directors, he found his head of security and The Guild's historian waiting in his office.

Parker must be dead, he thought gleefully. This called for a drink.

"Care to join me?" Preston asked, reaching for his bottle of Pappy Van Winkle. "The board is thrilled with my earnings projections, and it looks like we have something else to celebrate."

He turned, bottle in hand, and saw their dour expressions. His glee evaporated.

They had failed.

"We think they're in Virginia," Frank told him.

Preston took a deep breath, and then set the bottle down.

"How did you miss them?"

Newlon studied the plush carpet.

Keplar glanced at Newlon, then cleared his throat. "They found the listening devices we planted. Before we put the bomb on her car, Dr. Carr, as you heard, requested an extra day to verify her findings. Dr. Newlon and I watched her vehicle all night, but when there was no activity through the evening and into this morning, we went into her office."

Vogel didn't need to hear the rest.

"We found a television on, and anything with a bug on it was still inside her office."

"A college professor tricked you."

228

Newlon stared at a spot six inches above Vogel's head, unblinking.

"And while you two were scratching your asses, the three of them got a head start on their search." Preston had to admit it was a shrewd move on her part.

"I put a trace on Erika's cell phone," Keplar said. "We're able to trace any call she makes."

"Call her, Alex," Vogel said. "Ask her some stupid history question or something."

"I already tried. She didn't answer. I'm worried she's suspicious."

"Then I suggest you kill her." Preston walked behind his desk and sat down. "Here's what you're going to do." Preston pointed at Keplar. "Take five men you trust. If you think that the group are in Mount Vernon, go down there and find them. I don't care how you do it or how much it costs. Find Parker Chase and Erika Carr and kill them. Do you understand? I cannot afford for either of those people to interfere with my plans."

Keplar nodded, while Alex Newlon walked to the bar and poured himself a tall glass of whiskey. Several drops spilled as he drained it in one gulp.

"What does it matter if they find anything?" Newlon asked. "It will be a fascinating historical discovery, but how could it possibly affect us? I don't know if I can do this, Preston. They've got a CIA agent with them, for God's sake. What do you think will happen if we kill a federal agent?"

"What could happen?" Preston said, his voice rising. "You know damn well what will happen. If Erika Carr finds legitimate, documented proof that Samuel Chase murdered George Washington, what do you think that will do to us? Whatever she finds may implicate our ancestors, and from there it won't be much of a stretch to connect it with the two of us. Can you imagine the public outcry? Even though we were born two hundred years after the crime, what do you think would happen to my drilling permit?"

Newlon was silent, twirling the whiskey bottle slowly in his hand.

"I'll tell you what would happen," Preston said. "Congress would revoke my permit, which would cost me *billions*. Now, does that sound like it matters?"

Newlon poured himself another drink before walking out into the hall, closing the door softly behind him.

"I'll gather my men immediately," Keplar said.

"Call me when you find them. I have some questions I need to ask Dr. Carr before this is finished."

Keplar left the room. Preston fell into his chair and squeezed his eyes shut. No matter how slight the chance, he couldn't afford to risk it. Not when there could be a two-hundred-year-old smoking gun hidden in Virginia.

On the one hand, maybe there would be no way to tie Preston Vogel to the crime. Maybe he was worried about nothing.

And on the other, maybe two centuries of hard work were about to come crashing down around his ears.

Chapter 58

Erika had missed her calling as a tour guide. Beginning with the upper and lower gardens, she pointed out the estate's extensive variety of trees, which included boxwoods from Washington's day. From there they visited the simple tomb holding the remains of George and Martha. Other galleries brought out Erika's inner child, a passion for her country's origins that managed to draw even Nick out of his carefully constructed shell. For a few minutes, Parker forgot about the past week's events as Erika's contagious enthusiasm eased the tension he felt about the coming evening.

A short while later, the main attraction loomed in front of them. Sandstone walkways splashed with sunlight led to the mansion's front entrance, which they bypassed. Around back, groups of tourists stood on the grassy banks of the Potomac River. Behind them, eight towering columns supported an overhanging roof.

"We have to go over our plan one more time before this evening," Nick said. "This is the last stop."

"I'll make this quick."

An expansive red door stood open, inviting visitors inside. Fifty feet above them, a golden dove weathervane rotated in the breeze.

A wide staircase framed with dark wooden handrails dominated the central passage. Period furniture whisked visitors back in time.

"For the home of a president," Parker said, "these rooms aren't very big."

231

They passed through a downstairs dining room. A table set for five nearly filled the space. The general's study, leading off the dining room, was larger, more befitting a man of his stature.

"Two hundred years ago, this was a mansion with no equal." Erika brushed her fingers over a polished bookcase, next to which was a chair Washington had used. "At the time it was completely normal for an entire family to live in a single room. Everyone shared the same bed, and if it was really cold outside, they might bring the animals in so they didn't freeze to death."

A bust of Washington sat on a pedestal in the corner. Parker had to check twice, but the plaque underneath stated it was an actual plaster mask taken from Washington's face.

The second floor contained several additional bedrooms, including the master chambers. Inside that they found a writing desk, clock, and table, all authentic pieces used by George and Martha.

Next, they filed up another wooden staircase, with hand-hewn banisters supporting the rail, to the third floor. Erika led them into the mansion's pinnacle, a hexagonal cupola offering a three-hundred-sixty-degree view of the grounds. To one side, the Potomac's glistening expanse swept by, whitecaps gliding on the water's surface. A brisk wind buffeted the windows, and the cool air raised the hairs on Parker's arms.

He glanced at Erika, whose nose was inches from the window glass.

"The view is fantastic," she said. Barren limbs flared out from dozens of trees. Parker could only imagine how it would look in the fall, an explosion of color.

"Good view, but I feel trapped up here." Nick tested a window, which didn't budge.

"You could always climb out on the roof and jump down," Parker joked.

"Until one of those tiles slides out and you're lying on the front lawn with a broken neck. No, I'll stick with the stairs." Nick moved toward the winding staircase and signaled their time was up.

Once they were outside, with the sun beating down, Erika grabbed Nick and handed him a camera.

"Will you take a picture of us on the front lawn? Please?"

"Do you think it's a good idea to document our visit?" Nick asked. "In case you forgot, we're planning on breaking in here tonight."

"I know, but one picture of us won't hurt. I'll keep it on the memory card and delete it tomorrow. Please?"

Nick looked at her, then to Parker. "I suppose. If we get caught, this picture won't matter."

Erika ran back to Parker and pulled him in front of the mansion.

"Stand still." Nick snapped the photo, which Erika promptly ran over to inspect.

"Oh, I like it."

Wispy white clouds dotted the light blue sky above the mansion, a perfect backdrop for the shining golden weathervane atop the cupola.

She leaned her head on Parker's shoulder as they studied the picture. "It's beautiful. I hope we can put this all behind us after tonight."

"Who knows? You may be a celebrity tomorrow," Parker said. "Indiana Carr, celebrity historian."

"I would be happy with things going back to normal. I miss those days." She leaned back and looked up at him, her eyes coming alive with radiant flecks of iridescent light.

"Come on, you two," Nick said. "We need to move."

Parker looked up, and Erika's hand fell from his shoulder.

"He's right. We'd better get going."

Erika's phone started ringing as they walked. "Hi, Mom. Yes, I'm fine. I'm with Parker right now. Yes, *Parker.*"

He shook his head as she walked ahead. Her mom was going to grill her for all the details, wondering if they were back on. She'd always been his biggest fan.

As they headed toward the parking lots, Parker glanced at the magnificent home and wondered if it would appear so inviting in the moonlight.

Chapter 59

"We found her," Frank Keplar said.

Preston breathed a sigh of relief into the phone. Maybe his head of security wasn't totally useless. "How?"

"An incoming cell phone call. Received two minutes ago in Fairfax County, Virginia."

Mount Vernon was located in Fairfax County. Keplar was currently five miles from George Washington's estate.

"What did she say?"

"Not much, but we confirmed she is with Parker Chase."

As long as Preston knew where they were, he had the upper hand.

"Do you want us to grab them now?" Frank asked.

"No, not yet. Follow them, see what they're up to, but don't make contact. I want to know if there's anything to their little theory." Preston clicked off and considered their position.

Frank had a half-dozen men armed with enough firepower to vaporize anyone in their way. No reason to go in shooting when they could hang back and let Erika keep searching.

So far, Vogel's so-called expert had failed to provide one single shred of useful information. If Dr. Carr could do the hard work, Preston would be more than happy to wait.

Preston hit the intercom button on his desk phone.

"Brooke, get Senator Hunter on the phone."

A few moments later, Hunter's voice came through in a whisper. "Preston, what can I do for you?"

"Speak up. I can't hear a damn thing."

"I'm in session right now." Booming voices in the background faded to nothing, and Hunter cleared his throat. "That's better. Now, what can I do for you?"

"When the hell are you going to get my approval formalized?"

"Preston, I can't push the vote to an earlier date than it is now. It looks like a vote will occur within two days, but you know how long-winded my venerable colleagues can be."

The two-faced politispeak was infuriating. These pompous bastards tended to forget they served at the will of the people, and Preston had the money to make sure Hunter would continue to serve.

Or not, if the senator failed him.

"Make this happen, Hunter. Every day I wait costs me money. Money, which I shouldn't have to remind you, that will cover any checks I happen to write."

"Preston, you have my full assurance this will be handled in the most expedient manner possible."

"Do you think I'm just some pissant citizen who believes your bullshit?" Vogel said, his face growing hot. "You can fool the sheep who vote for you, but not me. I have the money, Hunter. If I don't want you to be reelected, you won't be. Don't patronize me like all your other yes-men. Make this happen, and make it happen now."

Preston slammed the phone down. How dare Hunter treat him in such a manner. Who did he think he was dealing with? Men like him, and there were precious few, weren't bound by the rules of normal society. If Hunter couldn't be counted on to follow through with his promises, Preston would find a new mouthpiece to do his bidding.

Chapter 60

"Again," Nick said.

Parker rubbed eyes that felt like sandpaper, an after-effect of his short-lived nap. They were in a hotel room ten miles from Mount Vernon, paid for in cash.

"Nick, we went over this three times already. I know what to do."

"Do you know why soldiers are able to break down an automatic weapon under fire with no problem?" Nick asked. "It's because they practice. We can't practice our plan, so the best way to make sure you don't screw up is to say it out loud, over and over. If we get in a tight spot tonight, I don't want you to freeze up. Now, do it again."

For the past hour Nick had presented their plan of attack for the evening, with Parker and Erika reciting their roles again and again.

Parker sighed. "Once you make sure no one is around, we park the car a quarter mile from the entrance and off the road. We follow directly behind you, no talking. When we reach the parking lot fence, we follow it to the gallery. The gallery's rear wall is two hundred feet from the fence line."

"Correct." Nick stopped Parker and turned to Erika. "What's next?"

"I follow you with Parker behind me to the rear wall," she said. "After you disarm the front door, we keep our backs against the wall until we get to the door. Go inside, head straight for the letter. You open the case, and then I go to work."

"Right so far. Parker?"

"After Erika is finished, I help you put the glass cover back on, you relock it, and we go back to the front door. You go outside first, then we follow you all the way to the car and get the hell out of town."

"Correct. In and out in thirty minutes."

Nick stood and opened the black duffel bag that had been stored in his trunk since they left Philadelphia. "Where's the gun you took from Independence Hall?"

Parker pointed to a dresser drawer. "Underneath one of my shirts."

"Wrap it in a towel and throw it in the trash out back. That weapon could have been used in any number of crimes."

"What if I need it tonight?" Parker asked.

Nick's steely glare shut him up.

"If we run into trouble, the only thing you're going to do is put your hands up," Nick said. "What are you going to do, shoot a cop?"

"If I didn't have that gun at Erika's apartment, I'd be dead right now."

"If I'd been there, you would have been fine without it."

He had a point. Not that Parker would admit it. "What if you get hurt? Are we supposed to just lie down and die? I'm not leaving it here, not when she's coming with us."

Nick stared at him, but finally removed several handguns from the bag. "Listen. I'm only doing this to protect you. I know you don't agree."

Parker held his gaze and didn't respond.

"All right, how about you take this?" Nick indicated one of the pistols on the bed. "And don't take the safety off unless I say so or unless I'm down."

"That would work," Parker said.

"Fine. Under no circumstances do you draw that if law enforcement shows up. This is only for defending your life, mine, or Erika's. Understood?"

Parker said he did. Score one for the good guys.

"Sunset is in one hour," Erika said. "Forecast calls for clear skies and a light breeze tonight. We should have plenty of moonlight to work under."

"It could be worse. Cloud cover would help with the cameras or any security guards, but motion detectors and electronic locks don't need light to work."

Nick finished concealing an impressive assortment of firearms about his body, holstering one on his back, another under a shoulder, and another one on his ankle. He, Erika and Parker all wore dark shirts and pants.

Parker looked across the room at Erika. She caught his eye and quickly looked down, feet tapping as she studied the computer on her knees.

Nick zipped the duffel bag and set it by the door.

"We leave in one hour."

Chapter 61

Mount Vernon, Virginia

A gentle but no-nonsense feminine voice came over the PA system, reminding visitors that the people dressed like servants and farmers wanted to get home to their families.

"All visitors, the estate will be closing in five minutes. Please make your way to the parking lots. Thank you for visiting Mount Vernon."

A red sun touched the horizon, the final rays of light sending shadows up the walls of every building.

Frank Keplar had been over the entire estate and found no sign of Parker Chase or Erika Carr. He stood at the rear of the exiting crowd listening to departing tourists recounting in wonder the sights they'd taken in. A group of schoolchildren barreled past, nearly knocking Frank off his feet as they raced out.

After the last visitors had departed, Frank drove his armored Escalade to an office complex north of the estate. Vogel Industries maintained a suite in one of the buildings, and it would serve as the staging point for his operation this evening.

Franking parked next to an identical SUV outside a nondescript three-story building nestled among a dozen other similar structures. Inside, opaque glass doors opened to a hallway lined with suites.

V. I. was stenciled across one of them. A keycard opened the magnetic lock to reveal six heavily armed mercenaries seated at a small meeting table. Throat microphones dotted each man's neck. Every man carried a suppressed Heckler & Koch MP5 submachine gun. It was hard to tell them apart, with each man dressed in muted green fatigues.

Frank took a seat at the table and laid out a map of Mount Vernon. "My best guess is that the targets will go to this building." He indicated the only gallery in which he'd been able to find a letter to Bushrod Washington from his uncle. "The estate's security consists of pole-mounted cameras on the grounds, electronic locks and motion detectors inside the buildings. All operations are run from this building." He tapped a guardhouse next to the mansion. "And there are two night guards, neither of whom leave this building unless an alarm is activated. Your team will establish a perimeter outside the grounds. Even if the targets access the area via the Potomac River to the east, they'll have to pass one of us to get inside."

A man whose beard stretched halfway down his chest spoke up. "What's the procedure if we spot them?"

"Detention prior to elimination."

Frank passed out photos, one each of Parker, Erika, and Nick. "My superior wishes to speak with them prior to disposal. This man"— he pointed at Nick's headshot—"is a Central Intelligence agent."

Six sets of eyebrows went up, their equivalent of an uproar. "Agent Dean is a former Navy SEAL, and during his time in the service he was the heavyweight boxing champion of the entire naval fighting force. He will kill you before you can blink."

Frank pointed to the next photo. "This is Parker Chase. He has survived at least four prior attempts at neutralization, including one I conducted. Mr. Chase is adept at Krav Maga and capable with a firearm, and has shown unexpected resourcefulness and resiliency. Underestimate him at your peril."

A glance outside found a clear sky, no cloud cover at all. "The final target is female, Erika Carr. She is both intelligent and resourceful. You should consider all three targets armed and capable of using deadly force."

Leaves skidded across the window, a few final remnants of last fall's colorful tenure. "I repeat, do not use lethal force unless your life is in danger. I trust that you will not allow a situation to progress that far. Our mission is to detain and confiscate any items they may possess. Again, my employer wishes to speak with the targets before we dispose of them. Any questions?"

No one spoke, and when Keplar turned to leave, the men followed him to their vehicles. Thirty minutes later, each parked out of sight down an oil well access road south of Mount Vernon. Without a word, the silent figures disappeared into the dark woodlands, melting away like ghosts in a fog.

Chapter 62

Mount Vernon looked different in the moonlight.

Parker stood beside Erika along the fence line surrounding the estate. Nick knelt in front of them, surveying the grounds through a pair of high-resolution night-vision binoculars. He'd let Parker use them after they stowed Nick's vehicle in the woods, and the things had knocked his socks off. They were unreal. Pitch-black surroundings burst to life in vivid shades of green as miniscule sparks of light, invisible to the naked eye, reflected off every surface and made it seem almost as clear as day.

He and Erika each carried a red LED flashlight to preserve their night vision while not interfering with Nick's binoculars. So far, their trek had gone smoothly, though now was the point of no return. Once they crossed over the wooden fence, they were officially trespassing.

"I can't see any movement," Nick said as he lowered the binoculars. "Are you two ready?"

Parker's heart hammered in his chest. He felt like he could jump over a tree or run through a building. Sort of like he used to feel before football games. "Ready to go."

"You know what to do. Follow me, handle your responsibilities, and no talking unless it's absolutely necessary. If I motion for you to get down, hit the ground and don't move until I say so."

With that, Nick slipped through the wooden fence and headed toward the nearest building. Even bent over, he still blocked out the moonlight. Erika followed directly behind him and Parker brought up the rear, their footsteps silent on the thick grass.

They soon reached the rear of the gallery and followed Nick's lead, pressing their backs to the wall. Nick peered around the corner, and then disappeared. Parker concentrated on his breathing: in and out, slow and steady. *Easy. Stay cool and don't trip.*

"Move."

Nick's whisper floated on the night air. Parker followed Erika, hugging each turn until they were on the front side and facing the estate. It wasn't hard to imagine burning torches replacing the yellow walkway lights on the dark nights two centuries ago when George Washington had still lived here.

Nick worked the lock before they slipped inside, and with a sharp *snick*, the front door was locked again.

"We're clear." Nick backed away from the alarm box, from which two additional wires now protruded. "As far as the guards can tell, nothing ever happened. Use the red lights to see, but only when necessary."

Every window had been shuttered for the night, which kept them hidden from any passing security guard, but also kept out the moonlight.

Erika's light blazed to life, aimed at the display case they sought. Time to find out if the small piece of paper contained a hidden message worth killing for.

"Whenever you're ready," Nick said.

He knelt at the stand's base, a metallic black box in hand. Several wires snaked out from the small case, which was barely larger than a deck of cards. One wire from his scanning lock-pick attached to the top portion of the lock, the other to the bottom. A red light on the box blinked as the device attempted over five thousand combinations per second.

Parker blinked, and the light flashed green.

"It's open."

Parker took the flashlight from Erika. She lifted the glass cover, and then stopped.

"Here goes nothing." Erika removed two small bottles of liquid from her pocket. "We'll test a corner first."

One small drop satisfied her. "Most secret writings from this time period have the hidden message written between lines of visible script."

"Keep it moving," Nick said.

She held the dropper over Washington's letter. Liquid slid from the glass tube, hung by a thread, and finally fell onto the paper below.

Erika grabbed the other bottle and squeezed out a second drop on the same spot. The combination should reveal any invisible ink, but who knew if it would work after two hundred years.

The second drop spread quickly through the dry paper.

Nothing.

"What if the hidden message was only a few lines long?" Parker asked. "It might not reach the bottom."

"I didn't want to destroy the letter," Erika said. "Smudges on the bottom might go unnoticed. A huge splash in the center will be hard to miss."

Parker shrugged.

What can you do?

There was a sharp crack at the window, and Parker nearly dropped his flashlight.

"It's just the wind picking up," Nick said.

For the second time that night Parker had to remember to breathe.

"I'll try the center lines next," Erika said.

She repeated the process, with the first drop going between two lines directly in the middle of the letter. The ink bled at once, blending parts of the message together.

Erika steadied her hand and applied a drop of the second liquid to the letter.

As it spread, a ghostly word emerged.

INSIDE.

Chapter 63

Erika gasped. "It's there. It's really there." Then she got to work.

The first set of drops ran horizontally across the page, irreversibly damaging the president's writing. Erika didn't hesitate as she dumped the second chemical.

Five translucent words came to life.

ADAMS ACCORD INSIDE RAKESTRAWS DOVE

Erika's jaw tightened. She knew that name.

Rakestraw.

Erika looked up. "His dove ... but that means ..."

"Means what?" Parker asked.

"That means it's here."

"What's here?" Nick asked.

"It was right above us," Erika said.

"*Rakestraw,*" Parker said. "That's the guy who made the mansion's weathervane."

"A weathervane in the shape of a dove," Nick said. "But what does *Adams accord* mean?"

Erika flashed back to their inspection of the president's journal, and she quoted the line.

"Today completed agreement to end the injustice within our borders."

"What does it mean, though?" Nick asked.

"This might be the answer," she said. "An agreement, or *accord*, may have been what it took to entice Washington out of retirement. If anyone had the power to cut a deal with him, it would have been his replacement."

"Adams is John Adams. The second president," Nick said.

"What kind of accord would Washington have struck?" Parker asked.

"Well, based on what we've read, I'd guess—"

"That we're about to find out." Blinding light flashed into her eyes as the harsh voice pierced the room's quiet. "You two are impressive, I'll give you that."

Six men in camouflage battle gear stormed in and surrounded them as the man spoke. Six automatic weapons painted red dots on Nick's chest.

Erika's heart froze in her chest. The man who'd spoken walked toward Parker. The same man who had chased them on a motorcycle, who had tried to kill them.

The man who had killed Detective Nunez.

Chapter 64

Mount Vernon, Virginia

Keplar's men had the estate surrounded for less than an hour when they spotted flashlights in one building. Within minutes, his team disabled both watchmen in the guardhouse. After that, it was easy. Once Parker Chase and his crew were detained, Keplar called Vogel.

"Three targets acquired and contained, sir."

"Are they alive?"

"Yes, sir."

"Did you locate anything in their possession?"

"Affirmative." When Frank relayed the hidden message that had been uncovered and the location of this mysterious accord, Vogel fell silent. "Did you copy, sir?"

"I copied," Vogel said. "What is the security situation right now? Are there any private contractors or guards on site?"

"Two guards, employed by the estate. They're taking a nap for a few hours."

"I assume there are surveillance cameras?"

"Affirmative."

"Is the footage backed up remotely or stored on site?"

"Stored on site, sir. The servers are in an adjacent warehouse."

"Excellent. Have one of your men ready to take them offline. Also, prepare Mr. Chase to inspect the weathervane. I want to see this personally," Preston said. "Mr. McHugh will call for the details."

James McHugh was Vogel's private helicopter pilot, responsible for the operation of Vogel Industries' Sikorsky S-92 VVIP, a bird capable of traveling at two hundred miles per hour, fast enough to bring Vogel to Mount Vernon within the hour.

If the Virginia skies were as clear as the heavens above Philadelphia, there was a chance Parker Chase might not break his neck climbing in the moonlight. If he did, well, that's why Vogel paid Keplar so well.

Chapter 65

Parker didn't find much to be positive about in the manuscript gallery.

There was little to do but stand and watch. All three of them were patted down, their weapons and cell phones confiscated. The group's leader, the man who had killed Detective Nunez, reappeared from outside where he'd been on the phone.

"Mr. Chase, you will be assisting us tonight," the man said.

A sharp retort rose in Parker's throat, but the gun barrel pointed at his chest stopped it short.

"Dr. Carr has been kind enough to analyze her discovery. Now it's your turn to contribute."

Parker could almost have grabbed him, he was so close. And then what? Get shot by six guys. *Great idea, dummy.* "How the hell am I going to do that?" Parker asked.

A grin devoid of mirth spread on his captor's face. "You're going to climb onto the roof and retrieve the weathervane for us. If she is correct, and there is something inside, I will let her live. If not, she dies first. Her fate is in your hands."

[A guard trained his gun on Erika, who glared at the other man leveling his gun her way.

"What? We don't know if—"

"I suggest you stop wasting your breath and figure out how to retrieve the dove. It's windy tonight. You wouldn't want to slip." The man turned and walked outside.

A rifle smashed into Parker's back and sent him stumbling toward the door. A second guard gave Nick a shove. They walked out, with two guards behind them. Outside, gusts of wind blew leaves and rustled branches; the wind had picked up since they'd arrived. Two guards walked ahead of them and two behind, rifles pointed.

Parker leaned close to Nick. "Can you call your buddies to come save us?" he whispered without moving his lips.

"This is a non-official mission," Nick whispered back. "No one knows I'm here."

"You're the CIA. They won't just leave you here to die."

"If I can somehow make a phone call, I'll have to explain myself, but they'd send help."

"They have our phones, and, unless you've got a gun stashed where the sun doesn't shine, all the weapons."

"We need to buy time," Nick whispered. "I suggest you find what they want."

"Shut it!" barked one of the guards, jamming his rifle into Nick's back for good measure.

At the mansion's front door, a strong hand grabbed Parker's shoulder and another grabbed Nick. They now stood directly beneath the soaring golden dove. The cupola wasn't so pretty when you were about to climb it, Parker observed unhappily. One of the guards bent and began to work the front door lock.

Two of their captors set off into the nearby woods and returned after a few moments, each carrying a length of rope and a pack. One of them tossed his into Parker's chest; metal clinked as he caught it.

"That's a belt with carabiner attachments," the man said gruffly. "Put it on."

Parker reached into the bag. With shaking hands, he extracted a waist harness, larger than a belt and constructed of thin, synthetic material. Several metal clips hung from the straps, all of it joined together by two interlocking buckles.

After a few misfires, Parker got the contraption around his waist. One of the guards opened the second pack and put on his own belt, with considerably more adeptness. When he finished he stepped over and tightened Parker's belt until his hips ached in protest.

"That's tight enough," Parker said.

"If your belt isn't secure, the harness won't hold you if you fall. I don't care about you, but you'll be attached to me."

The front entrance was unlocked now, and the leader directed everyone inside. "Mr. Chase, you and David"—he indicated the guard in the belt—"are going out onto the cupola to secure the weathervane. As long as you follow his instructions, you will survive. If you try anything foolish, your girlfriend gets a bullet in her leg."

The staircase creaked as they walked up to the mansion's third floor. Shadows danced on the walls as tree limbs bounced outside, the wind whistling around Washington's home.

The leader turned to the tall, wiry man next to him, clearly his second in command. "Come with us. You three secure the area for arrival and keep your eyes open. ETA is thirty minutes."

Parker caught Nick's eye, and the big man made a circling motion with his hand, which morphed into a flattened palm slowly descending.

A helicopter? Who could possibly be flying here?

Then it hit him. These guys were just the muscle. They had a boss, and he was on his way.

The man who had killed his uncle.

David motioned Parker up the narrow staircase towards the roof, Nick and Erika trailing behind, each with a rifle in their back Once they had ascended into the cupola, David uncoiled the length of rope and attached one end to his safety harness. Opposite end in hand, he opened a window and grasped several loops of rope like a cowboy as he leaned out. The cold air brought everyone's breath to life.

With a grunt, the man hurled the rope through the air, up and over the cupola until it looped around and landed outside the opposite window.

"Grab that end and attach it to your belt."

Parker did as ordered. Once he'd tightened it, David gave the other end of the rope several sharp tugs. He grunted, then jumped out the window and on to the mansion's roof.

"Come outside," David said through the open window. "I'll pull you up to the bird, steady you as you work. Don't do anything stupid or I'll cut you loose." A knife flashed in his hand. "When you get onto the upper roof, wrap this rope around the weathervane and drop it down."

The other man attached another rope to Parker's belt and handed the rest to him

"How am I supposed to get that thing off?" Parker asked.

"That's your problem."

The leader shoved him out the open window. Parker tumbled, flipped over and started sliding down the slick rooftop. Tiles scraped his backside before he reached out and grabbed a chimney and stopped moving. He scrambled to his feet as gusts of chilled air buffeted him from every direction, threatening his balance and numbing his whole body.

Once he made it back to the open window, his partner leaned back and started pulling slack through his hands. The rope at his waist tightened, and then began pulling him up toward the cupola's tiny roof.

The second length of rope nearly threw his already treacherous balance off. Half-climbing, half-slipping, he rocked back and forth, moving inches at a time until he reached the roof's apex. The cupola's overhanging roof was at eye level now, conveniently offering a gutter for him to grab. Parker bent down, then jumped and hauled himself onto the upper level. As he did so, however, his right foot kicked for momentum and he felt the glass window beneath him shatter.

Someone shouted inside. Damned if he could make out who it was. The wind was picking up every second, shouting in his ears. He wrapped both hands around the dove's narrow support spire and then stopped. *Take a second. No need to hurry.*

"Tie yourself to the pole," David shouted over the wind.

Parker wrapped the second rope around the spire, and then David reached out for the rope's end and snagged it.

Parker looked up. The weathervane was directly above him. Tantalizingly close, but that was a mirage. He had a problem.

It was completely out of reach.

There was no way he could climb the tiny support pole, and unless he grew five feet in the next five minutes, the dove was too far above him to grab.

He leaned against the pole and closed his eyes. If he didn't get this weathervane down, they would shoot Erika. These guys probably planned on killing them no matter what, but he could at least buy time for Nick to act if he retrieved the dove.

He leaned his head against the pole. Now what? He smacked it in frustration, his hand stinging in the cold, but in that moment he forgot all about the wind. The pole had moved. Only a few inches, but enough to notice, even on top of a house buffeted by increasing winds.

The support pole wasn't secured very tightly.

Parker grasped it with both hands. Now he had an option, but not a good one. His second rope, the one that would break his fall from the cupola roof, was wrapped around the pole. On top of that, the metal pole was the only thing he could hold for balance.

His safety weighed against Erika's life wasn't much of a battle. Gently at first, then with more force, he leaned back on the pole and pulled. If it broke loose now, nothing would stop him from tumbling onto the roof below. And from there, it was a short slide to eternity.

The pole moved a bit, enough that the dove atop it swayed to one side. He reversed direction and pushed. This time the bird moved away from him, but not very far.

The hell with it.

He wasn't getting anywhere like this. A quick tug on his main rope was answered with a responding pull. Hopefully this David guy was strong. With a wide stance, he pushed and pulled on the metal pole, slowly at first, but more with each effort, and the bird began rocking. Back and forth, he threw himself into the task. Each effort yielded a few more precious inches. Parker's thudding heart reverberated through his skull, and just as his feet started skidding on the slick roof and his hands went totally numb a cracking noise filled the air and the pole toppled over.

He went airborne, momentarily weightless as he fell and landed with a solid thud on the roof. The pole clattered next to him, then skidded away. Parker flipped over and grabbed one end before it could slide from view.

I did it.

He turned back over and sucked air greedily, waiting for his heart to slow. The intense beating failed to subside. *Wait a second.* Parker sat up and realized it wasn't his heart making the deep thumping noise.

Like a demon descending into hell, a helicopter ripped through the sky and touched down on the front lawn of Mount Vernon.

Looked like the boss was here.

Time was up, and he had no idea how to escape. Panic crept into his chest, a tight grip threatening to overwhelm him. *Stay calm,* he told himself. *Your chance will come.* Worst case scenario, he had the metal pole. Maybe he could brain one of the guards and steal his gun. A terrible plan, but better than nothing. He closed his eyes, took a deep breath, and his chest loosened. *You can do this. Just stay focused.*

Then he rolled over and looked through the open window into the cupola.

His climbing partner, David, was slumped out of the window with a jagged shard of glass protruding from his neck. He wasn't moving.

Inside the cupola Nick engaged the other guard in hand-to-hand combat.

Parker jumped to his feet, immediately slipped on the blood from David's neck and started sliding toward the roof's edge.

Chapter 66

Nick knew they were in serious trouble the moment Parker stepped out onto the roof. Whoever they were, these guys were pros. All business, with military-grade equipment.

Their best chance at survival was to escape. They were outnumbered and outgunned, a recipe for disaster. When Parker's foot came through a window everyone jumped, but only Nick seemed to notice the razor-sharp pieces of shattered glass strewn about the floor. He grinned in the darkness. That's when the helicopter arrived, and three men ran across the lawn toward it as the roaring rotor blades rattles his brain. Meanwhile, Parker was out there being buffeted by the winds.

One mercenary had a gun trained on Nick, but he was watching the helicopter. In the dark room, it was easy to grab a piece of jagged glass without anyone noticing.

"He's on to something," Parker's climbing partner shouted through the window. The man leaned into the window frame for balance and pulled on the rope around his waist, exposing his neck within arm's reach.

Time to move. Nick stabbed at the exposed flesh. Blood spurted, covering the floor as the man slumped back out onto the roof.

The second guard saw his partner go down an instant before Nick punched him, sending him to the ground but also knocking his gun out a window.

Before the group's leader realized what had happened, Nick lifted him off the ground and threw him down the twisting stairs.

"Parker!" Erika leaned out the window. "Get in here."

Nick grabbed her from the window ledge. "Don't let them see you. We don't want—"

His knee buckled as the guard he'd punched kicked it and knocked him down.

Nick fell and rolled into a fighting stance as the guy got up and pulled a knife from his boot. No time to stand around now. Nick feinted one way, pushing the man back. The guy slashed at him, and Nick dodged back out of range. The man raised his knife, took one step toward Nick, and then fell over to reveal Erika holding a rifle by the barrel with a patch of blood on the butt end where it had smacked the guy's head.

"Thanks," Nick said.

"Don't mention it."

Two men were down. There had been three to start.

"Where's their boss?"

"I don't know," Erika said. "He never came back upstairs after you threw him down there."

A scraping sound came from one open window. The rope to which Parker had been attached was stretched tight, moving back and forth over the window sill, still connected to a dead mercenary. The other end disappeared over the gutter.

Chapter 67

Parker couldn't stop looking at the ground as he swung. Forty feet was a long way down with only air under your feet.

"Parker!" Erika's face appeared above him. "Hang on." A moment later, the rope around his waist went tight, pulling him up toward the roof, inch by inch, until Parker grasped the gutter and hauled himself to safety, the metal pole attached to Rakestraw's dove clutched in one hand.

"Are you guys all right?" Parker asked once he got loose from his belt. He'd never go rappelling, not if he lived to be a hundred. The hell with that sport.

"Yes," she said. "Are you?"

"I'm fine. That was close, though. How did you do ... *this*?" Parker swept a hand over the room, indicating the two bodies.

Nick held up a shard of glass. "Thanks for the weapons."

"We need to—"

The windows. Bullets flew through the room, hornets of death zipping all around them. Nick dove forward, knocking them down and out of harm's way.

"Take the stairs," Nick shouted.

Parker crawled down the winding stairs, but not before he grabbed a pistol off the ground. Only once they'd made it to the safety of the floor below did they stop.

"Where can we go?" Parker asked. He still clutched the weathervane, waving the bird through the air.

"There's nothing around here for miles," Nick said. "We need to get to the car."

"What about the estate guard?" Erika asked. "He had to have driven here."

"Good point," Nick said. "Unfortunately, the employee parking lot is right next to that damn helicopter."

Parker risked a glance out of a window, then inspiration struck. "How good are you with that gun?" he asked Nick.

Nick's eyes narrowed. "Very. Why?"

"I have an idea." Parker held out the weathervane. "They aren't after us. They want this. It's our best bargaining chip."

"Our only one," Nick said. "You can't give it to them."

Erika chimed in. "Don't do it, Parker. Not after what we've been through."

"Is it really worth our lives? We don't even know if there's anything in here."

She reached for the dove. "Then why don't we find out? I'm not going to let those bastards have this."

"Do you realize what you're saying?" Parker pointed to the window. "Those aren't street thugs. They're serious killers who have no problem putting a bullet in us." He stepped toward her. "I'd rather take them on myself than risk you dying." That got her attention. "Now listen to me for a second. This isn't up for debate." He turned to Nick. "You know more about this than I do. Tell me if it's a bullshit plan."

"Make it quick," Nick said. "We don't have much time before they come in after us."

"They want this dove and whatever might be inside," Parker said. "They're not stupid, so we can't break it open, take anything we find and glue it back together before we hand it over. If I walk out there right now and get their attention, will you have time to get her out of here before we take these guys out?"

Nick sidled over next to the window and cautiously peered through the blinds. "They're all still standing around the helicopter. If I go out the rear exit and move around to the north woods, I might be able to get alongside them, say within fifty yards."

"Can you hit them from that far away?"

"I could shoot the cigarette out of someone's mouth from fifty yards."

"What about Erika? She can't stay."

"Like hell I can't." She wasn't going down without a fight. "We're in this together. I'm not leaving without you."

"I'll be fine," Parker said. "Nick will get close while they're distracted with this weathervane. Those guys will never know what hit them."

"What do you think they'll do when he starts shooting?" Erika asked him. "You'll be dead before he can get them all."

"I'm still pretty fast. I'll get out of there before they know what's going on. Nick finishes them off, we grab this dove back and bail."

Nick put a hand on Erika's shoulder. "He's right. It's the best chance you have to survive, and if we don't move now, we won't have any options at all. If Parker can stall them long enough for us to get in position, I'll take those guys out. While they're distracted, you can get to our vehicle."

She started to speak, but her voice caught before she tried again. "I'm not leaving you two behind."

"You won't help us by dying, Erika," Nick said. "And like he said, don't worry about us. I'll take care of them."

"Then let me help," she said. "I can do something."

"Getting to the vehicle *is* helping," Nick said. "If we split up, our odds of getting past them go up. You're not running away. You're helping us survive."

Erika's face fell, but she finally nodded. "Tell me what to do."

Nick studied their enemy through the window for a minute, before his fingers let the blinds fall shut. "Pay attention. We only get one shot at this."

Five minutes later, Parker walked out the mansion's front door.

Chapter 68

As his helicopter touched down on George Washington's front lawn, Preston still couldn't believe this day had finally arrived. For generations his family secret had remained buried, lost in the passage of time. As they landed, he thought about when his father had told him of the terrible act.

Given that the old man had waited until he was in his nineties to talk about it, Preston had a few reservations about how much of his tale was fact and how much was legend. His old man was sharp as a tack, but the story had bordered on the absurd. Nonetheless, Preston had tucked the information away, aware that should this legend ever come to fruition, it could easily lead to his downfall.

Fortunately, Keplar had everything under control this time, and The Guild's dark past would soon be buried along with the three people who had found it.

Except for the fact that moments after he touched down, everything went to hell.

Preston threw open the cockpit door. "Where's Keplar?"

"Retrieving the weathervane, sir."

He looked at the mansion but couldn't see anything. The pilot had turned off the front spotlights to avoid blinding Keplar's men.

"Get me a pair of binoculars." The mercenary disappeared, returning shortly with a high-powered pair of military-grade glasses. A surreal scene greeted him when Preston lifted them to his eyes.

The CIA agent and one of Preston's commandos were locked in

combat. Parker was hanging by one hand from the roof, a weathervane clasped in his grasp. Keplar was nowhere to be found.

"What's going on up there?" Preston muttered to himself. "You idiots better not have screwed this up."

He shoved his binoculars at the mercenary, who peered through them for a second and immediately grabbed his radio. "Team two to leader, team two to leader, do you copy? Over."

Preston took the lenses back in time to see Parker hauled onto the roof, weathervane in hand. Everyone on Keplar's team had vanished.

The soldier repeated his call. Crackling static was the only response.

"This is leader," Frank Keplar finally replied. "I'm coming out a side door. Do not fire. I repeat, do not fire."

"Copy leader. Holding fire."

"Don't just stand there," Preston told the soldier. "If you have a shot in that room, take it."

The soldier dropped to one knee and a flurry of shots rang out. As the cupola disintegrated, the government man knocked Parker and Erika to the ground and out of sight.

Seconds later a camouflaged figure appeared from the gloom, running low to the ground. Keplar headed directly to Preston. "We've had some complications, sir."

"This gets better and better."

Keplar relayed how Nick had caught them by surprise, killing one man and knocking Keplar down the winding staircase.

"I saw them handle the other guy just as easily," Preston said, arms flailing about. "Why the hell didn't you get back up there and take them out?"

Keplar responded in a flat monotone. "That man is a trained operative. He had the high ground and several automatic weapons. I have a pistol."

"Fine. We can't undo it now." As much as Preston hated to admit it, Keplar was better equipped to handle this than he. "How do you propose we handle this mess?"

"The three of them are inside the house. We have superior numbers, weaponry and night-vision. I recommend a two-pronged assault, frontal and side. The less time they have to prepare, the better. That's a large house, sir. If we don't move now, they could easily hide that golden dove well enough that we won't locate it tonight."

That made sense, Preston reasoned. Go at them full force, and if a few of these men died in the process, so be it. None of them was worth losing the weathervane over.

Before Preston could tell them to move, though, one of the men shouted. "Someone's coming out the front door."

Preston didn't need the binoculars to see that Parker had indeed just walked outside. Erika and their companion were nowhere to be seen as he closed the mansion door behind him.

Parker carried the golden dove in one hand; the other was raised, empty.

"Should I shoot him?" Keplar glanced at Preston.

"No. Either this kid is nuts or he's up to something. I want to find out."

"Hold fire," Keplar said. "I suggest you turn the spotlight on him, Mr. Vogel. Take away his vision in case he is armed."

"Put the headlight on him," Preston said told the pilot.

A brilliant beam of light focused directly on Parker as he stood on the mansion's front porch.

"One of you go around each side," Keplar told his men. "Get in the woods and keep an eye on the rear entrance. If you see the woman, detain her. If you see the CIA man, shoot to kill."

They all ran off, leaving Preston and Keplar alone with the helicopter pilot.

Parker walked toward them, apparently in no hurry to get there, one hand shielding his eyes from the spotlight's glare. Twenty feet from the chopper, he stopped.

Preston signaled his pilot to cut the engine. Keplar moved around to flank Parker, a snub-nosed machine gun in one hand. Parker looked over at him but didn't move.

Preston stepped in front of the light. He'd be nothing more than a black outline to Parker.

"You have something I want, Mr. Chase."

"I want to make a deal."

"Why would I deal with you?" Preston said. "You're surrounded, alone, and unarmed."

"Call your men off and let my friends leave," Parker said. "Do it and I'll give you this weathervane and tell you where Washington's journal is."

The damn journal. Preston had never actually seen it, had only heard Parker and his group reading from it. There was no telling what else was in the book. If it contained anything implicating his ancestor, Samuel Chase, Vogel needed it.

"How do I know you're not bluffing? That journal may not even exist."

"I took it from Samuel Powel's fireplace," Parker said. "It contained the original agreement between John Adams and George Washington."

Agreement? What was he talking about?

"The one in here is only a copy," Parker said. "If you let all of us leave, I'll tell you where to find the original."

Fear's cold hand raced up Preston's back. Did the kid really have stones like boulders? Either that or he was telling the truth. "Say you're not lying, that you have an agreement of some kind. How do I know you didn't copy it?"

"Do you think I wanted any of this?" Parker said, shaking the golden dove. "Do you think I wanted to get shot at, to spend the last week running from shadows, to lose my uncle? Whoever you are, you can have this. You can have everything we found. I just want to be left alone."

With that, Parker threw the dove to the ground.

For the first time in a long while, Preston didn't know what to say. What was this kid's game? He could have Keplar shoot Parker now, but that left Erika and the CIA agent unaccounted for.

"Where are the other two?" Preston asked.

Parker hesitated. "Inside."

Preston opened his mouth as gunshots rang out from the woods. Keplar dove to the ground, training his weapon on the tree line.

Preston ducked back behind the helicopter and found his pilot lying on the floor, covering his head.

"McHugh," he barked, "get up and be ready to leave."

Captain McHugh nodded, though he made no move to get up.

Preston shouted around the nose of the chopper. "Mr. Chase, I don't believe you've been honest with me." He reached up and pulled a pistol out of the helicopter's side door, a custom .45 Smith & Wesson with solid gold lettering along the barrel. A wealthy man's gun. Preston grinned. He loved it.

He faced Parker again. "It sounds like your friends are not inside the mansion. I believe they ran into my men in those woods."

Preston walked slowly out in front of the helicopter. Parker was ashen-faced, head twisting from the woods back to Vogel. Preston took a few steps to one side, moving out of the spotlight.

"I don't want to make a deal with you, Mr. Chase. It sounds like you are the only person left who knows where Washington's journal is, and you can keep that secret."

"Who are you?" Parker asked, squinting as his eyes tried to adjust. "Why are you doing all this?"

What the hell. He'd been dying to tell someone for years.

"My name is Preston Vogel."

Parker frowned, his lips moving silently. "As in Vogel Industries?" he finally asked.

"That's correct."

"What are you doing here? Why do you care about all this?"

"I'm going to tell you a secret, Parker. Something only one other person on earth knows. Does the name Samuel Chase mean anything to you?"

"What is he, my long-lost cousin?"

"No, you fool. Samuel Chase was my ancestor. He was one of the original Supreme Court justices, appointed by none other than George Washington. He was also a successful businessman. My ancestor was content with his life, until 1799, when George Washington conspired to destroy what he had worked so hard to build. Washington was going to undermine his life's work, so Chase decided something had to be done. He and a small group of like-minded individuals took matters into their own hands."

Parker's eyes went wide. "Are you serious? Your ancestor murdered the first president of the United States?"

"You could say I'm deadly serious, Mr. Chase."

He turned as one of his men trudged out of the darkness, headed toward them. Erika Carr half-walked, half-stumbled along in front of him.

"They killed Nick!" Erika shouted. "Parker, they shot him."

That was all Preston needed to hear.

"Well, it looks like this is the end. Thank you for retrieving this beautiful dove for me, Mr. Chase. I will think of you when I destroy it."

Preston raised his gun and aimed at Parker's chest. Erika's screams pierced the night.

Chapter 69

I'm going to die.

The words sprang into Parker's head with utter finality. With the spotlight in his eyes, Parker hadn't seen any of their assailants slip off into the woods. Nick and Erika must have been ambushed.

The broken weathervane pole lay on the ground where he'd thrown it, just out of reach. If he dove, he might be able to grab it and then … what? He'd have a broken stick to plug one of the bullet holes in his chest.

This was really it. *Fine.* If I'm going to die, at least give Erika a chance.

She was screaming, trying to run to him, but an armed man held her back and pushed her roughly to the ground. Vogel laughed as she fell, and then he turned back to Parker, taking aim with an enormous pistol.

Everything seemed to slow as Vogel's finger tightened. Adrenaline and fear set his body on fire. Parker dove toward Erika as a shot rang out.

A second blast roared before he hit the ground. Pain lanced through his shoulder as he landed. He reached for the wound, expecting to see a shredded mass of muscle and bone where his shoulder used to be.

Instead, there was nothing.

What the hell? Did Vogel miss?

More shots rang out. Parker looked up and saw Erika lying where she had fallen. But she wasn't dead. Quite the opposite: a gun was in her hands, the barrel spitting fire as she pulled the trigger.

The man who had captured her was on one knee, submachine gun blazing.

It was Nick.

Vogel was screaming, on the ground clutching his arm. The leader of the mercenary group stood across from them for a moment, silhouetted against the chopper and then staggered backward as half a dozen holes opened in his chest. When the guns fell silent, he slumped to the ground and didn't move.

"Get over here," Erika shouted and waved at Parker.

He jumped up and ran. "What the hell happened? How did—"

"Shut up and take this," Nick said as he shoved a pistol into Parker's hands. "The safety's off, so be careful where you point it."

An automatic weapon sounded, the bullets coming rapid-fire. Clumps of dirt kicked up at Nick's feet. "Shit. Follow me." He took off toward the mansion. Parker followed with Erika's hand in his until they reached the house and dove around a corner.

Parker wrapped his arms around Erika. "I thought you were dead."

She grabbed him and held tight. "Hey, get it together. We're not out of this yet."

Nick pulled Parker toward him, out of her arms. "Listen to me. There are still two guys on the other side. That one with the big-ass pistol is hit, but not down."

That huge gun. *They're not gonna believe this.* "That's Preston Vogel."

Nick and Erika stared at him. "As in Vogel Industries?" Erika asked.

"Yes. He's related to Samuel Chase—"

"The Supreme Court justice?"

"Yeah, that guy. Vogel's after us, after that weathervane, really, because he thinks it contains proof that his ancestor *murdered George Washington.*"

Even Nick's jaw dropped at that. "That's what this is about?"

"Everything is about that," Parker said. "Joe's murder, Detective Nunez, everything."

Nick's jaw took on a harder set, if that was even possible. "We can worry about that later. Right now, we need to get out of here."

Intermittent shots came from around the corner.

"Here's what we're going to do. Erika, take this gun." Nick handed her the automatic weapon. "This is the safety. Keep it off. When you run out of bullets, press this button, pull out the magazine, and jam a new one in."

He pulled two full magazines from his jacket. "Keep firing around the corner. Don't expose yourself, just stick the gun out there and shoot. If they stop shooting back, get over to Parker."

"Where am I going?" Parker asked.

"Over here." Nick pointed to the opposite end of the wall. "Get on the ground, behind that brick column. If anyone walks around the corner, shoot them. Don't think, just shoot."

One week ago, that would have sounded insane. Now it made sense. "All right."

"I'm going in here." Nick tapped the window behind him. "If you can keep them occupied, then they should be there when I get through the house. No one will expect an attack from inside. Then we can find Vogel and finish this."

Nick reached up and broke the window enough to reach inside and unlock it. He scanned the interior before deftly hopping over the sill and disappearing from view.

A jumble of thoughts rushed through Parker's mind, each worse than the last, and none what he wanted to say.

"Erika, I …" His voice trailed off.

"I know." She leaned in and kissed his cheek. "Be careful. Now get over there before someone sneaks up on us."

The house was wider than he remembered. Parker crept over thick grass until he reached the safety of a brick column. Moonlight chased long shadows from the nearby trees nearly to his feet.

Ongoing gunfire mean Erika was all right. He didn't dare poke his head around the side. A dumb mistake like that could be the last one he ever made.

Erika's gun went silent.

"Shit," he muttered. He turned to see her struggling with a magazine, trying to jam it into the gun. Just as he moved to help her, the piece snapped into place and she kept on firing.

He turned around again and came face-to-face with a rifle barrel.

Or rather, the tip of one. It jutted out from around the corner. Whoever was carrying the gun hadn't noticed him yet.

Parker willed his body to stay still as the gunman came into view, focused on Erika. At the same time as Parker put pressure on his own trigger, the man caught sight of him.

Parker's weapon fired and the mercenary rolled away, foot coming up in a blur to send Parker's gun flying through the air. The man fell back, one hand covering his eyes, his gun spraying bullets aimlessly.

Parker dove at him, grabbing for the gun. Randomly aimed bullets were not what he wanted here. It flipped around and out of reach, the muzzle spitting fire as Parker struggled to get at it, to avoid the bullets flying out. Parker brought a knee up into the guy's side and knocked the weapon loose. The metal was slippery, hard to hold, and it twisted in his hands and fell to the grass. The guy was getting up now, coming for Parker. He had a pistol on his hip, and he reached for it. Parker grabbed the automatic weapon, brought it up just as the guy pulled out his pistol and aimed for Parker's chest. He was running at him, coming too fast, and he crashed into Parker to send them both tumbling down. The machine gun bucked against Parker's chest as they landed in a heap.

He couldn't breathe. The guy was crushing him, pinning him down until Parker rolled away from beneath him. The gun was too big for this kind of fight, too large to aim, and he couldn't get a shot off, not until he flipped the whole way around.

The other man stared vacantly at the clouds. Bullet holes pockmarked his chest.

Erika appeared above him, brandishing her gun. "Are you all right?"

He took a deep breath, felt for wounds and found none. "I'm fine." He took her outstretched hand and gained his feet.

A fresh round of gunshots came from around the front corner of the house.

"Nick may be in trouble." Parker ran over to where Erika had been shooting. Before he glanced around, the open window caught his eye.

"Let's go through the house, the same way Nick took," Parker said. "We'll find him inside if he never made it out, and at least we'll have some cover."

They scrambled through the open window into the first floor, moving through the side room toward the main staircase.

No sign of Nick.

"Looks like he made it outside," Erika said.

Parker squinted, willing the dark shadows to come into focus. He could hardly see anything but shadows and lines in this gloom. Erika followed him to a front window, where they each crouched on one side and peered out.

"Glad you could make it."

Parker nearly shot himself and everyone else. He turned to see Nick standing behind them, a bemused expression on his face.

"You're lucky I didn't kill you," Parker said.

"What's happening on your side of the house?" Nick asked.

Parker relayed their activities, and Nick let out a low whistle.

"Nice work," Nick said. "But we still have to find Vogel."

Parker thought back to his standoff in front of the helicopter. "I lost sight of him when you two started shooting."

"Same here," Nick said. "He could be anywhere, so stay alert."

The sharp whine of an engine turning over came from outside. Deep thumping followed as the helicopter's rotors began to turn.

"Shit," Erika said. "We can't let him get away." She moved toward the front door and was only stopped from going outside when Nick grabbed her.

"Don't go out there. That headlight is right on the front door. You'll be a sitting duck."

"We can't just let him get away," Erika said. "What about your partner? What about Joe?"

"He's not going anywhere. We need to be smart so we don't get killed. Erika, you and Parker go over there." Nick pointed to the window he had snuck out of just minutes ago. "Shoot at the helicopter, get his attention."

"We can't bring that thing down," Parker said. "I can't hit the engine or the rotors from here."

"You don't need to hit anything, just get his attention. Keep him occupied while I go out the other side and circle around."

Nick darted away, and Parker and Erika opened fire. The angle was tough, but with Parker standing and Erika crouched below, they were able to bounce a few rounds off the machine.

Vogel returned fire, his rounds spraying wildly across the mansion's façade. Every so often one whizzed past them, close enough to hear.

The helicopter wobbled. "Where's Nick?" Parker muttered. "Vogel's getting off the ground."

The blades pulled at the air for lift, getting one skid off the ground.

Vogel was getting away.

Chapter 70

From the helicopter cockpit, Preston could see muzzle flashes bursting in the darkness as the rotors began to churn. He returned fire at random, his bullets slamming into the stately mansion as clouds of brick and plaster puffed under the headlights. Whoever was inside took cover and the shooting slowed.

Preston pulled the trigger at any flash of light. Maybe he'd get lucky.

At least the night wasn't a total loss.

Keplar was dead, along with all of his men. Their equipment was lying around the estate, though none of it could be traced back to him. The only problem was Keplar himself, well-established as Preston's head of security. There would be some questions to answer about why his corpse was among the carnage.

However, Keplar could be replaced. Deny everything and paint him as a rogue criminal, operating of his own accord with an unknown agenda.

Preston had the only thing that mattered.

The golden dove. And whatever it contained.

If Parker's story was true, if evidence of his ancestor's crime was inside, Vogel would burn it. Destroy the only possible link between Preston Vogel and the greatest unsolved crime in American history. You didn't have a crime without any evidence.

"Get this damn thing up in the air," Vogel shouted. He fired at the mansion again, cursing his terrible luck.

Just as Preston was about to shoot Parker Chase, that CIA bastard, disguised in a stolen uniform, had blasted the gun from his hand, a bullet nicking his forearm, burning like hell. Before he could grab his gun again, they had disappeared.

Return fire flashed in the dark and several bullets bounced off the chopper in a shower of brilliant orange sparks. Two different shooters firing, but mostly missing.

Preston leaned out of the copilot's seat and unleashed a barrage, flipping the fire button to full auto and burning through a magazine in seconds.

"Get us out of here. I'll hold them off until we're in the air."

His pilot shouted something inaudible, the turbine's increasing whine drowning him out.

Preston slammed home a fresh magazine and peppered the house. As the hammer clicked down on empty, the helicopter lifted off the ground. Preston reached for another magazine, but it fell from his hand when the metal bird suddenly dropped back down.

"What the hell are you—"

Oh shit. His pilot was slumped on the steering column. Blood covered his shirt and chest. And that wasn't the worst part.

The enormous CIA agent had one foot inside the cockpit and a machine gun leveled at his face.

Chapter 71

Nick circled around the chopper as the firefight raged.

Preston was firing madly from the passenger seat, too fast for the small-capacity clips. When the telltale sound of a hammer clicking on an empty chamber sounded, Nick pulled the trigger.

Two rounds ripped into the pilot, and the man slumped over the steering column as the aircraft bounced back to earth.

"Don't move," Nick said. "Drop the gun."

Preston complied, disbelief on every feature.

"My name is Nicholas Dean. You're under arrest for the attempted murder of a federal agent. I don't know what the hell your game is, but it's over."

A switch seemed to flip. Vogel laughed. "You want to know? Fine. You're in the way of something bigger than you, bigger than you can imagine."

"Why did you kill Dr. Chase?" Nick asked. If the madman was going to talk, he'd listen.

"He found something he shouldn't have."

"What are you talking about?"

"This."

Nick nearly shot him as Preston snatched up the golden dove.

"I had to stop him," Preston said.

"You killed all those innocent people for that, that *dove?*"

"Do you have any idea what this could do to me? How much I stand to lose?"

"Keep your hands where I can see them," Nick said. "Climb over the pilot and get onto the ground. Do it slowly."

Vogel didn't move. "You have no idea who you're dealing with."

"You have three seconds until I put a bullet in your head," Nick said.

Vogel's expression lit up. "You know what? I don't think you're really a federal agent. If you were, there would be dozens of drones like you out here. Where are all your friends?"

Nick didn't bite. "One."

"In fact, maybe I should call the cops and tell them that a man impersonating a government agent just shot up Mount Vernon."

"I'll take you to them. Two."

Preston finally realized he wasn't kidding. "Don't shoot. I'm coming."

He stood from the passenger seat and, as he stepped toward Nick, reached down to balance himself on the pilot's corpse. Nick blinked at the same time Preston tripped on the dead guy. Preston went down, and then stood and shoved the corpse at Nick with surprising speed.

Nick went down under McHugh's weight, the corpse taking each bullet Nick fired as he fell outside onto the grass. He landed on his back with the body on his chest. His arm, and his gun, was trapped underneath it.

Preston stood over him, aiming a pistol at Nick's head. Wind roared from the chopper blades as Preston grinned above him. "Tell Dr. Chase I said hello."

Preston pulled the trigger.

And then his head exploded.

Chapter 72

Vogel's body remained upright for a brief second before gravity took over and his knees buckled. The body fell to reveal Parker standing behind it with an upraised pistol.

That's for you, Joe.

Parker stepped down from the helicopter cockpit, then reached back with his free hand and shut off the spinning rotors. He offered his hand to Nick, who grasped it and hauled himself out from under McHugh's body and onto his feet.

"Nice shot," Nick said. "You saved my ass."

"Don't mention it. Thanks for distracting him. It's easier when they're not looking."

Erika ran around the helicopter and stopped when she saw Nick. "Are you hurt?"

"No, I'm fine, thanks to this guy."

"Good." She jumped into the cockpit and emerged a moment later with the golden weathervane in hand. "Well? What do you think?" she asked Parker.

Parker couldn't help but grin; since when did Erika ask his say-so to do something? "What are you waiting for?"

Erika laid the dove down. "It's made of copper and banded with iron strips. I need something to break them apart."

"This should do the trick." Parker grabbed an oversized pair of pliers from behind the pilot's seat.

She took it and started twisting and pulling, two centuries of rust and debris cracking under her efforts.

The first metal strip gave way with a shriek, and after she pulled off three more, Erika tossed the tool aside and picked up the bird. "Does anyone have a knife?"

Nick tossed one to her, and Parker knelt, leaning over her shoulder as she worked. A small line, so thin as to almost be invisible, ran the length of the sculpture.

Erika tapped on the metal. "Hear that? It's definitely not solid."

"Can you get the blade in there and lever it open?" Parker asked, holding a flashlight over the dove.

"Keep the light steady."

She wiggled the razor blade back and forth, trying to breach the seal. A chunk of copper broke off.

"Be careful," Parker said. "You don't know what's in there."

"Be quiet." Erika wedged the blade inside the bird with care. Soft creaks of stressed metal accompanied her progress, until finally the welds gave way all at once with a crack.

The halved sculpture fell apart to reveal a leather scroll inside. A length of knotted string held it together.

Erika pulled the knot free, and she unrolled the leather to find a note inside, attached to the leather backing.

1 December, 1799

Bushrod,

I must apologize for utilizing such obfuscating methods of contact. You have done well to locate this letter, and for that I thank you.

I recently learned that a contingent of men exist who wish to do me harm. Several months ago, I was approached by President Adams. He urged me to return to service in our nation's defense, in anticipation of a conflict with France. You are aware of my desire to live a peaceful, simple existence on the grounds of my estate, and I conveyed these intentions to President Adams. He persisted, however, and in his desire I saw an opportunity unlike any other.

In return for my service, Adams entered into an agreement concerning the forced labor of negroes, a copy of which I have enclosed.

I fear that I may not live to see the implementation of our accord. Samuel Chase, with whom you are intimately familiar, has learned of our agreement and wishes to see me dead prior to the issuance of this Executive Order.

I know not what he plans, only that he and several cohorts conspire to end my life.

Bushrod, if such circumstances should come to pass that I no longer live, I implore you, take this agreement to Philadelphia and ensure Adams fulfills his oath.

For too long our dark brothers have suffered an unjust enslavement. This new nation, our nation, was created so that all men, regardless of color, could pursue happiness while enjoying our God-given right to freedom. I trust you will assist me should it prove necessary.

Thank you, and I remain,
Truly Yours,
G. Washington

Erika found a second sheet of paper underneath the first.

25 April, 1798
A contract between G. Washington and J. Adams, as representative of the United States of America.

It is hereby agreed that George Washington will assume the position of Commander of the Armies of the United States, effective 1 August, 1798, at a rate of pay of Ten Thousand Dollars per annum. Washington will serve at the pleasure of the President and the United States Congress, his position to be held until such service is no longer necessary, as deemed by a majority of said body.

It is also hereby agreed that as a stipulation of Washington's service, President John Adams shall ensure passage of an Amendment to the United States Constitution, banning the practice of slavery in each of the thirteen states, effective 1 January, 1800.

Agreed and Executed on the Twenty-Fifth Day of July, in the Year of our Lord One Thousand Seven Hundred Ninety-Eight.
G. Washington
John Adams

"This would have changed the world," Erika said.

"No wonder Vogel was after it," Parker said. "If word got out that his ancestor murdered Washington, his company would be finished. He'd never make another dollar."

"I don't want to interrupt," Nick said. "But we have to get out of here. I'm not trying to explain all of this to the authorities."

He pointed to the bullet-ridden façade of Washington's mansion and the bodies strewn in front of it.

"You're right," Erika said. "Let's go." She rolled the documents back into their protective scroll and held it tightly.

Nick walked toward the surrounding forest without looking back. Parker followed with Erika at his side. Her hand slid into his as they walked, and for the first time in a long while, the future looked bright.

Epilogue

"Yes, I understand. I don't agree with it, but I see your point. Let me know if you hear anything else."

Erika slammed her desk phone down for the third time in three days.

"Those idiots have no idea what they're doing. This is the single most important discovery about our nation's founding and all they want to do is bury it. Knowledge is meant to be shared, not hidden."

Parker acknowledged her rant by running his fingers along the back of her neck, tickling the skin. Her efforts involving the scroll and what it contained had been rebuffed at every turn, and by now she'd had enough.

After leaving Mount Vernon, he and Erika had given statements and hoped Nick could sort everything out. Before they could do anything in Philadelphia, a half-dozen government agents walked through her front door and took them to the Philadelphia FBI field office.

They were grilled for ten hours about their activities over the past week.

When the no-nonsense agents started asking about what happened at Mount Vernon, Parker had begun to sweat, seeing as how they'd basically murdered over a half-dozen people. Thankfully, Nick had come in with a senior agent and assured them that everything they had done was under the guidance of a government agent with explicit authority to use lethal force. Under the circumstances, Parker and Erika figured it was best to cooperate, so they explained everything. The rest of the interview went smoothly until the subject of Washington's accord came up.

Erika refused to hand the document over. She didn't want it to be suppressed and had no faith the federal agents would do anything but that. All things considered, she did pretty well until they threatened to charge her with murder if she didn't cooperate.

Parker wasn't sure what strings had been pulled, but after the interviews a vague notice had been posted on Mount Vernon's website that the estate would be briefly closed due to a termite infestation. Unofficially, Nick told them a team of restoration specialists had been flown in to repair the mansion.

The business world had been shocked to learn that Preston Vogel, CEO of Vogel Industries, had died of an apparent heart attack while mountain biking. As condolences poured out from around the globe, his organization's permit to drill in the Arctic National Wildlife Refuge was quietly shelved pending further review.

In the week since they'd discovered Washington's hidden accord, no other mention had been made of the events at Mount Vernon.

"How can they justify keeping this discovery under wraps?" Erika asked Parker as they sat in her apartment. A week had passed since they gave their statements. "People should be allowed to make their own conclusions about the relevance of this agreement."

"I agree with you," Parker said. "But those guys are only doing what they think is best."

"What's best is telling the truth."

"Maybe there should be a mob with pitchforks and torches outside Vogel Industries calling for his head," Parker said. "Well, maybe not, because he's dead, but calling for a boycott at least. Either way, we'll have to wait and see what happens. Those agents promised you and Joe would be credited with the discovery when they decide to announce it."

"I'll believe that when I see it," Erika scoffed. "Those pricks can't agree on anything. I'll probably be dead before the accord is released."

Despite her angry bluster, Parker had little doubt Erika realized that the implications of their discovery stretched far beyond covering up Vogel's death.

Before they had been hauled in for interrogation, they'd discussed what would happen if the accord became public knowledge. History books would have to be rewritten. America's birth would be called into question. Would the country have even survived such a tumultuous change to the social order while still in its infancy? And who else would be put under the spotlight? Several prominent corporations traced their roots to a time when slave labor had been utilized to maximize profits. Was it fair for executives now to face questions about what their companies had done during the Civil War? And that was just the start of it. Something like this would take on a life of its own, and there was no telling where the issue would go from there.

"Easy," Parker said. "You'll have a heart attack if you keep worrying about this."

She stood and stretched, reaching for the ceiling. "By the way, what did Nick want when he called earlier?"

"He asked if I'd ever consider joining the CIA."

"Are you kidding?"

"Dead serious," Parker said. "Nick thinks I would be a good fit and wanted to know if I'd be interested in working with him. He said he could arrange for an opening in the Philadelphia office."

Her eyes narrowed. "What did you say?"

Parker recognized a loaded question when he saw it. "I told him that I'd consider it, but being in Philadelphia didn't sound so bad."

Erika tried and failed to suppress a smile. "I suppose you'd need a place to stay until you got settled."

He took her hand. "I suppose I would."

GET THE ANDREW CLAWSON STARTER LIBRARY

FOR FREE

Sharing the writing journey with my readers is a special privilege. I love connecting with anyone who reads my stories, and one way I accomplish that is through my mailing list. I only send notices of new releases or the occasional special offer related to the Parker Chase or TURN series.

If you sign up for my mailing list, I'll send you a free copy of the first Parker Chase and TURN novels as a special thank you. You can get these books for free by signing up here:

DL.bookfunnel.com/L4modu3vja

Did you enjoy this book? Let people know

Reviews are the most effective way to get my books noticed. I'm one guy, a small fish in a massive pond. Over time, I hope to change that, and I would love your help. The best thing you could do to help spread the word is leave a review on your platform of choice.

Honest reviews are like gold. If you've enjoyed this book I would be so grateful if you could take a few minutes leaving a review, short or long, on this book's Amazon page.

Thank you very much.

Dedication

For my parents
Thank you, for everything

Also by Andrew Clawson

Have you read them all?

In the Parker Chase Series

A Patriot's Betrayal

A dead man's letter draws Parker Chase into
a deadly search for a secret that could rewrite history.
Free to download

The Crowns Vengeance

A Revolutionary era espionage report sends Parker
on a race to save American independence.

Dark Tides Rising

A centuries-old map bearing a cryptic poem sends Parker Chase
racing for his life and after buried treasure.

A Republic of Shadows

A long-lost royal letter sends Parker on a secret trail
with the I.R.A. and British agents close behind.

A Hollow Throne

Shattered after a tragic loss, Parker is thrust into
a race through Scottish history to save a priceless treasure.

In the TURN Series

TURN: The Conflict Lands
Reed Kimble battles a ruthless criminal gang
to save Tanzania and the animals he loves.
Free to download

TURN: A New Dawn
A predator ravages the savanna. To stop it, Reed must be
what he fears most – the man he used to be.

Check my website AndrewClawson.com for more details,
and additional Parker Chase and TURN novels.

Acknowledgements

My sincere appreciation goes out to all of the people who assisted in this process. Without your aid, this book would have never come to fruition.

First of all, I have to thank all the folks who read the manuscript while it was still a disaster. My heartfelt appreciation goes out to Kevin, Steve, Mrs. B., Emily, Becca, Rags, and all the other wonderful people who offered their invaluable advice on this journey.

A special thanks to Kelsey for putting up with me.

Most importantly I have to thank my mom and dad, without whom this would not have been possible.

Praise for Andrew's Novels

Praise for *A Patriots Betrayal*

"A Patriots Betrayal had me hooked from the first page!"

"The characters were well developed and authentically true to life. The story was incredible, realistic, and historically intriguing."

"The mystery and suspense had me so intrigued that I had to keep reading."

Praise for *The Crowns Vengeance*

"Moments of sheer intensity make it hard to put this book down."

"This one is just as exciting and fast paced as the first, with new adventures flying at the couple in every turn."

"Be sure you set aside enough time to finish this one, you'll not want to put this one down until you read the last page."

Praise for *Dark Tides Rising*

"Yet another gem-filled yarn weaving fact and fiction."

"A story that is so well written it keeps you from putting the book down."

"Very fast and action-packed. Can't wait for the next amazing tale."

About the Author

Andrew Clawson is the author of the Parker Chase and TURN series.

You can find him at his website, AndrewClawson.com, or you can connect with him on Twitter at @clawsonbooks, on Facebook at facebook.com/AndrewClawsonnovels and you can always send him an email at andrew@andrewclawson.com.

Made in the USA
Columbia, SC
14 October 2020